PRAISE FOR *INTEI*

From a bakery fire in Minnesota to gun shots fired near a Montana alpaca ranch, *Intentional Heirs* will keep you wondering what's going to happen next. In this debut novel, Rebecca McLafferty creates a delightful mix of action and intrigue with a delicious dash of romance.

   - Becky Melby, *author of more than 20 Christian fiction titles*

Rebecca McLafferty weaves together a suspenseful novel that keeps the pages turning. This action-packed rendezvous stretches the confines of providence and law, but in the end, it will expand your faith and heart. *Intentional Heirs* makes an exceptional debut in the Sunrise Crik Series. Highly recommended.

   - Kate Jungwirth, co-author of *The Mystery at Point Beach Series*

Intentional Heirs is a story of forgiveness, belonging, and healing wrapped prettily with the raw beauty of Montana. Rebecca McLafferty's debut novel wooed me into caring for her wonderfully diverse characters, small-town life, and furry critters before scattering my senses with worry and suspense! Hope for the heroine and hero kept me tethered to these pages to the very end. I find myself grateful and full of anticipation as I await the second of this Sunrise Crik Series.

   - Susan Marlene, *author of the debut novel, Sisters & Friends*

INTENTIONAL HEIRS

Sunrise Crik Series

Rebecca McLafferty

COUNTRY
MEMORIES, LLC

Intentional Heirs

Country Memories, LLC
416 Turtle Creek Drive
Delavan, WI 53115

Cover by Roseanna White Designs

This novel is a work of fiction. Names, characters, businesses, places, events, locales, and incidents are either products of the author's imagination or used fictitiously. All characters are fictional, and any similarity to people living or dead is purely coincidental. Certain long-standing institutions, agencies, and public offices are mentioned, but the characters involved are wholly imaginary. Any brand names, places, and trademarks remain the property of their respective owners, bear no association with the author or the publisher, and are used for fictional purposes only.

Library of Congress Control Number: 2020908707

ISBN: 978-0-578-70341-1 (paperback)
        978-0-578-70342-8 (eBook)

ACKNOWLEDGMENTS

L OTS OF SPECIAL PEOPLE contributed to make my debut novel, Intentional Heirs, a reality.

Before all else, I thank God for gifting me with the love of story. The characters, with their own complex backgrounds and heartfelt desires, became my dear friends. Their personalities blossomed as the story evolved. When my husband and I visited Montana, the story's location became real. I cherish the moments when a story idea would pop into my mind—one that I would never have imagined. I would smile and say, "Thank you, Lord. This story is yours."

I must thank my wonderful editors, authors Kate Jungwirth and Delores Leisner. Kate's comprehensive edit and Delores's preliminary edit were critical to the story's success. And to my daughter, Colleen Bauer, for giving feedback and cheering me on, I so love and appreciate you.

To my friends in the Pens of Praise Christian Writers Group, I give my utmost thanks for their support, suggestions, and listening ears.

To my friends in the Crossway Communicators writing group, especially Becky Melby and Cathy Timmons, I so appreciate your guidance and wisdom.

To my dearest and most treasured friend, Susan Marlene Kinney, without your nurturing encouragement, critiques, shared learning, and unwavering faith, my journey would not be as dear to my heart. We are true kindred spirits, sisters in God.

To my supportive husband Joseph, you have shared this journey by wearing many hats—my manager, organizer, co-editor, and brainstormer. You are my partner in every way and I thank you for allowing me to pursue my dream and encouraging me along the way. I love you with all my heart.

I am honored and humbled to be able to create stories that give glory to God, stories that intermingle romance, suspense, and faith journeys. I hope my readers will benefit from the story's interwoven messages of forgiveness, redemption, and love.

"Lord," he said,
"if I have found favor in your eyes,
then let the Lord go with us.
Although this is a stiff-necked people,
forgive our wickedness and our sin,
and take us as your inheritance."

Exodus 34:9 NIV

CHAPTER ONE

Bakery chef Evah Rois stood transfixed, staring at the dark wisps slithering from beneath the storage room door. The ominous curlicues danced before her, choking the sweet cinnamon aroma and turning it into pungent, eye-burning fog. Her mouth went dry.

This isn't a drill.

"Carolyn, come quick!" She screamed, "Donald, call 9-1-1! Fire!"

"What?" Carolyn Turner, the bakery's owner and Evah's good friend, rushed from where she and Donald worked on the front display.

An intern near the floor mixer tore off rubber gloves and headed toward Evah. "I'll help."

Donald punched numbers into his cell phone. "Get everyone else outside and make sure no one comes in."

Evah reached for the storage room door. Hot. She thrust her hand inside an oven mitt and flung the door open. Smoke clouds billowed out, hot and suffocating. She choked.

"I'll get the fire extinguisher." She covered her mouth with the mitt and stepped into the miniature thunderhead. Stench clawed at the back of her throat.

"Wait for me," Carolyn called from behind her.

Evah paused and wiped her eyes. Fine white particles filled the air. She ran her hands across her face. Flour?

1

A plastic garbage container lay tipped on its side against the rack's bottom shelf. A marred, dark-rimmed hole exposed the melted path. Flames and smoke rose from stacks of cardboard circles, bakery bags, and boxes lining the shelf.

Evah's foot ricocheted off a knee-high box, sending it skittering across the floor. Other boxes lie empty. Why were cardboard boxes strewn across the floor?

"We've got to put this out," Carolyn coughed. "I'm going to grab a couple of wet towels. I'll be right back."

Evah's fingers traced the rough wall until she felt a smooth cylinder. She lifted it down.

"Carolyn?" Donald shouted.

"I'm here." Carolyn once again sounded close. "Are the interns outside?"

"Yes. And I called 9-1-1. Are you okay?"

"Yes, thanks. Stay outside and watch for the fire department!"

Evah yanked the pin from the extinguisher and squeezed the handle.

Nothing happened. She tried again. Nothing. *I thought the fire department conducted a safety inspection last week.*

She tossed it into the double sink and exhaled, trying to push smoke away from her face. Instead, she coughed, jagged and deep.

Across the room, something exploded. She covered her ears and the world spun. Rock-hard concrete closed in.

She opened her eyes and discovered an air mask covering her mouth. Crisp spring air tickled her arms and she felt soft grass beneath her. How had she gotten outside?

"Relax and breathe," said a fireman wearing Mankato, MN, gear.

Evah struggled to sit upright. "Carolyn?"

He looked down at her. "She's right there, on the stretcher. You're both okay."

Another fireman approached. "Which of you ladies is the owner?"

To Evah's right, Carolyn removed her mask. "I am."

"Why wasn't the fire extinguisher used?"

Evah pulled off her mask. "I tried it, but it wouldn't work."

"I remember being here to inspect it." He retrieved the extinguisher and studied it. "This isn't the one I approved."

~~~

Siren blaring, Police Chief Nolan Quinn peeled out of Woodridge, Montana's Police Department parking lot. His Patrolman, Luke Young, believed himself to be in pursuit of a drug drop-and-run vehicle.

"You there Bosco?" Nolan spoke into his shoulder mic.

"Affirmative, Chief." Captain Aiden Bosco's voice blasted. "Young's a few miles ahead. Still hasn't identified the vehicle."

"Roger that. Get there. Patrolman Young, do you copy?"

"Here, Chief. Screaming west on 91. I can't read the plate. It's a white pickup truck. They fishtailed a minute ago so I caught up a bit."

"Ten-four, Young. Bosco, what's your ETA?"

"Five minutes."

Nolan's heart thumped. "Young, keep the vehicle in sight. And keep your distance until help arrives. These leads are too far and few between."

Nolan hit his mic button. "Moss, you there?"

"Here, Chief."

"They're heading toward Bozeman. Call Gallatin County. Have a spike strip deployed on I-91, east of Jackson Creek Road. ASAP."

"Right away."

"Shots fired! Shots fired!" Young yelled. "They've turned onto Elk Ridge Road. Their truck's all over the place. It's spinning."

Ping, ping. Bratatat.

Gunfire exploded over the mic. Young's voice quavered. "We're nose to nose, Chief. I'm hit."

Nolan's stomach roiled at the fear in Young's voice. "We're almost there. How bad are you?"

"Shoulder. It hurts, Chief."

Nolan controlled a skid and then hit the gas, maneuvering East Lake Road's never-ending curves. Praise God there weren't any pedestrians. "Young, don't force it. Wait for backup."

His youngest officer yelled over gunfire, "They're getting out."

"Move back," Nolan screamed into the mic while gripping the steering wheel with his left hand. His car ricocheted over a pothole. "Do not exit the car. Retreat, right now."

Silence.

"Young, are you there?"

No reply.

"Bosco, where are you?"

"One minute out."

"Young. What's your status?"

Silence.

Nolan felt gut-punched. He turned onto the frontage road, thankful for a straight stretch. He hit the gas, a scarce moment later to slam the breaks to turn onto snakelike Elk Ridge Road. Lights flashed ahead. Bosco? Or Young?

Nolan rounded another curve and skidded to a dead stop behind Bosco's car. Ten yards ahead, Young's car was pitted with bullet holes. Broken glass glittered on the ground.

Nolan drew his weapon and ran to the scene.

Sobbing, Bosco knelt next to Young's body. "He's dead, Chief."

Blood covered Young's chest and legs.

Nolan tensed. "Did you request an ambulance?"

"It's on its way."

"And the suspect car. Did you see it? Hear anything?"

"No car. No one."

"Did Young say anything? Was he alive?"

Sniffling, Bosco looked up at Nolan. "No. I can't believe it. We were tight, Chief. Like brothers."

"I see that he pulled his weapon. Did he get off any shots?"

Bosco lifted the pistol and examined it. "Yeah. One."

"Cancel the request for the spike strip." Nolan clenched his fists and jumped to his feet. "Why didn't he stay in the car?" He shook a fist in the air and glared at the M-16 shells littering the ground. Young hadn't had a chance.

CHAPTER TWO

Nolan hadn't slept in three days. Thursday came anyway, and he sat alone with his thoughts during the short drive from Woodridge to Bozeman. He wasn't looking forward to the two-hour flight to Minneapolis-St. Paul. His agitated and somewhat sour disposition made him uneasy. Mankato, Minnesota hadn't been list. Not for the funeral of Patrolman Luke Young, age twenty-six.

He arrived at Gallatin Field in Bozeman and met Sergeants Gray and Eicherman from Park County.

"I appreciate your service." Nolan said. "If you need anything, let me know."

"Yes, sir. Guarding the casket of a fallen officer is our privilege, sir." One of the two guards spoke up.

They stood next to the flag-covered casket until it was on the plane. Nolan headed to board. They followed him.

Nolan's silencing headphones didn't help the distractions from within, memories of a young patrolman with an infectious smile and a heart for helping. He felt worse than ever.

The Mankato Police Department's car and driver would allow him to concentrate on funeral arrangements and memorials. On his return trip back to Minneapolis-St. Paul, he would meet up with Keith Strickland, his mentor from Campbellsville University's Criminal Justice Program. College in Kentucky felt a lifetime ago.

Half way through the flight, the pilot announced that the plane was transporting a fallen policeman. The passengers went silent. Nolan turned to his window, the lump in his throat larger than ever.

The plane began its descent. Minnesota's browns and greens gave way to industrial and residential terrain. He already missed Montana. God felt closer in the mountains.

Nolan waited until the plane landed. He walked with the two guards as they removed the casket from the plane and loaded it into the hearse.

The plane's passengers were still in their seats, watching.

Nolan collected his bag and headed to the terminal door.

An officer wearing sergeant stripes on a light blue shirt with navy epaulettes and pocket flaps approached. "Chief Quinn, I'm Sergeant John Alvarez, St. Paul Police Department. I extend our Chief's condolences. He was detained and couldn't be here. I am assigned to be your driver for the duration of your stay. Just name it and I'll get you there."

"Thanks, Sergeant. May I call you John?"

"Yes, please."

"I appreciate your service. Let's get these bags loaded and get to the hearse. A small motorcycle escort is to accompany the casket to the mortuary. You can brief me as we go."

"Yes sir." He popped the trunk of the squad car and tossed in Nolan's bag. "You travel light."

John maneuvered through thick traffic. Once he got onto the highway, he turned to Nolan. "Everything on track, Chief?"

"Yes, thanks. Both the mortuary staff and the organizing detail have been helpful. They've covered everything as discussed."

"Glad to hear it. As I mentioned earlier, the mortuary is just over an hour from here."

Nolan's cell buzzed. "Chief Quinn."

"Chief, I hope I'm not disturbing you. This is Evah Rois on behalf of the American Legion. Do you have a moment to talk?"

"Yes, Evah." She sounded compassionate and businesslike at the same time. "What can I do for you?"

"I have a hiccup in today's schedule. Would it be possible to push back our meeting by a half hour? I don't want to inconvenience you."

"I hate to admit it, but that would help my schedule. Is there a problem?"

"I'm meeting with tomorrow's volunteers and the timeframe is too short. It's nothing for you to concern yourself with. I hope you are doing well."

"We just left the airport."

"Are you fighting traffic?"

"No. I have a driver. I'm glad to hear from you." He liked her calm demeanor. "I'll see you at four o'clock."

John offered a few details and then they rode in silence.

Nolan had hoped to talk to Skip from the mortuary, but he and his assistant were out for the afternoon.

Upon arrival at the mortuary, Mankato's Police Chief waited in a chair inside the front door. After a lengthy discussion about tomorrow's formalities, he dropped his head. "The town is upside down with grief. Luke was a popular kid in school. Sports and all that. But when he went out of his way to make Mankato his first assignment, he was admired. It's so unfortunate."

"May I ask a personal question?" Nolan asked. "If everyone loved him, and I assume it was mutual, why did he apply for work in Montana? Again, don't answer if you prefer not to."

"It's okay." The well decorated police chief sat back and let out a sigh. "Nobody talks about it. Luke and his wife—"

"What? He's married?" The words tightened in Nolan's throat.

"And divorced, against his every wish. I'm not surprised that he didn't tell you. He and Jenny were married for no more than a year. She lost a baby. Couldn't live with him anymore. He couldn't deal with that. Said he was going 'as far away as he could get'".

Nolan blew out a breath. This was something he hadn't expected. Did the guys know?

John drove him to meet Pastor Janson at the Mankato Community Church. Nice guy and personable, but spread thin with commitments. From there, he met two representatives of the Eagles

Club. Their property would host the staging area where the procession would gather to proceed to Calvary Cemetery.

At last, he visited the place where everything became real, final. He noted the angel grave marker near the entrance and the limestone chapel in the middle. His heart felt like dead weight.

John dropped him off at the American Legion at four-o'clock on the dot.

~~~

Evah looked up when a uniformed police officer entered. He would be attractive in jeans, but the uniform made her breath catch. He removed his hat and placed it between his forearm and jacket. His strong features gave him an air of confidence and strength, that of a police chief.

His shiny black shoes clicked on the linoleum as he strode toward her.

"Police Chief Quinn?" She ran her fingers over her French twist.

"Yes. Eve? Am I pronouncing that correct?"

"Almost. It's Evah."

"Good. Please call me Nolan." He smiled and shook her hand, which tingled at once. Her face warmed.

"Where would you like to sit?" She gestured at the spacious room of linen covered tables.

"Is that your paperwork on the table there?"

"Yes, but we can sit anywhere. Coffee?"

"Please. That sounds great."

"Which? The sitting down, the table, or the coffee?"

"All of the above," he grinned.

She hesitated. Her pulse quickened. "Please make yourself comfortable and I'll get us both a cup." She walked toward the coffee station. What was she doing? She was a bakery chef who represented the church's hospitality team, not a ditzy school girl.

Evah returned to the booth. A spreadsheet and tablet lay near his linen napkin. He looked tired.

"Where shall we begin?" She lowered the steaming cups onto the table and took the seat facing him.

"Tell me about yourself. I like to know who I'm dealing with."

"I can get my credentials—"

8

"No, no. Just talk to me. Tell me about yourself."

"Like a background check?" How serious was he?

"That's not what I had in mind. Um, this tastes good."

Evah squirmed. "I'm a bakery chef employed at Carolyn's Bakery, here in Mankato. And I act as a liaison or representative for my church's hospitality team. I've appreciated you taking my calls. I can't imagine how busy you've been."

Beneath his gunmetal blue eyes lie an inconspicuous veil of sadness. He was handsome, yes. And he cared.

He lowered his cup. "Banners and signs line the streets. I didn't know what to expect."

"It seems like everyone knew him. Or knew of him. Even back in high school."

"Did you know him?"

"Just in passing. He was two years ahead of me and a sports star that everyone swooned after. Yet, he never seemed too caught up in all that. At least that's my take from a distance."

He looked toward the street traffic and then back at her. "That's the way he was as a cop. Charismatic. He could relate to kids and teens like nobody else. And he was conscientious, working to make things better."

"You did know him well." Evah cradled the cup in her hands. "I'm guessing he respected you as his chief?"

"Yeah, we got along good. Real good. He was like a kid brother and on-the-mark patrolman all in one."

They sat in silence until Nolan said, "I'm sorry. It's been a long day."

"And tomorrow will be longer."

He pulled the spreadsheet closer. "Shall we finish going over these details and grab a quick bite? Or is it too late for you?" He drew a breath. "Sorry, that was rather forward of me."

"It just so happens that I haven't eaten, either. I'd love to." Had she said that aloud?

They dove into calculations and logistics. Forty minutes later, when they packed up their belongings, Nolan's mic squelched.

"Chief, this is Dawn. Patrolman Moss has an update. Can you talk?"

Evah felt like an eavesdropper and looked away.

"Negative. I'll call you back in ten." Nolan frowned. "I'm sorry, Evah. I've got to deal with this. There's a lot at stake. His killers are still on the loose."

"It's okay, Chief. Tomorrow will be a busy day for both of us. It's been a pleasure meeting you."

Disappointment slapped her like a wet dish towel.

CHAPTER THREE

Nolan exited the church behind Luke's family. They followed the flag-covered, guarded casket. Crisp uniforms, white gloves, salutes, and tears.

"Nice eulogy." Someone patted him on the back. He'd struggled to keep his composure.

Feeling numb, he sat in the squad car, watching the last of one hundred plus police motorcycles lead the way to the cemetery. Their deep roar announced the otherwise silent procession, followed by the hearse, flanked by one motorcycle in front and two on each side, lights flashing.

Mankato Police Department cars pulled into place behind the hearse. John pulled in behind them. Nolan fought the bitter confinement of the procession.

"Good turnout," John offered.

Nolan stared ahead. "There are at least four hundred law enforcement personnel in the procession, not counting units along the route."

"Look at the photographers. Families, too. And there's another unit," he pointed. "They've come from all over Minnesota and the Midwest."

"And Montana."

"Yes sir."

John ran a hand over the black elastic dividing his badge crosswise. "The elastic's shot on my band."

Nolan stuck his hand into his coat pocket and retrieved a new mourning band. "Here. This should last the full month."

"Thanks. You okay, Chief?"

"I'm good. The pipe and drum corps and color guard are waiting at the cemetery. The bugler, bagpiper, firing detail . . . everything is set."

~~~

Evah stared out the American Legion window. "Listen. They're getting close."

The rumble of police motorcycles brought the staff forward. They stood quiet until a cell phone buzzed, followed by a ripple of hushed conversations.

"Have some respect for the fallen officer. Turn that off." Someone snapped. "He gave his life."

Evah closed her eyes. *Like you gave your life for us, Jesus.*

She opened them and saw Carolyn standing beside her. Her boss and friend nodded in understanding.

Evah turned to the employees, "If anyone wants to watch, or pray, you've got fifteen minutes. Otherwise, return to work. We'll be on in about an hour."

A worker appeared at her side. "We know the timetable. Relax."

"I know. But I won't stand for disrespect."

Three hours later, Evah noticed the crowd beginning to thin. She stood transfixed, watching Mr. and Mrs. Young and their adult daughter. Four policemen and Chief Quinn escorted them out the front door.

A few volunteers headed toward the side exit. Evah strode toward them and motioned for them to wait.

"Thanks, everyone. Your help was appreciated. Regardless of how long you volunteered or what you did, you made a difference."

When the place had cleared out, she headed home.

Wearing a sweatshirt, jeans, and fuzzy socks, she sprawled onto the brick red futon in the living room. The outside screen door creaked open and banged shut.

"Was it that bad?" Her houseguest-turned-live-in friend, Cassie, stood on the door mat and removed her shoes. "You look beat."

"Funeral receptions are somber moments, visitor reunions, and tall tales. Today's reminiscing ranged from neighborhood stories to police stuff. It was very emotional."

"Was his family there or just policemen?" Cassie sat in the plaid chair next to the futon.

"Both. The immediate members had their own gathering, but his parents and sister showed up for a while. They were appreciative of the procession and all the details. I heard everyone talking about the 21-gun salute and casket guards. Hundreds of patrol cars and motorcycles drove by the American Legion with lights flashing. It went on and on.

"But, when the officers came in, it felt different. All the uniforms . . . light blue, dark blue, tan, dark brown. They all showed respect for each other."

"You liked that?"

Evah nodded, picturing the handsome police chief from Montana. Whenever their paths had crossed, his warm smile gazed upon her.

"Here is today's mail." Cassie lifted a handful of envelopes off the side table and handed it to her.

Evah read the top envelope. "From Attorney Nicholas Angeli in Montana?" She slit the top and pulled out the letter.

"Dear Evah Mae Rois, duh, duh, duh," she scanned the page. "Uncle Regan is dead." She blew out a breath. "And it says, 'Real estate deeded to Marilyn McCormick and Evah Mae Rois as joint tenants with right of survivorship and not as tenants in common.' What does that mean? Blah, blah, blah. And 'Your presence is requested at the office of Attorney Angeli, located at blah, blah, Livingston, Montana, on or before . . .'"

Cassie looked at her, wide eyed. "You have to go to Montana? To inherit property?"

"No way."

"But aren't you obligated?"

"When it comes to my now-deceased Uncle Regan, I'm not obligated to do anything."

13

Intentional Heirs

Evah stood up, pivoted, and walked outside.
Uncle Regan.
God, I can't go through this, again.

CHAPTER FOUR

E vah lifted the latte to her lips, careful not to disturb the intricate mocha art. She scanned The Cup's mirrors reflecting Owatonna's street traffic and animated conversations beneath rows of Tiffany-style ceiling lights. "So, I overreacted a bit."

"A bit?" Cassie stirred froth into her cappuccino. Her bronze nails tapped the china. "It was more than that. But I appreciate the opportunity to dress up." She fingered the lace sleeve on her mustard yellow dress.

"I'm sorry, Cassie. It feels good to me, too." Evah gestured toward her navy and white floral dress. Her smile faded. "I wasn't prepared to ever hear the name Regan McCormick again. Even if he is dead."

"I didn't know you had an uncle. Something went sour?"

"That's what makes me angry. I don't know what happened. He must've had an argument with mama. I don't like talking—or even thinking—about it."

"Who made a coffee date to talk things through?"

"I know."

Cassie's caramel-streaked bangs blended into her black hair. "We're friends. We both have our pasts. If you can't talk about it, I get it. But I would like to know."

Evah squirmed in the hard-backed chair. "I've tried to deal with this for years. Since you got me reading the Bible again, I've felt Jesus helping me, a little. After mama died, Uncle Regan and Aunt Marilyn forgot about me. I waited in foster homes, one after the other. They never came."

"Weren't your foster parents, your last ones, nice to you?"

"Yes. I loved them both. But—"

"Did you ever try to contact your aunt and uncle?"

"I was a kid."

"In the last five or ten years?"

"No. I've been preoccupied."

Cassie raised her arched eyebrows. "For all these years? Maybe it's time to get over it. You could use this opportunity—going to your uncle's place—to your advantage. Maybe it's a blessing in disguise. God's looking out for you."

"God wouldn't send me to Montana." Evah stretched her fingers. "At least, not to deal with anything to do with my Uncle Regan."

"I get that. But you've been talking about wanting a bigger place, to have animals. What if your uncle's place is bigger than what you have now? And you've been commiserating about Carolyn's situation. And after what just happened at the bakery . . ."

"You have a point but I don't know much about Uncle Regan's place."

"What do you remember? How long since you were there?"

"I was eight. That would be twenty-one years ago. I rode a pony through a cornfield. There was a big red barn. That's all I remember." *Except that he smiled and we laughed. I thought he loved me.*

"Cornfields. Does that mean it's big? Don't they say that everything is big in Montana?"

"I think that's Texas."

"Well, out west anyway. Why don't you call and check it out?"

"I don't want the attorney to know I'm interested, if I am. And they wouldn't have left me anything anyway."

"You can't know that."

Evah had avoided the topic for years. How could she explain without divulging her past?

"Did I tell you the latest about Carolyn's Bakery?" Evah set her napkin on the table. "The Mankato Fire Department is investigating the cause of the fire."

"You told me and nice try. Changing the subject won't make your problem go away."

Their gazes met as they collected their purses and rose to leave. Cassie moved ahead and stopped at the cash register at the end of the teakwood counter.

Kaboom! Metal crumpled and glass exploded. Evah whirled to see the windowfront crash in, followed by a compact car, its engine roaring. Evah covered her ears. Tiny pieces of debris flew across the café. She covered her face. Screams rang in her ears. She ducked under the counter's overhang. Breaths bounced off her arms and steamed her face.

Glass shattered. She peeked and ducked lower when jagged shards spewed across the room like airborne razor blades, shattering against everything in its path.

A sharp pain shot through her bicep. She grabbed the spot and felt something hard and sharp. Glass. And wet, oozing between her fingers.

Stinky vehicle exhaust filled the air.

A car door slammed. People cried, murmured, and shuffled their feet.

"Is that her?" A man growled.

"Yeah, I think so." A deeper voice responded.

"Stop that!" A lady screamed. Glass shattered. Wood snapped. Cassie?

Alarm jolted her body. Little by little, she stood. A white cloud exploded into her eyes and the vehicle's wheels squealed in reverse. She fell to the ground, squinting through tearing eyes. She yelled, "Cassie are you okay?"

No one answered. Crushing fear paralyzed her.

"Cassie? Where are you?"

Approaching sirens stirred hope.

17

"Cassie?" she called out.

"We've gotta go. They're almost here." A man hissed.

"Take care of business. Hurry."

A shrill scream cut through the air.

Cassie?

Hot tears ran down her cheeks. Where was her friend?

Voices muddled. Time stood still until someone took Evah's elbow.

"Let's get you up and away from this counter," a man said. Sturdy hands guided her backwards and then upright. "Are you injured?"

"My arm hurts and there's glass or something on my face. I need to find my friend. Please help me."

"Be still." He pressed something on Evah's arm. Sharp pain made her breath catch. "Hold this here and keep pressure on it." Her fingers bumped something hard. "Don't touch the glass, just the cloth. You have multiple pieces in your arm. You don't want to break anything off or push it in further."

His fingers touched Evah's hair. "There is glass in your hair. You'll need to—"

"I need to open my eyes. Please hurry."

"Your face is covered with . . . I think it's sugar."

"What?" Evah blinked. "Ouch." Her eyes stung and watered. "Sugar?"

"Keep them closed for a minute." He wiped her face with something soft. "Okay. Try now."

She opened her eyes a little at a time.

A burly man with a short beard watched her. "Your arm needs attention. Glass is lodged and needs to be removed. You will most likely need stitches."

"I have to find Cassie." Evah held a blood-soaked cloth on her bicep.

People huddled against walls and sat on the floor. Two ladies remained at a far back table, their hands on their heads. Rescue personnel wearing red polo shirts moved among the patrons.

She spun around. "I don't see her. She's wearing bright yellow. She was a couple feet from me." Panic overtook her. "Cassie?" she yelled.

"Come over here," a lady motioned.

People moved. Whispered. Cried.

Evah gazed at her white tote lying on the floor. She picked it up. Its pristine cloth, splattered with wet blood, made her stomach lurch.

"Over here," the lady called again, standing near the restaurant's open door. Evah's view locked onto the bright yellow dress. Cassie lay crumpled on the floor. Blood oozed across her back. Something protruded from her right shoulder.

A knife.

~~~

The doctor's curt voice continued, "The row of absorbable sutures under the skin will keep the tissue together. The lacerations were clean, so they should heal well. Follow the instructions and come back in fourteen days to have your sutures removed."

Evah walked out of the hospital and toward a small diner. Her eyes adjusted to the street lights, but her head throbbed. The pill bottle rattled in the small paper bag. She never took pills.

Cassie was stable. Evah gave strict instructions that no visitors be allowed. The staff looked tentative and she didn't blame them. She couldn't tell them why. She didn't know herself. It was Cassie's unspeakable past. Evah prayed that the "week or thereabouts" in the hospital would keep her friend safe.

The waitress poured steaming coffee while Evah ordered split-pea-and-ham soup. Lunch with Cassie seemed days ago. Everything blurred.

She needed to get home, clean up, and sleep. It would take a few minutes to locate the car somewhere near the emergency entrance.

Her thoughts returned to the letter. How much would it cost to fly to Montana? She pulled out her phone and shoved it back in her pocket. Poor Cassie, her thoughts jumped around.

Her brain felt fuzzy and her eyes hurt.

She couldn't decide. Decisions could wait until tomorrow.

After a long, restless night, Evah rose at first light. She ached all over, but her arm throbbed. She popped two Ibuprofen tablets and poured a cup of steaming black coffee. She wandered to her favorite chair and sat transfixed as thoughts leapt from one thing to another.

Her decision couldn't be frivolous. If she needed to make the trip, she needed to get back as soon as possible. She would need to be home before Cassie was released.

She scrolled her phone's contact list. This would be a rational way to help with her decision making, nothing more.

"Woodridge Police Department. Can I help you?" a lady asked.

"Chief Nolan Quinn, please."

"May I ask what this is regarding?"

"It's personal." That sounded bad. "I'm calling from Mankato."

"You have good timing." It sounded like she was smiling. "He just walked in. Could I tell him your name please?"

Evah responded and waited.

"Evah Rois from Mankato, Minnesota?" Nolan's tone flowed warm, surprised.

"Yes, it's me. I wasn't sure about calling you."

"To what do I owe this honor? Is it my birthday or is this official business?"

Evah smiled at his humor. "I don't know the date of your birthday."

"Pick a day, whatever you choose." What was it about his tone? Warm, caring. "So, if it isn't my birthday, is this a reception follow up?"

Embarrassment flooded through her. She wanted to tell him about Cassie but she didn't dare.

"I received a letter from a lawyer in Livingston. I looked on the map and it doesn't look too far from you. My uncle owned a ranch somewhere around Woodridge. He's passed away. I wondered if you could tell me anything about it."

"I'm sorry to hear that news. Who was your uncle?"

"Regan McCormick."

~~~

Nolan sat stunned. *Regan McCormick?*

"Hello? Are you there?"

"Yes, I'm sorry. I can't believe that you have relatives here."

"Had."

Nolan settled back in his chair. He had to ask.

20

"Were you aware that his funeral was weeks ago?" Regan's long-time housekeeper, Jane Martin, said there were no relatives.

"I just received a letter about probating his estate." She ignored his question. "That's all I know. Are you familiar with his house—ranch—or whatever?"

She's calling me instead of the attorney?

"I haven't been there in a while. He has a house and barn a couple miles southeast of town. A few animals. I remember a dog." And Jane.

"I'm supposed to go for the probate hearing to meet some condition or something. I don't know if it's worth the trip."

"It would be great to see you. I could show you around, if you would like."

Nolan wanted to ask if she knew about Jane, but he didn't. Would Evah come here, to Woodridge, a small dot within Montana's one hundred fifty thousand square miles?

An hour later, Nolan sat across from City Manager Edwin Riser. His boss's fake tan announced a vacation. A past or future trip, Nolan couldn't keep track. Riser's cherry wood desk and credenza gleamed in the afternoon sun, a far cry from Nolan's steel relic.

"I hope you understand what I'm saying," Riser continued. "The committee wants surveillance upped on Sunrise Crik Trail, at least until after the grand opening."

"There's been no sign of trouble and my guys are spread thin, working on Young's case. At the trail, workers are adding finishing touches. Walkers are using it and its distance from downtown is averting vandalism. I've checked plenty of times, even walked my dog there."

The City Manager's forehead wrinkled above wavy eyebrows. "That's fine, but don't let the taxpayers think you've got nothing better to do."

Nolan's ears felt warm. "I walk my dog when I'm off duty, either lunch break or after work. I want people to know it's safe." He rose to leave.

His boss tapped a folded newspaper. "Did you see yesterday's Letter to the Editor?"

"No. More bashing?"

"My head against the wall. One corrupt employee dipping into fundraiser accounts and we all have our hands in the pot."

"It'll blow over."

"Not soon enough."

~~~

Coffee in hand, Evah left the grab-and-go bar in Terminal One. She found a seat near Gate D6 and settled in. The airport clattered with people walking, talking, and pulling suitcases. She loved to people watch, but the appearance of a boy with a casted arm brought her thoughts back to Cassie.

Her friend had a few days, or maybe a week, before being released. Evah hoped to be back by then. If not, Evah had arranged for a neighbor lady to care for her in the interim.

Evah pulled a folder from her bag. She'd hastily collected an array of tourist information on Montana. She poured over pages until a speaker squelched.

"Delta flight 2521 now boarding at Gate D6."

CHAPTER FIVE

O nly a weak security light greeted Evah at the shadowed two-story country house. She'd tried the door twice and found it locked.

At 10:30 at night, she'd like to call the lawyer to give him a piece of her mind, but he probably wouldn't get a message until morning. She'd left him details of her arrival. He should have had it unlocked.

Maybe it served her right for not catching an earlier flight, but she'd needed to run errands, visit Cassie, and talk to Betsy about helping with Cassie, if needed. Arriving in Bozeman late wouldn't have mattered if the attorney had done his part. But now, she peered into crisp darkness. She couldn't see mountains, but she felt their presence, towering over her thoughts, her very soul.

She looked at her rental, a blue Toyota, gleaming under the yard light. At least she wouldn't be stranded if she couldn't get the place unlocked.

Frantic dog barks sounded nearby. She descended the steps and peered at a lit cabin some fifty yards away. She didn't like bothering anyone at this hour, but someone living nearby might have been contacted by the attorney. She headed that way.

She climbed the steps and knocked.

Moments later, the door swung open. Light gave way to a barking, tri-colored dog bouncing behind a silver-haired woman wearing a camouflaged outfit. A dark brown sofa and straight-backed rocking chair in front of a fireplace reminded Evah of a cozy photo.

"I'm sorry to bother you," Evah explained. "I notified an attorney that I was arriving tonight and that I needed the McCormick home unlocked. He must have forgotten. Would you know anything about it?"

"And you are?"

"Evah Rois." Evah held out her hand. The lady didn't budge. Evah put her arm down.

"Oh, it's you. I forgot." She rubbed her wrinkled forehead.

"You knew that I was coming?"

"I guess I did."

And you didn't have the house unlocked for me?

Evah tried to hide her surprise at Jane's revelation. "Do you have access to the house?"

"I'm the only one that does."

"Good." Evah stepped back. "If you will unlock it, or allow me to, I'll get my bags."

"You're planning to stay, are you?" The lady's petite frame seemed to stretch taller.

"I am, for now. I've been requested to be here by an attorney. And who are you?"

"Mary Jane Martin, Senior Master Sergeant, retired." Her petite frame bristled. "I was Regan McCormick's housekeeper."

"Oh," realization dawned on Evah. "I'm sorry about his, Uncle Regan's, death. It's nice to meet you, Mary Jane."

Again, Evah held out her hand. Mary Jane hesitated, but shook it.

Evah pushed her purse back on her shoulder. "It's convenient that you live so close to your work."

"Call me Jane. And yes, ma'am. I live here on McCormick property. This is *my* place." She crossed her arms and looked Evah over from head to toe. "Welcome to Sunrise Crik Ranch."

~~~~

Three nerve-wracking days later, Evah walked through the kitchen's early morning shadows. The microwave clock glowed

5:30. She wasn't going to put up with Jane's heavy-handed presence this morning.

Listening to Jane babble about protecting Regan McCormick's ranch was getting old. From what, Evah had no clue. And trying to get information from her rivalled interrogating a war criminal. Evah just wanted to get home before Cassie was released.

Sitting atop Evah's stacked work clothes, a magazine now leaned against a pair of binoculars. She peered at the dog-eared issue and recognized the one Jane drummed on her thigh while waiting for Uncle Regan's corgi, Cash, to finish his business.

A marker bulged between pages but Evah flipped to the cover. Army Times. Addressed to Mary Jane Martin (SMSgt., Retired).

She flipped pages to the marked one and stepped into the night light's rays. A soldier held binoculars to his face, viewing a person drawn on a target and circled with red marker. Evah tossed it onto the counter.

Snap! It sprang back to its rolled-up position. Jane either had a warped sense of humor or contorted rationalization. Or both.

She scooped up the stack—sweatshirt, running shoes, and work gloves. The glass-paned door revealed predawn darkness. She opened it and walked into the crisp morning air.

Had Uncle Regan put up with Jane's military antics? Maybe they deserved each other.

Evah scolded herself. God wouldn't approve of combative thoughts.

How could she sooth Jane's ire? What if she couldn't? The lawyer should approve her request to leave without jeopardizing the probate. Evah's rationale would be solid. Cassie would be released from the hospital and needed help. They relied on each other and, even though they weren't sisters, Cassie said they were sisters in Christ. Evah liked that.

She hoped to grow a faith like Cassie's, even though it sometimes confused her. Like now, Cassie praised God that she hadn't been killed. She reasoned that the stab wound hadn't done as much damage as the resulting bone splinter.

Evah had never known anyone involved in a stabbing, but she'd heard stories. Cassie's paranoia about being around people lingered in her mind.

Crossing the porch, white puffs materialized near her mouth and dissipated in the breeze. She shivered. After so many sleepless hours, she needed to move, to do something.

The porch floorboards chilled her feet. She shuffled toward the swing at the far end of the wrap-around porch.

"Ouch." She pulled a wood splinter from her right stocking.

A shoelace twirled around a sweatshirt sleeve. She placed the heap on the porch swing and tugged. A gust teetered a glove. She caught it mid-air.

Thud. Both shoes toppled onto the porch.

Evah jerked toward the cottage's pitch-black windows. She didn't see movement or hear barking. Her cold fingers fumbled with the laces. Once untangled, she smoothed her hair back into a ponytail and secured it with an elastic hair band she'd slipped from her wrist. She zipped the sweatshirt, then slid her fingers into soft leather gloves.

Stars illuminated the sky. When mama brought her here to visit Uncle Regan so many years ago, they must have stayed for days. But she was little then. She didn't remember the stars or the mountains. Or Jane.

Whenever she noticed stars in Mankato, they were never sharp and clear, like now. The industrial park created a smoke screen of sorts.

The break of day would arrive soon, but not yet. The heavenly lights reminded her of Abraham. *Thank you, Cassie, for reintroducing me to the Bible last Christmas.* To think that Abraham had been promised as many descendants as stars in the sky. Well, she would be one star.

"Oh." A shooting star streaked across the sky, leaving a trail of lingering light. After a few moments, it disappeared. Evah stared in awe.

She crossed the C-shaped drive that led toward the barn. Brisk air mingled with fragrant dew-covered fields, putting Miss Corrine's Spa to shame.

At the two adjoining sixteen-foot square doors, she grasped a handle with both hands and tugged sideways. An immense door rolled open and released the sweet aroma of hay.

She inhaled a deep breath.

Thank you, God. You know what I love.

Her hand touched her bulging back pocket and she waited for the sneeze that didn't come.

She stepped inside and flipped on the light. Chicken pens. "Yuck."

She would earn her keep, as Jane insisted. She clenched her teeth and attacked the matted-down straw with a straight-edged shovel. After today, Jane could do her own chores.

The clucking and chattering Rhode Island Reds fascinated her, their red combs bobbing when they darted out of her path. Jane's acquaintance, Simeon, had shared feeding and cleaning instructions with Evah despite her lack of enthusiasm.

The clang of steel on concrete echoed within the barn. Over and over, she scraped the shavings and tossed them into a waist-high garbage can. Her shoulders and left bicep burned, but she tightened her grip on the shovel. There was no getting around what needed to be done, even if it hurt. She could take a couple Ibuprofen when she returned to the house.

The mixture of repulsive shavings and eye-watering ammonia burned her nose and made her cough. She flung clean cedar shavings across the floor and resisted the urge to use her puffer. Carrying it with her was habit. Maybe she was outgrowing her allergies after all these years.

"That smells better."

The chickens' dark reddish-brown feathers contrasted their red-orange eyes. She reached into the nesting boxes.

"Wow, three eggs. And here are two more. Thank you, ladies." She cradled three brown eggs against her midsection and grasped the remaining two. Facing the chickens, she pushed the pen door open with her back, stepped out, and closed it with her elbow.

"What nonsense is this, talking to chickens?"

Evah whirled to face Jane's scowl. An egg slipped through her gloved fingers and shattered on the concrete floor.

"Thought you had the chores under control," Jane smirked.

"They were under control."

"I see."

"You startled me and . . ." *Don't accuse.* "I've broken an egg."

"We have lots of eggs. Chores need to be done and done right. I told you."

Evah fought to keep silent. *Use the tongue to praise, not curse.*

Excited barks bounded as Cash rushed into the barn. His long, sturdy foot-high stature waggled from nose to docked tail.

"Hey, Cash." She petted the tri-colored corgi.

"Get that egg cleaned up quick, before he gets it." Jane tossed a rag to her.

"I will." Evah set the eggs between stacks of feed bags before scooping up the slimy mess and dropping it into the trash container an arm's length away.

"Eeuw." She turned toward the dog, with her hand outstretched.

"Watch out, the eggs are rolling."

Evah jumped. A second egg splattered onto the concrete. She caught the third egg midair.

Cash yipped and leapt.

Jane pushed him onto his haunches. "Stay." He wiggled but stayed.

Evah retrieved the used rag and hurried to clean her second mess. "Sorry."

"Sorry doesn't cut it. How did you expect eggs to sit there? They were bound to roll off." She pointed. "Use those cartons on the bench for unwashed eggs. Keeps them from breaking."

"If you knew they were going to roll off, why didn't you say something?"

Cash bounded toward her. Evah ran her fingers along his foxlike face and under his chin.

"You don't have the discipline to listen to details." Jane stood, hands on her hips. Her olive sweater bulged over green military pants. "Why would a city woman like you care?"

"City woman?"

"Mankato is a city, isn't it?"

"I don't live in the inner city. And I work, but I've never done ranch chores. Simeon gave me pointers, but if you want things done a different way, please tell me."

"I'm telling you now. Don't put eggs there or else they'll roll off." Her mouth twitched. "And don't forget our appointment with the attorney tomorrow."

"At one o'—"

Jane's black boot tapped the floor.

"Sorry. Thirteen hundred hours. You've reminded me twice. I didn't know attorneys worked on Saturdays."

"He made an exception."

"I'm glad he did. And just so you know, I don't plan on doing chores after tomorrow."

"Is that right?"

"I'm hoping."

"And where will you stay after tomorrow?"

"What do you care, as long as it's not here?" The words froze between them. Evah regretted her tone. "I'll manage."

Jane wiped her nose with a tissue. "It isn't your place to be here. You haven't a clue as to what you're doing."

"It appears that the lawyer thinks it *is* my place to be here. I'm Regan McCormick's niece. And I have been doing chores for almost a week now, as you told me to do." She glanced at the wet floor.

"Cleaning chicken pens isn't doing chores. And you've done a mighty good job of not tending to the alpacas."

"I've fed them every day. And I've remembered to close and lock every gate behind me, going in or out. Close and lock the gates, close and lock the gates." Evah thumped her palm against the wood pen frame. "I'm not stupid."

"Maybe not, but you're human. So, don't forget."

"You insist that I do chores. I don't have to, but I'm doing them. What's your complaint?"

"People don't learn chores overnight. You learn from someone. You practice. You become efficient."

"How difficult can it be?" Evah stood up and moved a stack of egg cartons. "In this time, I've become somewhat efficient."

"That's what you think. You need to clean better. Use that." Jane pointed to a tall, plastic bottle containing amber liquid.

Evah picked up the bottle and knelt down on the concrete. She reached for a clean rag. "Like I said, if you tell me how to do things, I'll do them as you want. Simeon helps you with chores sometimes. Do you want me to ask him to come tomorrow?"

"Why should I pay him? You're free."

"Until tomorrow."

"Hmph." Jane looked to be standing at attention, as tall as her five-feet-three-inch frame would allow. "I know what needs doing. I've been here for thirty-six years. You don't know anything. You didn't even know the McCormicks, your own blood."

"That's not *my* fault and I'm not here by choice. I shouldn't have to stay until the estate is settled. God willing, I'll be able to leave tomorrow." Evah sprayed the egg residue with cleaner and scrubbed, angry for speaking in such a tone. "I'll be gone as soon as I can."

"God willing." Jane's stare chilled the air. "I'll give you directions for other chores. Come in for breakfast when you're done." She strode from the barn, ordering "Cash, fall in."

Would it kill the woman to utter a kind word? And "fall in"? Would a dog know what that meant?

Help me, Jesus. I feel like Jane's prisoner of war.

Cash cocked his head to one side. He didn't move.

Evah petted her new friend.

A sinking feeling told her that she might regret having harsh words with Jane. Fifteen minutes later, she scuffed back to the house, Cash at her heels. The smell of eggs and toast greeted her, but a single plate embellished the table.

"Jane, I'm here. Where are you?"

Cash's nails clicked on the tile and quieted on the living room carpet.

The clock ticked.

Evah washed her hands and sat at the table. She bowed her head. "Dear Lord, thank you for today. I don't know what it will bring, but I'm grateful to have this new experience, for now." She paused. "And please show me your will. Amen."

Bright blue note paper next to the phone caught her attention. She walked to it. Jane's handwriting scribbled, "Attorney cancelled. Will reschedule."

Evah groaned aloud.

Three quick, bold knocks sounded on the front door. Evah listened for Jane's presence.

Cash bounded across the room, barking and spinning in circles near the door. Where had he disappeared to and then reappeared so fast?

Knocks sounded again. Evah crossed the living room.

~~~

Nolan listened to yips coming from behind Regan McCormick's door. He frisked his pocket for a dog treat and stepped back, anticipating a high-energy reunion with the "big dog on short legs".

He scanned the snow-capped mountain backdrop. In mid-June, the frosts would come to an end.

The bakery box crinkled beneath his grip. Delivering baked goods nurtured public relations. Being late defeated the purpose. And now a complaint. Leave it to Jane to dredge up a story about an undesirable houseguest. If Evah was the person in question, he wasn't taking stock in any civil dispute.

He knocked again. Barking escalated.

City Manager Edwin Riser's insinuations bothered him. He prided himself in serving the whole community. Riser knew that. If Jane had an intrusive houseguest, she should've reported it to his department. He strived to be proactive, not reactive. It didn't sit well with the City Manager and it gnawed at his own conscience.

And if it was Evah—

Creek. The door opened enough for a slender brunette wearing jeans and a long-sleeved tee shirt to sardine herself in the opening. Mid- to late-20s. Pretty.

He smiled. Her eyes reflected recognition. He could read her so well. "Evah Rois."

"Police Chief Nolan Quinn." Her smile dulled beneath a tentative gaze. "I wondered if or when I would see you. But you look—is something wrong?"

Was *she* reading *him*?

A blast of barks sounded. She whirled. "Cash, be quiet." The barking continued. She turned back to Nolan. "What were you saying?"

He returned the treat to his pocket and extended his right hand. "It's great to see you again. I brought a little something for Jane . . . and her visitor." He flashed a smile.

She shook his hand. "Thank you for remembering my name. I'm the visitor."

Her smile generated an electric pulse to his heart.

"It's great to see you." He held out the box and lowered his voice. "I'm sorry about your uncle's death. After your phone call, I wasn't sure if you would come."

"As you can see, I'm here." She took the box from his outstretched hands while gripping the storm door. She stretched to set it somewhere and turned back to face him.

"Get back, Cash."

Jane said Regan had no living relatives.

His memory flashed to Evah wearing her baking cap and stylish ensemble. How different she looked now, in jeans and tee-shirt— and a diamond-studded watch and bold earrings. And the frown she wore while squinting at his CHIEF badge. She snugged the door closer.

What was wrong? His senses went on alert.

"Is Jane here?" He stood firm instead of leaning against the porch pillar.

"She was earlier, but she didn't answer the door just now. Do you need to see her?" She pushed invisible hair off her forehead and checked out his police sport utility vehicle.

"No. If I need her, I'll find her. You're the person I need."

"I am?" Worry crossed her pale blue eyes. Eyes the color of his summer uniform shirt.

"I'm looking for a blue Toyota rented in Bozeman." He motioned to a car parked beside the barn. "Is that yours?"

"It's my rental car. Why?"

"I knew you didn't own the truck." He smiled and pointed to a green relic decaying at the far side of the barn.

She ignored his smile. "What about the car?"

He handed papers to her. "It is about to be towed. It was a one-day rental, which you have exceeded."

"What? That's crazy. It was an open-ended lease, for a week maximum." The papers crinkled in her grip. "They've made a mistake."

He checked out a passing vehicle. "The tow truck is on its way. That court order was initiated by your rental agency." He removed his hat and smoothed yesterday's haircut. "It seems that they need it back right away."

"I won't have any transportation. They can't just take it, can they?"

"It's their car. Maybe you can call them and make other arrangements."

"I'll call right now. Please don't take this car."

This isn't the Evah that I remember. "You can call, but even if there's been some mistake—"

"Oh, they have." She pulled her phone from her back pocket. "I'll straighten this out. Let me find the number."

"It doesn't work that way. The court approved and ordered the repo. Your car will be towed whether you reach them or not. It can't be released without court approval. They've been trying to reach you."

"I haven't received any calls." She looked at her cell phone.

"Could be bad reception. That happens in the mountains."

"That doesn't help. Listen, I rented the car for a week max. It's been rented for four days." Evah punched buttons on her phone.

Nolan's head shot up. How had they initiated legal action so fast? How could she be so beautiful, even angry?

His welcome had backfired. A dead uncle, a wacky housekeeper, and a towed rental car.

Nolan watched her slender fingers cradle her phone. "There's more. The City Manager requested that I follow up on a complaint."

"About me?"

Nolan nodded.

"What have I done?" She blushed. "I'm Regan McCormick's niece. I was requested to be here, a provision of his will. You know that, kind of."

Nolan wanted to bang their heads together, Jane and the City Manager. Repos evoked anger, but not the depth of sadness in her eyes.

"Excuse me." She walked away, phone to her ear. She returned moments later. "I got through. The person is waiting on someone. They'll return my call."

"I'm sorry about the complaint," Nolan sympathized. "Some people are suspicious-minded." *Or manipulative, like Jane.* "If you'll give me a few minutes, I'll finish this inquiry and be gone. I need to see your driver's license and registration."

"Do you have a search warrant?"

"No. I'm following protocol. You have the right to refuse—"

"Refuse what?"

Nolan looked into her eyes until she looked away. "How about you get your driver's license while I'm running your registration? We'll finish faster. The City Manager, my boss, requested this. It's nothing personal." He cringed. How cliché.

"It is personal. And not very hospitable from the City Manager." Her stockinged foot tapped impatiently. "So, Jane complained?"

"I'm not at liberty to divulge the complainant's identity. The person asked to remain anonymous."

"It's obvious, isn't it? And I even told her that I didn't want to be here."

Nolan's heart plunged.

"The attorney requested my presence. The bakery where I work, in Mankato, is in trouble. Carolyn is under pressure to sell. If she does, we'll be out of—" She stopped. "Sorry."

Nolan handed her his business card. "I'm being honest, Evah. That's what I know."

"She blew out a breath and glanced at the card. "I'm used to Minnesota cops. I'll get my shoes and keys."

Used to Minnesota cops?

Evah closed the interior door to within inches. Cash's barking escalated. "Sit down and behave," she ordered.

Nolan suppressed a smile.

Moments later, keys jangled. She stepped out and descended the steps. Sharp yips exploded from behind the closed door.

"Do you have a leash?"

"Maybe in the house, but I don't want Jane to get fired up."

They crunched across gravel and onto the grassy field. "I don't remember Uncle Regan having a dog. I like animals, or maybe just the thought."

Nolan inhaled her light citrus scent. Jane had obstructed justice, withheld information. What would Riser say?

"Did you know my uncle? Or Aunt Marilyn?"

"I met your uncle a few times. I'm sorry about his death. I didn't know him well, but he always shared stories about his llamas."

"Alpacas. He has, had, three."

"Yes, alpacas. Thanks. They are curious looking creatures."

"They are. I don't know quite what to think of them yet."

Standing next to the blue rental, Evah dug into her jeans pocket. She handed over the driver's license and rummaged in the glove compartment. She emerged with the registration and handed it to him. "I didn't think our next meeting would be like this."

Nolan didn't know what to say.

She continued, "I'm going to check messages."

"I'll be back in a few minutes. Please wait here."

She looked away, but not before he observed anguish in her eyes. He recognized pain and sadness that came from somewhere deep. There was something else, too.

He opened his SUV door, slid onto the seat, and pushed the mic button. "Chief to dispatch."

Evah. Beautiful. Professional. Compassionate.

Regan's niece.

He turned toward the back seat and petted his black and white border collie. "Almost done, Honey."

Radio static sounded. "Dispatch here, Chief." He recognized Patrolman Chuck Seamor's baritone.

"Chuck, I'm Code 6 at 2901 Straight Street. Running numbers on the license that I called in."

Nolan plugged information into his laptop, keeping an eye on the young woman near the alpacas. She leaned against a fencepost, the phone to her ear.

Attractive. Very.

But different than in Mankato. The voice in his head sounded a private alarm. Something was wrong.

He finished the record and background checks. Evah Marie Rois. Age twenty-nine. Mankato address. No outstanding warrants or records, not even a parking ticket. Yet, in his gut, there was something. He felt it. Maybe not on paper, but just as real.

He opened the door and watched her slide her phone into her pocket. She coaxed a tiger-striped cat closer.

He returned her driver's license and registration. "Any luck?"

"No."

"Do you plan to stay long?"

"That depends, doesn't it? Without a car, I have no choice." She pulled a strand of hair from her face. "I'm sorry. I know this isn't your fault. I have an appointment tomorrow with an attorney. I need permission to leave. It's not what I thought it would be."

"I'm sorry for that. These car issues are never a quick fix. Bumper Edwards, the repo guy, should be here any minute."

"Bumper, the repo guy? That's his name?"

"Yes."

Despite her anger, the edges of her mouth curved upward. "And you know him?"

"It's a small town."

"Can you ask him to leave the car here?" Her pleading eyes melted his defense.

"Not possible. The court order would need to be reversed."

"This complicates everything." Exasperation heightened her tone.

"Does it affect your return flight?" He hoped not.

"My ticket is open-ended."

"Why not stay a while? Get to know the area and the people."

She frowned and look up at the mountains.

Talk about something else.

"It looks like you're making a friend." Nolan motioned to the cat. "I need to ask you a few questions. How long have you been here?"

"Almost a week."

"When was the last time you saw or spoke with your uncle?"

She bent down and stroked the cat that was walking circle-eights around her ankles. "I was eight years old, so twenty-one years ago."

"You had no contact with him in all those years?"

"No." Her ponytail swung.

"Who contacted you before, or after, he died?"

Evah jerked her hand from the cat. "Nobody contacted me. The lawyer mailed a letter, remember?"

Nolan's collar felt tight. "Why were you requested to stay here until . . . what, the completion of probate?"

"I don't know yet."

"So, the document that you received—"

"I am so ready to be done with this court stuff." Her ponytail swung again. "Do you need a copy of the letter?"

"No. I'm sorry. I didn't want our meeting to be like this."

"Me either."

"How are you getting along with Jane?"

"What?"

"I wondered how you are getting along with Jane. She can be a bit abrasive."

"Abrasive. That's what you call it?" Long dark strands swished and again Nolan smelled citrus. What was it with that ponytail? He caught himself staring.

"Abrasive is as good a word as any." He walked with Evah, aware that she hadn't answered. "Your uncle's corgi quieted down."

"I read that Pembroke corgis are barkers."

"Exercise might settle him down. Did Jane tell you about Sunrise Crik Trail?" At her blank look, he continued. "It's a new trail a half mile down the road." He pointed across the street, to the east.

"What's a crik?"

"It's smaller than a creek. This time of year, most are full from melted snow."

"Oh." Her face warmed. "Is the trail dog friendly?"

"Yes, it's people friendly, too." He filled with optimism, wanting her to like the small town he served. "As a matter of fact, that's where I'm heading with Honey, my border collie."

"You have your dog in the police car?" She peered into his vehicle.

"I thought we'd stretch our legs after this call." *I'm talking too much.* "Thanks for your time. You should take advantage of the trail. I'll check on the repo."

He opened the door and slid onto the seat. Why had Jane complained to Riser? And why hadn't she been contacted by her relatives for so many years?

Evah Rois. A gorgeous mess.

A loud roar and sputter drew his attention. The cumbersome tow truck's long yellow boom creaked and bounced. Bumper waved.

Why would a car be towed that had just been rented?

CHAPTER SIX

S itting cross-legged on the bed, Evah picked up her ringing phone. A call at this hour from Carolyn's Bakery usually meant a crisis.

She hit the green button. "Hello?"

"Evah? It's Carolyn. I hoped you would answer."

"I'm glad your call went through. Reception is hit-and-miss here."

"I received a letter from the Mankato Planning Commission. They're holding a meeting next week at city hall. Get this. My bakery is within a larger piece of property that some developer, Bemka Enterprises, wants for a shopping mall complex. It looks like there are a few homes around the corner that they want, too. I'm in the middle of it."

"That's not good. At the meeting, will you be able to defend the bakery? They can't force you out, can they?"

"I don't know. Even if they would offer to buy me out, I have no desire to sell. I've worked hard and have a good customer base right where I am. I wish you were here," her voice cracked. "I never saw this coming. That's one reason why I wanted my own business, so I could be free from interference like this."

"Don't make any hasty decisions. I'll be back soon and will help."

"I appreciate that, but I'm the owner. I'll let you know what goes down at the meeting."

"How are the repairs coming along?"

"I'm hoping to reopen in two weeks. They're almost finished painting the back room."

Evah's heart felt heavy. "I wish I could help you. You know—"

"Yes, I do. But I don't want you to rush back. I need you, but you have to get things settled there."

"I appreciate that. I just had a thought. Will you take a picture of your correspondence from City Hall and send it to me?"

"Sure, but why?"

"It will help my bruised ego, that's all." She forced an optimistic tone.

"I'll send it later. I've got to get to the bakery right now. I'm trying to work around the restoration crew."

After saying their good-byes, Evah's mind raced. Could Carolyn be forced to sell? And what about everyone's jobs?

She headed downstairs. A note lay on the kitchen table. "Pick up alpaca food this morning." Jane included the vet's name but not the address. Evah punched the name into her phone and the address popped up.

Realization dawned. "You've got to be kidding." She had no car, yet Jane expected her to pick up alpaca food.

Keys dangled from the wooden key rack. She hesitated at the oversized R, lifted it and its vehicle key off the hook, and walked outside.

The old, rusty pickup truck looked as though it hadn't moved in ages. Would it run? All she could do was try. She slid onto the seat and bowed her head. *Lord, am I supposed to use this truck?*

She turned the key. Nothing.

She left the key turned, hit the radio button, and walked to the front of the truck. On the third yank, the hood creaked open. She checked the battery posts and cables. Still nothing. Come on! She removed a shoe and struck it over and over against the battery.

"Burning ring of fire . . ." Johnny Cash's bass-baritone filled the air. The truck rumbled and groaned.

She slammed the hood shut. It wouldn't close. She tried again. A little better. She hurried back to her seat and coaxed the engine to stabilize.

Her phone chimed. She picked it up but fumbled between screens. How could it have gone into voice mail so fast?

She hit "play message."

"This is attorney Angeli. I rescheduled your meeting to week after next. At that time, I will give a thorough accounting of the probate process. There are no exceptions to the provisions of a will. You will be subject to legal ramifications if you do not remain on the property as requested. Expect three or four months, total."

Three or four months? No way!

"It is to your benefit since, as I understand, you are unemployed. It takes time to allow creditors to file claims and—"

Evah hit the red button and drove. Cassie told her to stay positive. Cassie had never been to Woodridge, Montana.

Her phone signaled another missed call. Give me a break!

Cassie. She hit play. "Cassie here. Big surprise. I've been released from the hospital. Betsy drove me to the airport. Get this, girl. I'm on my way to you!" She laughed a weak laugh. "I'm under doctor's orders. I'll be there later today. I'm between flights."

Stunned, Evah punched the off button. Cassie was flying to Montana?

Smelling of gas, the truck growled, chugged, and sputtered down the road. She grabbed a blanket from the passenger side floor and shook it. A stiff, dirty top. Uncle Regan's? She threw it onto the floor and turned on the heater. Nothing. She clicked the switch off and on. Nothing.

"Could there be anything else?"

~~~

Nolan's chest brushed the underside of the grimy truck. His flashlight illuminated rust and debris. He kept his mouth closed in the event of dirt falling and stretched his arm upward and to the left, groping. Rough gravel scraped his back.

"Any luck, chief?" Don Simpson called from above. "I've gotta get to work. What am I going to tell them at the plant?"

"Tell them you couldn't drive your vehicle without endangering the life of an animal."

"That won't carry much weight."

"I'll vouch for you."

"That would help, but when? I need to get going."

"Okay." Nolan slid out from beneath the truck, its red color almost concealed by thick grunge. "We can't move your truck. Give me your keys. I'll have Stick drive you to work."

He turned to two men watching from The Coffee Pot's parking lot. "Hey Stick, will you drive Don to the paper plant? Tell them I'll stop by to explain."

"Sure thing." Stick stepped forward, coffee in hand. "Come on, Don."

Nolan called, "Stop at the Woodridge Animal Center and ask for a half cup of cat food."

"Okay, Chief."

A faint meow sounded from within the Chevy. Why couldn't the stowaway be behind the radiator grill or someplace he could reach? He'd already lost forty-five minutes of much needed office time.

Stick's vehicle backed out of the parking lot and headed down the street.

"Well, what have we here? Our tax dollars hard at work?" Curtis Bayfield, dressed in business attire, spoke while approaching. His new co-worker, Ayako Bertram, accompanied him in a floral dress. Curtis smirked. "I didn't realize auto repair consummated our police chief's repertoire."

She shot a disapproving look at Curtis and turned to Nolan. "It looks like you've been working under less than desirable conditions, Chief."

Nolan brushed loose debris from his grease-stained uniform and wondered for the umpteenth time why a beautiful lady like Ayako would associate, let alone work, with a bitter character like Curtis Bayfield.

"A kitten found its way into a truck. We'll get it out, but it's taking patience and ingenuity."

"Oh yeah, engine-uity," Curtis snickered. Chin in the air, he added, "If you're still here at noon, I'll request an oil change. Oh, and I hope you find a decent replacement for the cop that was shot. It's hard to find good help in such an insignificant location."

Nolan fought the urge to grab the guy by the collar and throw him in Don's truck bed. He watched them disappear into The Coffee Pot.

A cup of hot brew would taste good, but wouldn't sooth an insult like that. Luke Young didn't deserve it and neither did the department. He glanced at his watch. Eight-fifteen and already a long morning.

If he didn't want flak from others, he needed to step up the pace. His hands were dirty, knuckles bruised, and grease stained his dark blue uniform shirt. Good thing the department hadn't yet changed to summer's light blue shirt.

Riser expected to meet him at ten o'clock. He needed to find the kitten, shower, and change before then.

Stick approached. "I dropped Don off and then stopped at the vet's office. Got some grub for the cat." He flashed a crooked grin. "I met someone there. She's coming to help."

Nolan shot him a look.

"Hope you don't mind, Chief." His eyes glistened. "A real looker. I told her where to find me, us."

Stick fell for one lady after another. The interest was never mutual.

Nolan opened the container of kibble and jiggled it. "Come and eat, little one."

A faint thrum pounded in his head. He hadn't slept well and a busy day loomed ahead. He set the food beneath the engine. He needed coffee.

tuckaTHUCKtuckaTHUCKtuckaTHUCK.

Everyone turned at the sound of an approaching vehicle. A battered green truck came into view, old and dirty.

Stick waved. "She's here."

The truck squealed to a halt and Nolan glimpsed the driver. Then he shook his head and wondered what to tell Stick.

The door opened and closed with a creaky thud.

"Good morning, Chief."

Her voice sent his pulse racing. "Miss Rois."

She wore a tee-shirt, jeans, and leather gloves. Where was a sweatshirt or jacket?

"It's a mere 45 degrees, in case you weren't aware." His voice hinted at both scolding and teasing. A four-inch square bandage covered her right upper arm. She'd been wearing long sleeves yesterday and he hadn't seen it.

"Minnesotans are tough." She motioned to Stick. "This guy— Stick, is it—said help was needed to rescue a cat. He didn't mention a public scene."

Stick twisted his cap in his hands and looked at Nolan. "You two know each other? She's new here and I thought . . ." He turned to Evah. "I thought with you being new, I took the liberty to ask . . ."

"That's enough Stick." Nolan cut in and faced Evah. "I'm working on the cat situation. Your help really isn't needed."

His face reddened. That hadn't come out right. He didn't want her in this cold, dirty mess.

~~~

Evah turned and marched back to Regan's truck. How dare he insult her like that.

Did Nolan realize what he had said? Was he so chauvinistic that a woman couldn't help?

Heat coursed through her veins. She grabbed her gloves off the seat, pulled them on, and marched back toward the crowd.

"Where have you looked" She met Nolan's solid gaze.

"The cat is lodged underneath Don Simpson's truck. Somewhere around the engine, I think. Uh, I didn't mean that to sound so . . ."

Evah ignored his apology. She'd heard it before. She would slide under another bucket of bolts. The pavement would be cold and wet.

She pulled off her cap and plopped it onto the hood.

Nolan's shoulder brushed hers. Even covered with grime, he attracted her.

"Wait a second, I'll get you something," he offered.

In one smooth movement, Evah dropped to the ground and rolled onto her back. She pushed with her heels until she was under the chassis.

No sissies allowed.

In her memory, she saw long, thin tails dashing around the engine. Her head shot upward, cracking her forehead against hard steel. "Ouch." She punched the underside of the truck with her palm.

"What's wrong? Are you okay?"

"I'm fine." Perspiration trickled down her temple. "Give me a minute."

"You didn't let me tell you where to look."

"I know where to look. Just give me a minute!"

After all these years, I'm stuck here again.

"Where are you, baby?" Her voice shook. "Come out. Let me help you."

She groped the familiar places and shook off the memory. There. A fuzzy tail? She scooted further under the skid plate and tried to reach it, but it pulled away. Moments later, a head peeked around the edge of the skid plate.

"I see it." Her heart thumped. She reached forward and wrapped her gloved hand around soft fur. The kitten, small and helpless, meowed.

"I have it." She slid out from beneath the truck and grinned up at Nolan, Stick, and a small crowd. Nolan reached for her gloved hand and helped her up. Everyone cheered.

Nolan's eyes glistened. A pleasant feeling embraced her. She looked down at the black-and-white kitten, hoping Nolan didn't notice the blush she felt warming her cheeks.

He took the kitten from her and, after a quick look, placed it on the seat of his SUV. When the crowd thinned, he turned to her.

"Montana is colder than Minnesota. Are you frozen?"

Without waiting for her answer, he reached into his truck, retrieved a plaid blanket, and placed it across her shoulders. "I'll take the cat to the vet's office. Then I've got to get to a meeting. I'll make sure the cat's okay and see if anyone reported it missing."

"It's young." Evah shivered and pulled the blanket tight. "Its owner may not even know about it, if the mom roams wild."

"You did a great job. Do you need your forehead checked? You have a nasty scratch."

"No." She lifted her cap off the truck's hood. "I'm fine."

"What happened? How did you know where to look?"

"Luck, that's all."

"No, you knew. And you're driving Regan's ancient truck. Who started it?"

She looked down. He noticed too much. Her throat felt parched. "I did. I know some things about motors and stuff."

"You?" He looked at her incredulously. "For real?"

"Yes, me, for real."

His expression held questions.

"Please don't ask."

CHAPTER SEVEN

Evah watched Jane lift a gas can to the Zero Turn Mower. If she coaxed Jane into a decent mood, maybe she wouldn't fuss over unexpected company.

Cassie didn't know anything about Jane. It was going to come as a shock to her that they would return to Minnesota so soon.

"Can I help?" She approached Jane. "I didn't think the lawn was tall enough to cut."

"It's the first cut of the season. More to clean it up than anything. Get out the dead grass." Jane tightened the gas cap. "You wouldn't want to ride this. It takes practice."

"Can I try, riding it? I won't mow unless you say so."

"Have you ever driven one of these?"

"No."

Jane's forehead wrinkled like an amused bloodhound. "All right but listen close. This is a zero-turn radius lawn mower. The wheels turn independently."

"Meaning?"

"One side can turn forward while the other side turns backward, in reverse. You can spin or turn in place without moving."

Jane pointed out levers for the blades, throttle, and choke. "Don't move any of these."

"Okay." Evah lowered a hand to the shift handle.

"Not so fast. Cross the field in front of the barn and alpaca pens. Get used to steering and turning. Go around trees. Figure it out.

"When you pull back on the control arms, you're going to go backwards. If you push forward, you go forward. To turn left, push on the right and ease back on the left. To turn right, push on the left and ease back on the right."

"Push right to turn left?"

"Yes. Take a good hold of the control arms and keep them steady. Then, real slow, pull back on the control handles to move backwards."

"I've got it."

"If you move too fast, let go of the control arms. The mower will go back to neutral and you'll stop."

Evah started the engine, released the brake, and pulled back on the control arms.

The machine crept backwards. She then moved forward and, after a dizzying circular rotation, she bumped across the field. An immediate thrill raced through her.

She maneuvered around trees, careful to avoid their jagged above-ground roots. After a number of passes, Jane waved her over and showed her how to engage the mower. The cutting blade hummed and Evah rolled forward.

She looked up at the snow-topped mountains and wondered when the snow would disappear. The mower jerked over a bump. She tightened her grip on the control arms. Focus.

"This is great." The bumping motions lessened and Evah mowed in front of the barn and then, with great care, along the edge of the alpaca pens.

Who knew that operating a zero-turn mower rivaled a carnival ride? She mowed behind the shed and ventured into the backyard. Jane looked up from a stack of flower pots near the barn and, for once, Evah didn't mind.

A car pulled into the driveway. Bold lettering on the door announced TAXI. Evah's heart skipped a beat. A window rolled down and Cassie's grinning face appeared.

Evah let go of the control arm and waved. Then she pushed forward. The mower sped toward the driveway. She glanced at Jane, still working with the flower pots.

The car stopped.

Evah scooted past a flower bed and turned toward the tall, slim figure standing in the gravel driveway. A stack of luggage lay on the ground. Cassie handed the driver what Evah assumed to be taxi fare. As abruptly as it had appeared, the taxi left.

Evah pushed both control arms and darted next to a large tree sprouting rust colored buds. She pushed forward with the left control arm to turn left. The machine turned right. *Thunk!*

Evah's neck whipped back. She let go of the control arms and the mower sat motionless. Her vision spun.

A few moments later, her equilibrium returned. She reached for the control arms and moved away from the tree. Forcing a smile, she bumped her way past Cassie and into the garage. She turned the key and the engine sputtered to silence.

"You're here!" She ran to her friend and gave her a gentle hug. A dark wrap immobilized Cassie's arm or shoulder, securing it near her body.

"Seventy-five dollars for a taxi!" Cassie laughed. "I didn't expect to go sightseeing, but it came with the trip. What a view. These mountains are unbelievable."

"What's going on?" Jane approached. "What's all the hollering? I knew you'd crash."

Jane stood, feet apart, dressed in camouflage top and fatigues and black boots.

Evah forced a smile. "Jane, we have company. My good friend, Cassie, flew into—"

"Bozeman." Cassie interrupted. "Then I rented a taxi to get here. The drive was another thirty minutes."

"She flew in from Minnesota." Evah couldn't hide her excitement.

"This isn't a motel." Jane stood in front of Cassie and looked her up and down. She made no attempt to hide her displeasure but gazed at Cassie's injury. "What happened to you?"

Evah stepped forward. "Cassie's just out of the hospital. She was stabbed."

A look of horror crossed Jane's face. "What? You were attacked?"

Cassie's expression sobered.

Evah opened her mouth to speak, but closed it when Jane reached out and turned Cassie toward the house.

"You need to be off your feet, miss. Knife wounds are nothing to fool with. I'll set you up in the room next to Evah."

~~~

Sitting in his office chair, Nolan answered his phone. "Chief here."

"Decker here from Bozeman. I have news."

"What did you find?" Nolan stood.

"A possible match. A patrol car called in an abandoned Chevy Silverado. It was under a cover of trees north on Green Valley Way, about two miles southeast of Green Mountain. It's way up. A couple of four-wheelers came across it and called it in."

"Any blood or prints?"

"No blood. We're still searching for prints. It was wiped down. We did find a slug in the passenger's door. I'm betting it will match Patrolman Young's gun."

"Is the truck still on site?"

"Yes. I thought you might want to see it before it's impounded."

"I appreciate that. I'll expect a text with the exact location. I should be there in thirty minutes."

"It'll take you longer than that."

CHAPTER EIGHT

Evah's bulging travel bag leaned against the headboard. At two a.m., it had become clear. She and Cassie would return to Mankato. Cassie needed to be somewhere stable and Evah should be helping Carolyn. If the bakery closed, they would be searching for jobs.

Would there be repercussions over leaving during probate? Probably.

Evah padded along the hall and downstairs into the kitchen. She passed Cassie's closed door, glad that her friend was settled in the guest bedroom.

A plastic cup with matching lid and straw sat on the counter. Jane pampering Cassie seemed so out of character.

Cassie's physical condition dictated an early bedtime. Evah understood, but felt disappointed that they hadn't had time to talk.

Evah walked outside and crossed the porch. The sweet smell of grass and sounds of chirping birds made her smile. She tilted her face toward the immense mountains. If not for the probate turmoil and Jane, it would be peaceful here.

A chill ran down her frame. If she were home, she would be working through her five-thirty run, not heading out to shovel manure. God must have a sense of humor after all.

Maybe Jane did, too. After Evah's outburst, an oversized American flag magnet appeared on the refrigerator door, securing a ridiculous list of chores.

Evah pulled on her sweatshirt, cap, and gloves. She disliked waiting. Waiting to talk to Cassie. Waiting for the appointment. Waiting to see Nolan.

A mournful howl silenced the birds.

Her heart pounded.

She raced to the regular-size barn door, unlatched it, and yanked it open. It slammed shut at the same time she found the overhead light switch. She rushed from window to window, imagining wolf eyes, but she didn't see anything. After a half-dozen trips to and from each window, she stood still.

Why am I always afraid? She bowed her head. *Psalm 118 something, The Lord is with me; I will not be afraid.*

"Thank you, Lord." She turned her back to the window and tried to ignore her thudding heart.

At the rabbit cages, she opened the first wire door. "Are you waiting for breakfast?" The caramel and white lop-eared rabbit wriggled its nose. She scooped pellets into the feeder. "Pew, this food smells like dried spinach."

She ran her fingers through the soft fur and returned it to its cage. Next, she lifted out a black and white bunny. What fun it would be to have a pet like this.

She returned the bunny to its cage and pulled on her plastic gloves. *Remember day two.* Jane's neighbor, Simeon, showed her how to slide the drawer out from beneath the cages and dispose of its contents. She had gagged repeatedly.

Holding her breath, she dumped the urine-soaked pellets into a plastic waste bin.

"Argh."

The hair-raising howl replayed in her mind. She tried to steady her trembling hands and pushed the barn door open with her back. When she turned around, her heart rejoiced at dawn's sunshine illuminating the mountain tops.

She cranked the frigid water faucet and grimaced. Toxic waste dripped from the drawer and ice water splattered on her already-ruined sweatshirt. Eeuw.

She washed away the waste and, holding the drawer as far away as possible, she ran inside and slid the drawer on the rack.

Holding her arms out at her sides, she rushed back outside and wriggled her gloved fingers to shake off the debris.

Jail time would be better than cleaning rabbit hutches. Almost.

She followed Simeon's example and spread loose hay on the bottom of each cage. Then she filled the water dispensers and turned to the chicken pens.

Trying not to breath, again, she dumped soiled shavings into a barrel.

"Breakfast is almost ready. You coming?" Jane's crisp invitation cut through the quiet.

The front door wasn't open far enough to see Jane. "I'll be right there." Evah rushed to the grain bin and scooped pellets for each alpaca.

"It's ready, now."

"I'll be there in a minute." The fragrance of molasses cookies lost its appeal. Evah balanced the bowls while unlatching the interior barn door. She stepped into the holding pen and the alpacas jostled for position. As she poured pellets, they hummed and snorted. She dropped armfuls of fresh hay into the pens.

Simeon Pratt deserved a thank you note. He had showed her how to feed Uncle Regan's alpacas and told her their names.

Marcos, the light fawn-colored male watched Evah's moves with big brown eyes. And, unlike Princess Peachy and Cocoa Lady, she could pet his neck.

They reminded Evah of the llamas she had seen at the Sibley Park Zoo in Mankato. Had there been alpacas, too? These animals were smaller than llamas, like deer with ostrich-like necks and soft fiber that Simeon compared to cashmere. He said they were sheared once a year and some were worth a quite a bit of money. She would check that out when Jane wasn't stealing glances at her laptop screen.

Good thing I was researching rental cars and not military eccentricities.

Evah latched the holding pen door, picked up the carton, pushed the barn door closed, and turned toward the house.

Splat!

An object ricocheted off the barn next to her. Evah fell to her knees and crouched low. Shards of yellow plastic and chunks of white foam filled the air.

Bang! Splat!

Jane laughed from near the tractor.

Evah's mind flashbacked to punching fists and baseball bats. "Jane, it's me. What are you doing?

"You said you were ready."

Another plastic egg, this one bright pink, bounced off the barn and settled in the grass a few yards from Evah. Another egg flew and popped. And another.

"Jane, stop." Evah turned away from a hissing sound just as it exploded. Bits of white foam filled the air and covered the ground.

Evah crept around stacks of hay bales, toward where she had seen green camouflage. Reaching around the corner, she poked Jane's back. "Are you off your rocker?"

Jane sprung up, revealing a bucket half-full of plastic eggs. Camouflage paint streaks covered her face.

"Are you trying to scare me or convince me that you're crazy? Jane, you are, *" things that come out of a person's mouth come from the heart and defile them,* ". . . outflanked."

Heart pounding and knees shaking, Evah hastened into the garage. She set the egg carton on a table and pulled off her work shoes, cap, and gloves. She ran up the stairs as fast as her legs would allow. Her hands trembled, but she lifted her Bible off the end table and sat on the bed. Tears threatened. She bowed her head.

God, why does she hate me so much? Did Uncle Regan and Aunt Marilyn know what a terrible kid I was? Is that why they didn't want me?

She opened her Bible's thin, delicate pages. Psalms again. "They are brought to their knees and fall, but we rise up and stand firm."

She steepled her hands in front of her face. Was Jane full of hate or was she mentally unstable?

"Evah, is that you?" Cassie called.

She caressed the smooth, thin pages as she closed the book. "Yes."

"Jane came in a while ago. Said you were doing chores. Is that true? Have you lost your mind?"

"You have no idea." She walked to her friend's door and pushed it open.

Cassie's bright smile greeted her from atop a mountain of colorful pillows. A vase of fresh flowers graced the nightstand, along with a cup of coffee.

"I'm impressed with Jane's amazing hospitality."

~~~

Nolan parked his sport utility vehicle on the inclining shoulder. Tall evergreen trees surrounded him, blocking the sun. The place felt ominous.

Yellow blockade tape secured the perimeter. He ducked under it and approached the officer standing near the Park County pickup truck. Large gold letters announced SHERIFF across the dual cab doors.

"Chief Quinn?" The officer looked up.

"Yes," The men shook hands.

Nolan scanned the area. "I got here as fast as I could, but I underestimated the distance. Did your squad desert you?"

"I'm low on the seniority list. I am Deputy Sheriff Brian Redding, sir."

"Glad to meet you, Redding. Where's the suspect vehicle?"

"Back here."

Nolan followed him to an enormous pile of evergreen branches piled next to a scratched and dented white Silverado.

"These branches covered the truck. They hid it from view, even from overhead."

"With all this cover, they didn't have to hide much. But then again, the truck is white. I see tire marks there." Nolan pointed. "Did you get imprints?"

"The team did. It looks like the getaway vehicle was stashed under the same branches they used to hide this truck. There are some fresh branch cuts. The patrol is knocking on doors, but there aren't many people up here. If it was concealed well, it might've gone unnoticed."

"Registration?"

"It's reported stolen from Great Falls two months ago. We're checking possible connections."

"That's three hours away. If we can tie the owner into the drug-runner operation, it could be a good lead. We can't let anything fall through the cracks. What evidence do you have on the getaway vehicle, if this was it?"

"Just the tire imprints."

Nolan surveyed the area, crunching brittle grass and green sprouts alike. Other than the stack of evergreen branches, half on and half off the white truck, it didn't look like anyone had been there.

He walked between evergreen trees and crossed ground strewn with broken limbs, probably remnants of last month's wind storm. He ducked under the perimeter tape and into taller grass.

Some fifteen yards further, he spotted a distinct paw print. Perhaps a mountain lion from the size of its M-shaped pad. Stooping, he sized it next to his open hand. Must be three inches across.

He stood and turned to circle back. Something glistened in the sunlight. He pushed aside a stand of tall grass, exposing a set of worn false teeth. He pulled a plastic bag from his pocket and picked them up. This was a first for his career.

"Redding! Call your squad back here. They have more searching to do."

He crouched down. Prickles of disbelief chilled his senses.

A jagged piece of dark green cloth waved in the breeze, secured beneath fallen branches. The edge flapped, faded and dirty. A dark stain covered one corner.

CHAPTER NINE

E vah closed Cassie's bedroom door, crossed the room to the robin's egg blue vanity, and dropped onto its stool.

Cassie tried to sit up. "What's wrong?"

"I wanted to talk to you last night. We can't stay here. It's Jane."

"What do you mean?"

"It sounds so . . . not nice."

"Then don't say it."

"I have to."

"Have to or want to?"

"Have to. You need to know. She is crazy."

"That is a terrible thing to say."

"It's true."

"You're exaggerating."

"Listen to me." Evah explained what had transpired since her arrival.

Cassie looked stunned. "Those are intense accusations. And now your car is gone?"

"Gone."

"Well now." Cassie cleared her throat. "First off, you can't run from here. This is your uncle's ranch."

"We should both run."

"You can't. You're Regan McCormick's heir."

"I'm not."

"Who else? He won't leave this place to Jane—his housekeeper. You are his niece."

"It can't make sense to you, but he didn't want anything to do with me. He wrote me off years ago."

"Then why are you here?" The pillow crinkled under Cassie's head. "Let's take it one day at a time. No hasty decisions. I'll talk to Jane."

"Good luck there."

"She's treated me great compared to you." Cassie ran her free hand along her bandaged arm. "And, I have to ask. Who is this weekend warrior that we call Jane?"

"The housekeeper. That's all I know. What's a weekend warrior?"

"It's someone who does something when they have time, like a hobby."

"That doesn't fit. She's 24/7. Cassie, what if we aren't safe? We have no car. You need to get better. The one thing drivable here, and not even, is that old pickup truck. It's unreliable."

"Then you need to find a mechanic. That's our Beamer."

"You're asking a lot. And what about Jane? What if she's dangerous? Who's going to stand up to her?"

"You are."

~~~

Evah returned to her bedroom. She wouldn't run. Not yet. If Jane was trying to scare her into leaving, there must be a good reason.

Cassie said Jane wouldn't respect her until she stood up to her. How she could pull that off? The woman terrified her.

She finger-combed long strands of hair while staring at her Bible. What could she do?

She crossed her bedroom and past Cassie's closed door, and headed downstairs.

Jane stood near the kitchen's back door. She had replaced the camouflage face paint with blush. "You still here?"

"Where else would I be?" Evah's knees shook.

Jane pulled a black Army sweatshirt over her head. Her nails matched the lipstick and blush. "I'll be back in a few hours."

Just like that, everything was supposed to be normal?

Evah swallowed, her throat dry. "I thought we were having breakfast."

"That was an hour ago." Jane motioned to a plate of dark-crusted biscuits next to a small bowl of something unrecognizable.

"I see. What did you make?" Evah couldn't stop her nose from wrinkling.

"Do you have a problem with my cooking?"

"There's a bowl of mystery goo sitting here. What is it?"

"It's Army food," Jane's voice sharpened. "And, if it's good enough for the U.S. Army, it's good enough for you."

"Well, that explains the . . . metal dishes?" Evah picked up a stainless-steel bowl. "And what about Cassie?"

"She's your guest, not mine." Jane stuck her chin out. "If this is not to your liking, you can scrounge elsewhere. Or, if you think you can do better . . ."

"You would be surprised."

"I would like to see you try. I am not often impressed." Jane's boots clomped across the linoleum.

"I noticed."

"Don't be smart."

"It's true. You don't notice anything I do."

"You don't measure up. And I'm not assigned K.P. duty for you and your friend. Pitch in."

K.P. duty?

Evah swallowed. *Be not afraid.* The song's melody calmed her thoughts. "Well . . ."

"Well, what?" Jane adjusted a sponge roller dangling over her right eye.

Be brave. Say it.

"I will pitch in, but you called me for breakfast. I thought we were going to eat together." She looked into Jane's harsh gaze. "So, now we're not having breakfast and you're leaving?"

An amused smile appeared on Jane's face. "Unlike you, I have a schedule to keep. I have to do my route. I'll be back later." Jane turned to leave.

"Jane?" Evah's voice rose.

Jane whirled, her eyebrows pulled together, "What now?"

"You have a new hairstyle, I see. It's nice, but you missed one roller in your hair."

"Thanks. I'll pull it out when I get there." Her face transformed into a smug smile and she patted the roller. "It's a new style. I used the round brush first, like the magazine said. Then I used a little spray from the silver bottle. So, after I take out the rollers, my hair should be downright glamorous!" She turned and laughed all the way down the steps.

Glamorous? Was Jane attempting humor?

Would a doctor give Jane's medical information to a non-family member? No. What if she was forgetting to take medications?

Evah pulled her smartphone from her pocket, dropped onto a kitchen chair, and hit Carolyn's number.

Breakfast, shmeckfast.

"Hey there," Carolyn's cheerful tone tugged at Evah's heart. "Are you settled in?"

"No. So, what's the scoop?"

"About the fire, they say that the investigation is still pending. About the municipal meeting, I've been researching. There was a zoning request for part of this property a few years ago. It was approved, but it didn't change anything."

"Keep researching. You might find something important. I can send you some links to—"

"I'm doing okay, Evah. I've got a friend helping me research a bit while we're getting the bakery together."

"Who is that?"

"Just a friend. Listen, I have to go. Thanks for calling."

"I do miss the place. And everyone. Almost everyone." Evah pulled a piece of hay from her jeans. "If you hear anything about the fire, please let me know."

"I will, but people aren't saying much. Oh, Evah, you should see the new pumps I bought over the weekend." Her tone changed to light and carefree. "Leather t-straps with studs and my favorite shade of pink."

What is she talking about? She isn't into fashion like that.

"And you know they were on sale." She laughed, a tight, false sound.

"Sounds great, Carolyn. So, will you let me know if you hear anything? I have a couple of questions."

"I wish you could see my pumps." Her words came fast, falling over each other. "I'll send you a shot of my shoes. Watch for it. Too bad you're so far away. There's a new outlet next to The Golden Bolt. I can't talk right now."

Why was she babbling? She hadn't even asked about Cassie. "Okay.

It's great to talk."

Evah stared at her phone. What had just happened?

A photo came through on her phone. She clicked into the message.

Avoid the shoes. The price is too high.

Evah's mind whirled. Her hands trembled.

After an hour of emotional battle, Evah decided not to say anything to Cassie. She was supposed to be recuperating, after all.

Breakfast for Cassie. She had forgotten.

A generous portion of angel food cake sat on top of the refrigerator. She sliced it into cubes. At least there was no shortage of eggs. She broke them into a dish and marveled at the bright yellow yolks. She added spices and whisked the liquid. The scent of cinnamon and nutmeg tickled her nose.

Why had Carolyn . . . she . . . not now.

Butter sizzled in the cast iron skillet. Minutes later, she delivered breakfast to Cassie. The expression on her friend's face reflected hurt and disappointment, but Evah was in no mood for chit-chat.

She marched outside and gazed at the shrubs bordering the house. Shoots towered one above another. She studied the weathered mailbox post. Either project would show quick results.

She could tug at the shrubs without the precision of painting. She walked into the garage, hunting for scissors. Nothing. Back in the house, she rifled through drawers. Frustrated, she headed to the tool shed.

She muscled the door until it screeched open. Paint-stained cotton gloves sat atop boxes of rusty or broken tools. She shook them and peered inside before pulling them on. She wiggled her fingers. No holes.

Cobwebs gave her goose bumps. She snugged the cap on her head and proceeded to grab item after item. At last, she spotted wooden handles and pulled out ancient rusted shears. The blades stuck together.

Frustrated, she exited the shed and blinked in disbelief.

A tan truck pulling a long silver trailer sat next to the alpaca pens. A man wearing a western hat and a smaller person moved around the trailer—right on Uncle Regan's property. Evah tossed the shears onto the ground and walked forward.

They were trespassing. If they had gone to the house, Cassie would've phoned.

Warm adrenaline accompanied her rapid pulse. They stood in an empty pen, next to where Uncle Regan's three alpacas jumped and skittered.

"Hey there," she yelled, brushing herself off as she walked. "Can I help you?"

Neither responded.

Are they trying to steal Uncle Regan's alpacas?

Walking fast, she removed her gloves and stuck them in her back pocket. A plastic rake leaned against the fence. She grabbed it and squinted at the license plate. Colorado.

"Can I help you? Hello there," she called from five feet away.

A man hopped down from the trailer step and turned toward her. "That's what we're counting on." He flashed a wide smile and Evah didn't like the way he scanned her from head to toe. "Can you tell me where we can find . . ." He unfolded a paper against his thigh while smoothing creases, "a Mrs. Eve Rose?"

"My name is Ev-uh. Evah Rois. But, I'm not the person you're looking for. What's the address?"

"We've got the right address. Where do you want your animals?" He turned toward the truck. Heavy steel creaked.

"Just one minute." She stepped closer. "I don't live here. I'm visiting. Nobody here ordered any animals."

"Regan McCormick placed this order."

"He couldn't have. My Uncle Regan died three weeks ago."

"Oh. Well, I'm sorry about that." He and the boy exchanged a brief look and the man shook his head. "I've got paperwork telling me to make delivery to you. The directions read that I'm to contact a . . ." he held up the paper and squinted, "a Mr. Simeon Pratt, if you weren't here. But you are here, so we're good."

"No, we're not good. I don't know anything about this. Can we talk to Mr. Pratt?"

"No ma'am. He's the contact if you're not here. You are. The animals were purchased in your name."

"What do you mean?"

"It says right here." He tapped the paper with a gloved finger, "The alpacas are the property of Mrs. Eve, er, Evah Rose."

"Rois. And I'm a miss, not a missus. And I don't live here."

"Well, that's odd, being that you're here."

"It's quite by chance."

The man faced her. Evah stared at the largest belt buckle she had ever seen. Silver, decorated with a bucking horse and stars. Shiny lettering, "Colorado . . . something".

He put his gloved hands on his hips. The teenage boy moved behind him.

"Ma'am. This deal is not reversible. We just drove these alpacas from Colorado Springs and I'm unloading them. Now."

"You're delivering alpacas?"

"What did you think we were bringing? Bucking broncos?" He laughed and rocked back on the heels of his cowboy boots. The teenage boy laughed, too.

He rubbed his chin. "This here is an alpaca ranch and we're delivering your alpacas."

Evah's heart pounded. What could she do? Where was Jane? She didn't know what would become of the three alpacas that Uncle Regan had left. Now there would be more.

The man disappeared into the silver trailer and reappeared, leading two stunning alpacas. The freckled faced boy behind him had two more on leads. Evah watched, mesmerized. They repeated the process until ten alpacas wearing neck ribbons and silver identification tags had been unloaded. Ten more alpacas. Dark brown, fawn, white, black. Beautiful.

Ca-whomp! The trailer door slammed. Evah jumped.

"Are you all right, ma'am?" The boy asked over clanking chains.

Evah's face burned. She couldn't think.

The man thrust a paper in front of her, along with a pen. "Sign here."

"I don't think I—"

"Sign right now," he bellowed.

She scribbled her name. "I don't understand."

"Look, lady, I'm not the seller. The contact information is on the form, along with the contract guarantee and medical provisions." He handed her the yellow copy. "It amazes me, you city folk buying livestock. You don't know the first thing about anything."

He sounded like Jane. Was she that obvious? She looked at the plastic rake in her hand. Minutes later, the truck and trailer maneuvered out the circle drive and disappeared down the road.

Uncle Regan's three alpacas pranced about, as did ten new animals in the adjoining pen. Her alpacas.

How would she find them all homes? Jane would blow her top like an arctic blast.

Uncle Regan had purchased ten alpacas in her name. Why, after twenty-one years? He couldn't have known that she would ever come to his ranch. She hadn't known it herself.

She grabbed the cell phone from her pocket and dialed 9-1-1.

~~~

Nolan lifted a water bottle from his passenger seat.

"Dispatch to Chief," Murray's voice beckoned.

"Chief here."

"Keith Strickland from St. Paul wants you to call. And, Chief, the Deputy Sheriffs think they're going to crack our case."

"That's not going to happen."

CHAPTER TEN

Wearing a black half-zip training top and jogging pants, Nolan closed the back door of his sport utility vehicle and watched Honey settle onto the seat. He slid in behind the wheel and picked up his radio. "Chief to dispatch."

"Dispatch here, Chief." Murray's high-pitched voice contradicted his burly frame.

"I'll be at the new trail. I called Keith Strickland from home and am going to take a walk."

"Okay, Chief. Got your dog with you?"

"Yes."

"Enjoy your date. Ten-four."

He pulled onto Rock Street and crossed Main. Cars near Ellen's Café reminded him of his craving for flapjacks and syrup. Her 24/7 breakfast policy was a favorite with the guys. Maybe today was his day.

Two blocks later, he headed west on East Lincoln. The road ran adjacent to an immense grassy meadow surrounding Sunrise Crik Trail. ETA less than fifteen minutes.

"All units," sounded on his radio. County dispatch, not city. "Priority two at 2901 Straight Street."

Straight Street? Split jurisdiction. He pushed the button on his mic. "Dispatch from Chief Quinn."

"Dispatch here."

"I am three or four minutes from 2901 Straight Street. Reconfirming address."

"Address confirmed."

Nolan pulled up his computer aided dispatch and scanned the screen. 9-1-1. Caller Evah Rois. Why was his heart pounding?

He parked and exited the vehicle.

Peripheral vision caught movement to the left. The barn door burst open and Evah dashed toward him. Beads of perspiration dotted her forehead and her breathing puffed out in rapid, shallow bursts.

"I'm so glad you're here."

His stomach knotted. He didn't detect any bruises on her, other than the large square bandage on her arm.

"You called 9-1-1?"

"Yes. You need to stop a truck that just left. Hurry. They'll get too far and you won't find them. It's a tan truck pulling a big silver trailer. You won't believe what just happened."

"Okay, slow down and tell me."

Evah relayed the events. The rig wouldn't be difficult to locate. Nolan excused himself to phone dispatch. No need for emergency responders.

Not slowing between breaths, her tone rose and fell like musical notes. "And I had no choice but to sign the receipt. He slapped it in front of my face."

The thought alarmed him and excited him at the same time. "Ten alpacas? That's quite a gift."

"It isn't a gift. We're not talking about a cat or dog. These are alpacas. It's like being given horses or cows."

He wasn't going to argue the point. Not now. A gift from a dead uncle was one for the books.

And she had called 9-1-1. This was not a 9-1-1 emergency, but he didn't dare offend her further, not in her present state of mind.

"You signed a receipt?" He spoke in a soft, confident tone.

"Yes."

"That might not have been the best thing to do if you want to contest delivery."

"I'm not contesting delivery. They're here. But the driver flung the form at me and demanded that I sign it. It happened so fast. What I should've done is write on his receipt that I refuse delivery. Then they would've had to take them back."

A vision of Evah begging Regan's dog to behave flashed across his mind. "No, what you did was wise. In a situation like this . . . were you here by yourself?"

"I am capable of taking care of myself."

"It would've been unwise to put yourself in danger. You were dealing with someone, or in this case, two men that you didn't know."

"A man and a boy, a teenager."

Thank you, God, that she wasn't hurt.

Her index finger tapped her cheek. "I wish I hadn't signed it.

"If your uncle legitimately purchased them for you, they are yours to keep or sell." He looked into her eyes. "I don't want to be out of line, but you might consider keeping them. They're valuable."

"Shall I take them back to Mankato with me?" She snapped. "What I want from you is to get that truck back here."

Her tone stung.

"Were you able to get the make or model of the truck? Color? License plate number?"

"It was a tan Dodge Ram 3500. Colorado plate. I didn't get the number. There was too much happening." She turned toward him. "I'm not a ditzy city girl."

"I can see you're as intelligent as you are pretty. You have the receipt. The alpacas are yours."

Maybe he shouldn't have said that.

"I don't expect you to understand, but I expect your protection. Doesn't that include helping me?"

"Okay. Let me see what I can find out. I'll get a picture of this receipt and contact them."

"The truck drivers or the company?"

"The company."

"You're not going to let the truck keep going, back to Colorado?"

"I have no reason to detain them. They made a delivery. You signed for it. It's legal."

Evah punched the air. "You've got to be kidding. I panicked and signed. I'm getting burned, again."

Again?

The situation was too fresh. Receiving an expensive gift could not be considered getting burned. Maybe it was dealing with her uncle's death that she couldn't handle.

Evah raised her hands, palms up. "What do you suggest I do? I can't return them by FedEx, now can I?"

Nolan worked hard not to smile. *Lord, she's amazing when her eyes flash.* He cleared his throat. "No, that wouldn't be possible."

"I should have known better than to call the police. It never does any good."

Her eyes darted back and forth. Her breaths were fast and she held her stomach. Fight or flight.

"You've had quite a day. This gift from your uncle, you didn't expect it?"

"No."

"The animals are amazing. Beautiful."

She didn't answer.

"I hope you consider the possibilities before you do anything."

"My life is full of possibilities," she snapped. "Like the possibility that Carolyn's Bakery will be forced out and we'll all be unemployed."

Her look told him to mind his own business. He had overstepped his boundaries.

"I'm sorry to hear that. I'd best be going." He tipped his hat. "I'll let you know what I learn."

He clicked pictures of the receipt and warranty before returning to his vehicle. A quick call to dispatch initiated the inquiry process. Murray reported that Strickland had phoned again, requesting Nolan to call.

"Time for a walk, Honey." Falling temperatures and an opportunity to check out Sunrise Crik Trail might clear his thoughts.

He started the car and watched Evah, hands on hips, studying the animals. Or maybe she was thinking of something else and not looking at them. He needed to talk to Jane.

People expected police to fix everything, even personal problems. Evah's uncle posthumously bequeathed alpacas, which he guessed to be worth a chunk of money. Alpacas. How could she be so sure she didn't want them?

He took one last glance at the gorgeous lady staring at her alpacas and turned the vehicle around. What had Regan McCormick been thinking?

He glanced up in time to see someone move from an upstairs window.

~~~

Evah stared at the fluffy deerlike creatures munching on pasture grass. There's no doubt they were beautiful. And no doubt valuable. But they were another thing that she would have to deal with.

What had Uncle Regan thought she would do with them? And what were the chances that she would ever have known about them?

The money from the alpacas would help her financially, but how would she go about selling ten alpacas?

She sighed and stuck her hands into her jeans' pockets.

CHAPTER ELEVEN

Evah returned the puffer to her pink leather bag. "This place reeks. I can't wait to get outdoors. The scenery between Woodridge and here looked like a continuous calendar page. I'd like to look around a bit."

Jane wore black loafers, a black skirt, and an Army-green blazer. But she'd ignored Evah's suggestion to back brush her hair.

Evah crossed her arms and listened to the attorney ramble into his cell phone. Twenty-five minutes. Unprofessional. His salmon shirt looked slept in and the way he twirled his eyeglasses, Evah sat ready to duck.

"We'll meet at the courthouse prior to Wednesday's hearing," he continued.

Jane stood up and tapped her watch. "We've waited long enough. Hang up."

Evah smiled to herself. For once, Jane's irritation wasn't directed at her.

He looked at Jane and lip-synced, "I'm done." He spoke into his phone. "I must cut this short."

Evah coughed again. Between the dust and his atrocious cologne, her nose hadn't stopped tingling since she walked in.

Jane's composure softened, but the file folder in her hands bore creases. "If you don't feel up to this, I can brief you later."

"I want to stay."

Cheap lamps on rickety furniture made her tentative. Was Nicholas Angeli a legitimate attorney? She eyed the crooked frame displaying a certificate.

He placed the phone on his desk. "Sorry for the interruption folks, but I am very busy."

"You've made that obvious," Jane spouted. "I'm busy, too. You rescheduled our appointment. We didn't."

"But I fit you in earlier than I thought possible." He looked pleased with himself.

"That's fine, but we're here and you aren't."

He raised his eyebrows.

Jane struck the file on her knee. "We don't have all day."

Angeli licked his lips and nodded, his finger scanning a legal tablet. "I do understand and I apologize. Now, let's see. You inquired about the next course of action for this probate matter."

He clicked his pen. "I would say the next task should be a thorough inventory of all household items."

"Is that something I can do?" Jane gripped her armrests.

"Yes. An itemized list of assets is necessary to make sure there is adequate value to cover Mr. McCormick's debts."

"I'll write up the itemized inventory list," Jane declared. "What else?"

Evah's face warmed.

Nicholas Angeli smiled at Jane, showing glistening white teeth below a thin moustache. "I've found from previous experience that knowledgeable parties of interest, such as yourself, excel at inventorying outdoor items, like equipment and tools. Persons not familiar with such assets would have difficulty."

He stole a glance at Evah. "Perhaps the young miss would be more comfortable inventorying items inside the household. If you both agree, that is."

Evah waited for Jane's biting response.

Angeli scribbled on a tablet. "Sharing the inventory would be efficient. If you both work on your own area, it could be completed post haste." He looked from one woman to the other. "What do you say?"

Jane pulled her shoulders back. "Sounds as efficient as a left-handed monkey wrench, but we'll do it."

"Fine, fine." He nodded.

"Aah-choo!" Evah sneezed again. "Excuse me. Yes, I would like to help with the inventory process. What do you mean by 'finding value to cover McCormick's debts'? How much does, did, Uncle Regan owe?"

Jane shot Evah a sharp look.

Evah continued, "Does the amount of debt determine the length of the process?"

Jane spat, "That does not concern you."

Evah looked at Angeli. "I would like to know."

"How much money will be left for you?" Jane blurted.

"No." Evah gasped.

Jane didn't blink.

"A list of debts will be compiled after notice is given," Mr. Angeli responded.

"Meaning?" Jane interrupted.

"We advertise, giving a specific time period for people to file claims if the deceased owed them money. Now, concerning the inventory, everything needs to be recorded and appraised. Animals, machinery, everything."

"Appraised? Ah-choo!" Evah clamped the tissue over her mouth.

"Yes. Understanding the value of your uncle's estate is critical to knowing where you stand. And it will help me determine the feasibility of you selling select items one-by-one or auctioning everything." He looked up from his writing and directed his comments to Evah. "When Ja—Miss Martin—came to my office, she indicated that you wanted everything taken care of as soon as possible, so you could leave."

Evah tried to conceal her surprise. They had already met, without her.

Angeli smoothed his greasy, flat hair. "And then there is the matter of the llamas."

"They're alpacas." Evah corrected.

"It should be quite simple to ascertain the value of the animals. When Mr. McCormick purchased the llamas—"

"Alpacas." He's not listening.

"Yes, yes. The animals should be registered with an organization. You indicated they were quite valuable." He looked at Jane.

Jane shot Evah a mind-your-own-business look.

"Excuse me," he sounded irritated. "Don't you agree?"

Evah shook her head. "I'm sorry. What did you say?"

"That the animals are valuable," Jane hissed.

"Maybe. I just received the ten—"

"I know they're valuable." Jane reached in her folder, retrieved a piece of paper, and handed it to him. "I printed this off the Alpaca Owners Association website. It gives a lot of good information. And here are some links to breeders with alpacas for sale. The asking prices give an idea of value. Prices vary with breeding."

Since when had Jane become a walking encyclopedia?

"I would like a copy of that." Evah leaned forward. "Since ten alpacas are mine, I need to register them in my name."

"Why put them in your name? I'm going to sell them and use the money." Jane's cold look stifled her response. "You don't want them. You just want to leave."

"It sounds like you don't want them either," Evah argued.

The attorney looked from one to the other. "I'll make sure everyone has a copy."

Did Jane realize the amount of information they were giving to this stranger? They didn't know him. Or she didn't. Jane said that his business card had been left in their door. Now it turns out that he and Jane had already met. What was going on?

Angeli continued. "Registered animals are like vehicles. You must register it in your name to have authority for a sale to transpire."

Evah's head hummed with the onset of a headache. "Mr. Angeli, is there anything I can do to speed up this process? I am interested, as Jane knows, in leaving as soon as possible. I am not interested in the ranch, the real estate."

"There is one thing." He shared a look with Jane. "You could waive your right to inherit the ranch."

Evah hesitated. Why not?

"I'll do it."

Jane clasped her hands in front of her, leaned back in her chair, and nodded.

Angeli continued, "This waiver applies to any and all inheritance that you would receive. Do you want to waive your right to everything or just the ranch itself, the real estate? What about personal belongings? Is there anything that you might want?"

Jane shot him a warning look.

No, she didn't want anything. But, what if—

"What if I find something personal? Maybe something that belonged to my mother? We'll be conducting the inventory."

"You can specify a waiver of real estate only."

"That's what I would like to do, in case I find a few mementoes. I'll waive the real estate only."

"I will draw up the paperwork. Watch for it in the mail. You'll need to sign it and date it. Your signature must be notarized. You can accomplish that in Woodridge to avoid another trip here."

"How long will it take?"

He jotted notes on his tablet. "A week or two. After you sign the Waiver of Inheritance, it will be presented to the Probate Judge for authorization."

Weeks were better than months.

Jane headed to her vehicle to do errands. Evah walked along the main street, feeling like she had stepped into a western movie set. The breeze blowing off the mountains whipped a few loose strands of hair from her bun and thrashed them against her face. The air smelled fresh and clean.

She stepped up into the truck, shoved the city map into her pocket, and turned onto Yellowstone Street.

With the window rolled down, the breeze whistled in her ears. She parked and walked across Sacajawea Park. Memorialized in bronze, the famous woman held her toddler son while on horseback. She remembered it from a tourist magazine. Why did seeing it in person give her such a sense of awe?

She sat on a bench overlooking the view. How could Jane be so mean? She couldn't imagine Cassie and herself remaining in the house much longer.

Jane didn't get it.

Evah just wanted to go home. She hadn't heard from Carolyn. What would become of the bakery? How could Carolyn fight big business and did she really want to take that on? If her friend decided not to reopen, Evah would need to get job hunting. She'd worked hard to put money away. She didn't intend to use it up.

Uncle Regan hadn't contacted her after mama died. Strangers took Evah to the first group home. And now he was gone and she was back at his ranch. How ironic that Jane wanted her gone, too.

Lord, is there a purpose in this? Tears trickled down her cheeks. She pushed her hands into her purse, searching for a tissue.

"Look, Daddy. Boo-boo, boo-boo."

Evah gasped and looked sideways into the face of a young girl with arms latched around her father's neck. Her dark curls bounced and blew in the breeze. When he juggled the child to reach into his jeans pocket, she clutched a handful of his shirt in her chubby fist.

"Boo-boo, daddy. Boo-boo." Her large brown eyes studied Evah.

"Yes, Precious, the lady has a boo-boo." He handed her a fistful of Mickey Mouse tissues. He nodded. "I'm Jonathan Green. This is my daughter, Gemma. I call her Precious."

"Thank you." Evah took them from his outstretched hand. "How embarrassing. I'm Evah Rois."

Similar to his daughter, the stranger's hair formed a dark, shoulder-length cascade. He wore a headband and his dark eyes peered out from behind tinted glasses. He smiled between the dark moustache and goatee.

"We all have moments." He shifted the toddler's weight and smoothed her blowing hair. "Are you okay?"

Aware of his deep, calm voice, Evah felt flustered. "Yes, yes. I just lost control for a minute. I'm fine." She wiped her eyes and tucked the tissues into her pocket.

"Job papa, job?" The toddler squirmed in his arms and pressed her face against his.

"Hush, Precious."

"Job, papa?"

"No, Precious." He rubbed the girl's back and rocked her. "Not today."

Classified ads stuck out of a large cloth bag draped over his shoulder.

"Are you job hunting?"

"No. A job isn't my problem. I have a good one."

"Oh, I'm sorry. I thought . . ."

"It's all right. You wouldn't know. I don't need a job. I need community service."

"Oh." Evah scrambled to grasp what he had just said. "Are there parameters for what kind of community service you need?"

"Ordinary. Sixty days' worth." He removed his glasses and looked toward the moving water. "They had a job lined up for me at the courthouse. It fell through. And every local business I've approached has refused to help me."

"I hope they come up with more opportunities for you."

"I thought if I tried to find something, face to face, that I might speed things up. It seems that my fiasco—breaking and entering with the intent to steal—ticked off a prominent family."

Evah hoped she didn't look shocked. Breaking and entering? Had he just admitted to it?

He juggled Precious in his arms. "I'm not from Livingston. My wife and I moved here six years ago, to Woodridge actually." He rocked his daughter, his eyes dark with emotion. "And regardless of whether I did or did not do what they say, they're not going to let me find community service around here."

"What will you do?"

"Try to find placement in the outlying towns. It will be hard to juggle with day care."

"Can't your wife help?"

"She died last year. Leukemia." He turned toward Evah. "I've taken up enough of your time. I'm glad you're okay, but we'll be on our way."

He turned and headed toward town. Evah's heart melted at the sight of his daughter's face tucked against his shoulder. He neared a line of parked cars.

"Wait." She called, hurrying after them.

He whirled, a puzzled look on his face.

Self-conscious of her ragged breathing, she held up an index finger. "Just a minute." She rummaged in her purse and pulled out a tablet. Evah scribbled on the top page, tore it off, and handed it to him. "If you don't find anything, have someone from community service call me. You're welcome to work on my uncle's ranch. He's, uh, gone now. It's in Woodridge. We can use the help, if you don't mind that kind of work. And if it's acceptable."

Standing next to Uncle Regan's old truck, Evah recognized his gratitude. She had been there.

Gravel crunched and a familiar police vehicle pulled into the parking lot. Evah watched Nolan's handsome form step from the still running vehicle. His gaze settled on Jonathan.

"Good morning, Miss Rois," he said while watching Jonathan.

"Chief."

"Sorry to interrupt your conversation. You look familiar. Do I know you?"

"I'm sure you do, Chief, and I was just leaving." Jonathan Green, still shouldering his daughter, turned and walked away.

Nolan turned to Evah. "I received a phone call that concerns you. Seeing you here saved me a trip to the ranch."

"You just happened to find me here at the park?"

"No. I happened to see you leaving the attorney's office."

"Isn't Livingston out of your jurisdiction?" Evah tried to keep her tone light.

"The Park County Courthouse is here. I met with the Sheriff."

"Did you talk about the alpaca delivery people?"

"No, I had other business. But Bosco reported in and relayed that your uncle's death is being investigated."

"For what? He's buried."

"Yes, he is. But an autopsy had been requested prior to the burial. There are questions surrounding his cause of death and you are a suspect, the only suspect. For the record, I'm advising you not to leave Park County."

~~~

Nolan watched Evah stare after the familiar man. Once in a while, when she didn't think he was watching, she let her guard down.

The attorney had requested that she make the trip from Minnesota. Was that the only reason she was here?

He had no reason to suspect she was lying about anything, but signs of conflict crossed her expression, darkening her eyes and causing her to bite her bottom lip.

Like now.

CHAPTER TWELVE

E vah watched Jonathan Green disappear behind the parked cars. Then she turned to face Nolan.

"I don't know why Uncle Regan's death is suspicious. And after twenty-one years of silence, I don't care."

"There's more to it than that."

"No, there isn't. I couldn't have been in two places at once, could I?"

"Why not?"

His half-smile became wide and crooked. She smiled, too. Why did he have to be so good looking? And a police chief?

She studied the majestic mountains, now dark beneath a front of incoming clouds.

"This is standard procedure. That's all." Nolan removed his hat, revealing short dark hair, buzzed on the sides but a little longer on top.

"I'm glad to hear that because, as you can see," she pointed at the green truck, "I am not planning a getaway."

"I'm impressed you've been driving it." His eyes shown with . . . admiration?

Her heart did a mysterious flutter.

"It's been sitting by the barn forever. I assumed it was junk." Nolan looked startled. "Sorry. That was rude."

"I understand and, for the most part, I agree."

"Anyway, you need to remain in the County."

I'll be wearing an ankle bracelet next.

"Did you ever get to the trail?" His eyes glanced at something above her.

"No."

"Do you want a walking tour? I'm off at five. I'm taking Honey. You could bring your uncle's dog."

"Cash."

"Yes. I could show you the trail and we could enjoy the getaway, with the dogs." He smiled again.

Evah's cheeks warmed. She flexed her neck from side to side. Dreaming about a Police Chief was out of the question, but a walk sounded good and she could get away from Jane.

Cassie.

"I may have an obligation. I won't know until I get back ho- to the ranch"

"I'll be at the trail a bit after five. If you decide not to come, that's okay. But I would like you to. I'll wait until five-fifteen."

Back in the rumbling truck, Evah drove to the ranch. Inventorying house contents would get the process moving. She hoped that Jane would inventory the barn and equipment and leave her alone.

She found Cassie reading a book and sipping lemonade from her propped position in bed.

"Are you sure you aren't faking it?" Evah chided.

Cassie's soft laugh mirrored the pastel walls. "You've caught on. I found a way to legitimately miss work."

Evah sighed, "Work. I can almost smell the lines of pies, tortes, and cakes. My perfect world."

"Was it, Evah? Do you really miss it so much?"

"I love Carolyn's Bakery. She's hoping to reopen, but I don't know if it's going to happen."

"Has she told you that?"

"Not exactly. But I can sense it."

Cassie laid her head on the pillow. "I always dreamed of living . . . you know . . ."

"No, I don't know. What?"

"Like this, in a small town. People knowing their neighbors, caring. Stuff like that."

"What's come over you? You've been reading too many books. I'm right here with you and I'm not seeing any neighborly caring stuff."

"But you haven't given it—"

"Don't you dare say I haven't given it a chance. Jane rakes me over the coals every chance she gets."

"So, you're basing your whole country experience on Jane?"

"It's not just Jane, although she is off the charts."

"You might be right."

Evah lowered herself onto the blue stool. "I am right, aren't I?"

"It's obvious that she's a bit delusional, trying everything to keep you from wanting to stay here. She can be fierce and uncompassionate, but she's protecting her home, which happens to be Regan's homestead."

"Protecting? She's hostile. And what are you doing, marketing country life? It's me, Evah, remember?"

"I know. But, don't you see? Jane *is* country."

"I don't know what she is. And don't give me that look. You haven't experienced her insanity."

Cassie continued. "You're Regan's heir. You know it and I know it. Jane knows it. That makes you a suspect."

"That's ridiculous. What about Jane, his housekeeper? I could see her doing something off-the-charts."

"Maybe, but Nolan hasn't said anything to us about that. And some people must be wondering at your presence after all these years."

Evah headed downstairs. The aroma of blueberry coffee cake wafting through the house.

In the living room, she approached the large curio cabinet. How odd that Uncle Regan kept the collection of figurines and knick-knacks after Aunt Marilyn died. Had he been sentimental? No, more likely too lazy to get rid of them. By the accumulation of thick dust, they hadn't been touched since her death.

Evah rubbed her tingling nose.

A telephone ring cut the silence. Evah bolted into the kitchen and grabbed the receiver.

"Hello?"

"This is Krista Cox from the Blue Water Motel. Are you the owner of the alpaca ranch on Straight Street?"

"My uncle owned the place. He passed away."

"I'm sorry. This call is inappropriate in light of that news. I apologize for bothering you."

"I'm his niece. Can I help you?"

"Some business owners are creating a tour circle on the south side of town. I wondered if your ranch could be included."

"What's a tour circle?"

"When people stay at local motels, they ask about things to do. I'm highlighting local businesses, with emphasis on smaller places that offer attractions. I'm trying to up consumer awareness and help us all."

"That's a great idea."

"Do you think so?" She sounded surprised.

"Yes, I do. I don't expect to be here for long, so I wouldn't want you to put us on your list. But perhaps when the place sells, the new owner might be interested. That type of advertising opens doors."

"You're selling the ranch?"

"I'm trying. And if someone buys it as something similar to what it is, your idea will be perfect."

"Thanks. I didn't ask your name."

"Evah Rois." She felt the nudge. "I have a friend, a marketing consultant. She might have ideas to share. I could ask her, if you like."

"Would you? Professional help is limited here."

The enthusiasm in Krista's voice made Evah smile. It had been a long time since she heard genuine excitement.

"I would enjoy talking with your friend. Is she there?"

"Umm."

"I'm sorry." Krista back peddled. "I'm too forward. If she could contact me, I would appreciate it."

"I'll ask her."

Cassie might enjoy a marketing project. And if communications were by cell phone or email, no one would have to interact with her, face-to-face.

"Good luck with your efforts to sell. It's too bad you aren't staying. I would've enjoyed getting to know you."

Evah hung up the phone, the words ringing in her ears. Cassie would eat this up.

She retrieved a dust cloth and filled a bucket of warm, soapy water. Back at the curio cabinet, she unlatched the glass door and ran her fingers along the woodwork's intricate carving. The mirror reflected duplicate images.

She reached for the nearest figurine inside the door and wiped the rosy cheeked child. On the legal pad, she recorded M.I. Hummel from the bottom and its ID number.

Something rustled inside the quarter-inch hole in the base of the figurine. Paper. A receipt?

She set the figurine down and rushed to her bedroom and back to the cabinet. Tweezers in hand, she coaxed the curled paper through the opening. How many years had the stiff paper been inside the figurine?

She uncurled a corner. Uneven handwriting read, "Upon my death, this collection becomes the property of my dearest niece, Evah Rois."

"Dearest niece?" Evah touched the delicate message. She unfolded the scroll. The message continued. "Each figure holds a memory. Your loving aunt, Marilyn McCormick."

Loving aunt?

"Cassie," Evah ran upstairs with the figurine clutched in her hand. "Look what I found!"

She burst through Cassie's doorway and stopped in her tracks. Tears streamed down Cassie's cheeks, something that Evah had seldom witnessed.

"What's wrong?" she whispered.

"The Mankato Police Department contacted me. The car from the accident belonged to someone from the Chicago area. I don't know how, but after all this time, he tracked me. I've got to figure out what to do. I'll have to leave as soon as I'm well."

83

Nolan exited his SUV in the Sunrise Crik Trail parking lot. Two county squad cars sat nearby.

He recognized two in brown uniforms—Deputy Sheriffs Bob Grease and Al Witt.

Grease stepped forward, notepad in hand. "Glad you're here, Nolan. Just like old times." His smile resembled a toothpaste commercial.

"Good to see you, Bob. Al. We have a shooter?"

"Correct. Three shots at three-thirty, seventeen minutes ago. Believed to be twenty-two caliber. One shot missed. The other shot injured the walkers' dog." Al shook his head.

The deputy sergeant pushed up on the underside of his broad-brimmed campaign hat.

"Preliminary staging has the shooter near those evergreens in the center of the park." He pointed ahead and to the left. "Cory and Bernadette Jardan weren't injured. They had crossed Knowles Bridge, passing from the Green Trail to the Red Trail. It's thick back there.

"They figured someone was target shooting. But, the second shot struck their three-year-old golden lab. Hit him in a hind leg. They scooped him up and ran. They called 9-1-1 on the way to the vet."

Nolan scanned the terrain. "I'm familiar with the grounds and the trail system. A sniper could've picked them off in the clearing before the parking lot."

Deputy Sheriff Witt continued, "They're lucky they weren't nailed when running on the trail. Jamison met them at the vet's office and called it in. Here are some details."

While Nolan scanned the handwritten notes, two squad cars arrived. In minutes, yellow tape roped off the walking trail. An armed search team spread out to scour the area. Nolan recognized two guys from martial arts class.

"Thanks." Nolan returned the paper. "With a hundred acres of cover, the shooter could be holed-up, hard to find, or long gone."

Nolan made calls from his SUV. The City Manager would be livid. His campaign promoted a crime-free community. A shooter would set off a wave of panic.

The timing couldn't be worse. Scaring the public before the grand opening would be disastrous, to the trail and his career.

It was going to be a long night.

CHAPTER THIRTEEN

E vah snapped Cash's leash onto his collar and dropped dog treats into her pocket. The corgi's body waggled with excitement.

She leaned on the oak newel post and called up to Cassie. "Are you sure you don't mind? I won't be gone long, an hour max."

"Just go. Enjoy yourself."

"I'm taking the dog for a walk, a little exercise. Nothing more."

"Exercising your eyes." Cassie's cheerfulness sounded forced. "I know."

"What do you know, Cassandra Ballard?"

A string of labored coughs echoed down the stairs. Evah's heart plummeted.

"Are you okay?" She rushed upstairs. "I should stay here."

Cassie sputtered, "No, I'm fine." Her facial features relaxed as she regained normal breathing. "Don't look so pained, I'll have my energy back soon. And just so you know," she whispered, "he's a hunk. I saw him from the window."

"What? Are you crazy?"

"What did I say?"

"When did you see him out the window? He didn't see you, did he?"

"Of course not. You worry too much."

"Cassie, he's a policeman. He notices things."

"And I notice things, too. There's nothing finer than a man in uniform. Uh-huh." Cassie made a foolish face, but Evah didn't share her humor. How would she ever explain the stabbing and that whole mess?

Regardless of how Cassie's injury occurred, the locals would never understand. People judge.

Evah headed downstairs. Maybe Cassie wasn't so far off. Evah did want to see Nolan. She wasn't about to wonder why.

She secured her pink running cap over her ponytail and peeked in the mirror. The hot pink capris and matching top felt great. FedEx to the rescue.

They walked outside and Cash's pace shifted into high gear. For a long-bodied dog with short legs, he motored. His nose sniffed inches above the ground, but he stayed close to her and moved fast.

Leaf blossoms covered most trees, interspersing pale greens and yellows within the dark evergreens. It smelled sweet and wonderful, even if she didn't know what she smelled.

Realization swept over her and she bowed her head. "Thank you, Father, for showing me your beautiful creation." Maybe God wanted her to see this part of the country.

What would it be like to live like this, with a slower pace, close to nature? She quashed the thought. Her job was in Minnesota.

A rattling car approached. A belt squealed and its engine whirred. Evah pulled Cash off the shoulder and onto the grass. A beat-up Chevy Impala crowded the white line. It vroomed next to them.

So much for hot pink walking attire. If there weren't plans to install a safe walking path to the trail, someone should suggest it.

The car hit the brakes, did a U-turn, and headed back the way it came.

"Oh, oh." Evah yanked Cash from the shoulder into the grass and prayed that the vehicle wouldn't stop near her. To her relief, it rattled past.

She nudged Cash back onto the shoulder. Ten feet later, a siren sounded behind her. She tugged the leash and again moved off the shoulder. The car flew past. Park County Sheriff.

The police car braked hard about one hundred yards ahead and turned left. The siren quieted. Her heart thumped. She could turn back, but Nolan would be waiting.

She approached the trail sign and realized that this must be where the squad car turned. She passed two colorful trail signs, one bearing pictures of dogs and one mapping out the trail system.

She stayed to the far left of the park entrance. Towering evergreens created a dark, feathery umbrella overhead, making it appear much later than five o'clock. Walking through the dim tree-tunnel, she focused on a bright field up ahead.

She stopped. Cash whined and tugged at his leash.

Emergency lights flashed. Red. Blue. Yellow. She had never seen such a conglomeration of lights, even in Minnesota. She sought out Nolan's black vehicle. An anxious fear spread through her. Something terrible must have happened to warrant this many response vehicles.

"Hey, you!" A man called. "You in pink." She followed the voice to a large policeman standing near a squad car. "Come over here."

His brown uniform and Stetson were unlike Nolan's dark blue uniform and standard police hat.

"Who are you and what are you doing here?"

"This is a walking trail." She held up the end of the leash. "I'm walking."

He gave her a stern look. "The trail is closed today. What's your name?"

"Evah Rois."

"R-o-y-?"

"R-o-i-s."

"You from town?"

"No. I'm here to meet Police Chief Nolan Quinn."

"Oh, I see." His eyebrows raised with sudden interest. "You know the chief?"

"He was to give me a tour of the trail, but this doesn't appear to be a good time."

"You noticed."

Rude.

She hated to give him the satisfaction of asking. "What's going on here?"

"A shooter in the park."

Evah felt the blood drain from her face. "Is. Everyone. Okay?"

"No worries. Your chief is fine. Someone just shot a dog. You need to leave."

Her chief? And someone *just* shot a dog?

Evah's stomach flip-flopped. "I am leaving. Please tell Nolan that I was here."

"Oh, I'll tell him." He tapped his pen on his knuckles. "Sorry to interrupt your date with hotshot."

"What did you say?" Evah glared at his smug expression.

Jesus doesn't like razor sharp words. She closed her mouth before a reply could slide off her tongue. She turned, pulled Cash alongside, and headed to the ranch. After a few minutes of stomping along the shoulder of the road, she noticed Cash panting.

"Sorry boy." She stood still to let him rest.

Rude and crude. Typical police.

No, she couldn't say that anymore. She envisioned Nolan's blue eyes, kind and polite. He wouldn't approve of that man's behavior. If there was an advantage to small town living, she'd just thought of it. She would report the obnoxious public employee.

Her thoughts drifted to the endless sea of evergreens surrounding Sunrise Crik Trail. Nolan would have his hands full trying to find anyone.

What type of person would shoot at a dog? She glanced around resumed walking. The farmhouse wasn't yet visible a half mile down the road. Cash tugged.

Meeting Nolan would've been no more than a casual walk with their dogs. Still, she felt disappointed.

Thirty yards ahead, someone walked out of the woods. He looked like Jane's counterpart, clothed in green military garb. He waved and stood waiting. When she got close, he removed his camo cap, letting grey and brown shoulder-length hair fall helter-skelter.

He eyed the energetic corgi. "Hey, Cash! I recognize him. He's okay with strangers." He reeked of cigarettes.

"He wouldn't hurt anyone, as long as I'm controlling him." Why had she said that? For all she knew, Cash would lick him.

He moved into step with her, his head nodding in such a way that Evah wondered if he could control it. "Commotion over at the park, 'eh?"

"Yes. It wasn't the best time to go for a walk."

"Why is that?"

"Someone shot at a dog."

The man looked across the highway. "Too bad."

"I can't imagine why someone would do such a thing. Do you live around here?"

"Sure do. Why?" His eyes narrowed.

"You have military patches on your jacket and if you know Cash, you must know Jane. She has patches, too."

"Everybody knows Jane." He veered toward the centerline. "I've gotta' cross over to get home. Good to meet you."

Everyone knows Jane. Evah watched him cross the highway.

~~~

Exhausted, Nolan sat on the bench alongside the trail.

Six-forty. He'd walked every loop and scoured the terrain, concentrating on the rear area leading to the mountains. The guys were getting testy. There was no sign of anyone in the park. The County Sheriff had announced the search would cease at dark. That left an hour and a half of daylight.

He weighed the pros and cons of continuing. After two hours, he assumed the shooter to be long gone.

"Dispatch to chief."

Nolan pressed the radio clipped to his shirt. "Chief here."

"Good news, Chief." Seamor's baritone rose with excitement. "Shooter suspect is in custody. County picked him up in town. Repeat. Suspect is in custody here—at the city jail. Waiting for you."

Nolan sat stunned. Where had the shooter been apprehended and why hadn't he been notified? The suspect was already in jail. If County picked him up, why hadn't Bob Grease notified him?

"My ETA is fifteen minutes."

His face heated. Someone was going to get a piece of his mind this time.

On the good side, he wouldn't have to pull an all-nighter. He stood and stretched. Once everything was in order at the jail, he would update the waiting City Manager and head home.

Nolan walked the trail to the parking lot. The guys would be glad to head home. Everyone would be gone except Carmichael and Tungsten. He rounded the curved trail. His vehicle was where he'd left it. But now, it sat alone in the parking area.

Anger surged. Bob Grease had gone too far this time.

Nolan pushed the mic button and asked to be put through to the County Sheriff. Personal pettiness was one thing. Police procedure was another. No matter how much Grease resented Nolan moving from county to city police, this was out of line. He wasn't going to let it slip.

The Millers would feed Honey. All he had to do was let them know. He dug his cell phone from his pocket. She would have to wait until tomorrow for her exercise. He had put in all the miles he intended for one day. So much for planning a walk—

With Evah.

Nolan clenched a fist and punched his invisible opponent.

CHAPTER FOURTEEN

Nolan crossed the linoleum floor and stepped into the morning drizzle. He tightened his collar and held the heavy glass door open. The rapid click of Dawn Clements' heels on concrete announced his administrative assistant's arrival. Despite the dreary morning, she flashed a smile. Her plus-size frame moved past him and stopped inside the entrance to collapse her umbrella.

"Morning, Chief. Thanks." She stood in the entrance of the renovated two-story brick building that housed the Recreation Department on the main level and the Woodridge Police Department on the lower level.

"You had a late night. Bring you back a few years?" She gripped the front of her raincoat and gave it a shake.

"A few. I had no idea fourteen years ago . . ."

"What? That you would be the city chief and not a good-old county boy?" Her twang made him smile.

"Now Dawn."

She laughed, a deep heartfelt laugh. "I've known you for a long time, Chief Nolan Quinn. You knew being chief would carry a heavier load than a jail supervisor."

"Or patrol officer or detective. I know. And yes, it was a long day."

"I'm glad he's in custody. Who has the morning shift?"

"Chuck Seamor. I'm grabbing a bite and taking ten to let Honey run. I'll drop her off at the house and be back."

"Sounds good. I'll get at the report." She slipped off her raincoat and folded it over her arm. "And just so you don't make an unnecessary stop at the school office, I took care of the KIN account. I know you were concerned about it."

"Thanks. I appreciate it and so do the kids in need."

"Have you been down to the jail?" She pushed dark graying curls off her forehead.

"Yes. I'll be back after breakfast." He tightened his hat and headed down the wide concrete steps.

Dawn came off as all business, but since locating her two missing grandsons a year and a half ago, their mutual respect had blossomed into a solid friendship.

He marveled that she drove from work to the small low-income apartment where her daughter, Shenise, struggled to raise seven- and nine-year-old boys. From the sound of it, Dawn did everything from tutoring and preaching to hide-and-seek. The vision made him smile, but he sobered at the thought of Shenise working two jobs to make ends meet. His heart ached for single parents. Her ex-husband wanted nothing to do with the boys, except for rare occasions that caused more grief than good.

Driving toward Ellen's Café, he glanced at Honey in the rearview mirror. Her large brown eyes watched him. He felt sentimental. Must be the rain.

"You're a good girl, Honey. You have more patience than Deidra's elevator operator."

The thought of his former fiancé surprised him. No, he wasn't going there, not for a minute.

Nolan parked and exited his vehicle. He paused in front of a newspaper stand. The headline read, "Romeo shot in Woodridge."

Who would name a dog Romeo?

He sighed and entered the café. Giving short answers and nods to patrons, he made his way to a back-corner booth. He settled onto the leather-look vinyl, eager for hot food and coffee.

Without warning, Jane stood in front of him, hands on her hips and wearing a military green and tan ensemble.

"Morning Jane." He wasn't in the mood to smile, even though she looked ridiculous.

"Chief."

"What's on your mind? I'm trying to order breakfast. You look like the cat that caught the canary."

"I think it's swallowed the canary. And I need to get home. I've been doing my route."

Ellen poured Nolan a cup of steaming coffee and hesitated.

He looked up at Jane. "So, what is keeping you in town? Do you want to join me?"

"No. I saw you park and followed you in."

Lucky me.

Ellen still hesitated, the coffee pot in her hand. "You sure you don't want a cup? It's fresh."

"I said no."

Nolan met Ellen's gaze. She moved to the next table, but turned back to Nolan. "The special today is French toast."

"No thanks. I've been thinking about a stack of flapjacks for days. A tall stack."

She nodded, smiled, and walked away.

"So, what's on your mind?" He turned to Jane, smelled the dark brew, and took a sip. Hot and strong, just like he liked it. He cradled the cup in his hands and nodded toward the empty seat across from him.

Jane slid onto the bench seat and leaned forward. "Just so you're aware, Evah Rois is staying at the ranch."

"That's common knowledge."

"But this isn't. There's another lady, her friend from Minnesota whose name is Cassie." She sat tall and proud, as though she delivered classified information.

Nolan sighed, hoping she wasn't going to file another complaint.

"It appears that you're having a bumper season of visitors."

"You don't know about Evah's friend."

"I'm glad she has friends."

"Just listen."

"All right, then tell me." He sipped his coffee, irritated.

"Her lady friend came here to recuperate. From being stabbed."

Nolan choked and grabbed a napkin.

He dropped Honey off at home and drove to the hardware store.

Jane's thorns pricked time after time. He never knew when to believe her.

Right now, the media was screaming for answers. Had the slug been identified yet? And what about the false teeth? Was there a connection?

Kendra St. John greeted him from the register. "You're right on time, Chief. I have everything ready."

Her black hair fascinated him, bound back in rows of intricate braids. "Thanks. I have a few additional items."

"Did the ladies make the list for you?"

Nolan nodded and pulled the crumpled note from his pocket. "How are those children of yours?"

"They're good, thanks." She gave him a grateful smile. "The after-school program is making such a difference. Just what Tyrone needed."

"He's a good boy, even better with a little direction."

She limped around the counter and placed a hand on his shoulder. "I don't know how I can thank you."

Someone cleared her throat. They both turned. Evah stood, listening.

Nolan motioned her over and introduced Kendra. Then he moved away to finalize his order. Was she hiding someone from him? He simmered.

Genevieve's shaky handwriting was all but illegible. Three trowels, one shovel, and gloves.

One by one, he compiled a stack on the counter. Last item. He reached for pink flowered gloves.

"I'm assuming these aren't for you?" Evah spoke from behind.

"To be honest, pink flowers are one of my favorites." He felt tentative. "What do you suggest for senior gardeners?"

"They can be a tough crowd. I'm guessing that the gloves are supposed to last for a century and will be worn by everyone in the county?"

"Good guess."

"I suggest cotton instead of plastic. They can be washed often and they'll wear better. Besides, plastic gloves get sweaty."

"These?" He pointed to the plain brown stack.

"The yellow ones. Sunflowers look happy."

He wanted to ask her about the trail, but it had been a bust. This wasn't the place or the time.

He could kick himself for falling into Jane's trap. But the crux of what she said made him uneasy. It niggled at his mind that a friend of hers might have been stabbed. And she wasn't telling him.

Kendra approached Evah and the two walked to a display near the checkout.

He carried four flats of petunias and marigolds to his car, glad that Kendra had set them aside. He returned to the counter with potting soil. Evah was still there.

"So, you're gardening today?" Her tone didn't match her smile.

"I'm picking this up for someone. An assigned task."

"Aren't you the one to assign tasks?"

"Sometimes. I volunteered for this one."

Nolan paid for his order and pushed the cart to his car. He loaded his car, got in, and shut the door. Flowers were community service but what must the citizens of Woodridge think of their Chief when he toted petunias?

What did Evah think?

He grabbed his mic. "This is the Chief. I need that update."

~~~

Evah returned to the ranch, her mind reeling. Nolan hadn't mentioned the paper's headline or the fact that they weren't able to go on the walk. It left her feeling out of sync.

She set her purchases on the counter as the house phone rang. She grabbed it. "Hello?"

"Hi Evah. This is Krista Cox returning your call."

"Krista, hi. Is it too late to be included in the tour circle promotion?"

"What a great surprise. I would love to include you. I thought you weren't interested."

"I apologize for this last-minute change of heart. I came to the conclusion that promoting the ranch would be good for sales purposes."

"Good idea. I should have the flyers printed in the next few days. I never heard from your friend about the marketing."

"Sorry. I should've phoned you. She would love to help but has some medical issues right now."

"I understand. Please tell her that I can always use help."

She placed the phone on the receiver and noticed the message light blinking. She hit the button. A lady's voice said, "This message is for Evah Rois. I am phoning on behalf of the Woodridge Police Department."

About the alpaca delivery? Hope rose in her heart.

"We have a man in custody here at the city jail. Jonathan Green. It sounds like you know him. He is a single parent and doesn't want his young daughter involved with social services. He is hoping you might watch his girl until he can make arrangements. Please call me as soon as possible and let me know if you can care for his child."

Care for his child?

Evah stood, dumfounded. Had they arrested him for not complying with community service requirements? Maybe she could help by vouching that he had been searching for work. Maybe now he would be allowed community service at the ranch.

She had talked with him for only a short time, yet she remembered the affection he showed his daughter. How could he entrust the care of . . . what was her name . . . to Evah? Had he no friends or family?

That stung. She knew the ache of loneliness. She couldn't stand by and not help. She ran a brush through her hair and fastened mama's silver heart necklace around her neck.

She hoped to avoid Nolan. No matter how nice he seemed, what kind of person would arrest a single father trying to secure community service? It wasn't right and she would do whatever she could to help Jonathan.

She grabbed the key off the wooden rack and headed outside. Good thing Jane hadn't objected to her use of Uncle Regan's truck. And good thing she knew how to keep it running.

~~~

"Hey Chief, this is Fred from the DNR. I was asked to give you a call. You reported the mountain lion track?"

"Yes. I'm quite sure that's what it is."

"You're right. We checked it out. I had a couple guys scour the area. Next to a fallen tree about a quarter mile back, they found a partial carcass. Pronghorn. It was pretty bare. The interesting thing is that about ten yards from it, they found a torn green cloth with dark stains, similar to the one you found. We sent it to the lab."

CHAPTER FIFTEEN

The green pickup truck squealed to a stop in front of the two-story brick building. Large gold letters identified the Recreation Department and Police Department. Evah wondered at the strange combination in the same building.

Jonathan requested that she care for his daughter. Did that mean she had to talk to him, to go inside the jail? Her stomach fluttered. She grabbed her leather bag, dug for a comb, and pulled a few tangles out of her long hair. She used the visor mirror to touch up her makeup. Then she stepped out of the truck.

To the left, a large policeman in a brown uniform surveyed her movements. The smirk on his face made her breath catch—the policeman from the trail. He leaned against a gold patrol car two over.

She looked away, but he'd seen her. She gathered her purse and fumbled with her keys.

"Well now, look who's here." His voice teased, but not in a good way.

Evah's grip tightened on the key as she locked the truck.

"I wouldn't worry about locking that pile of scrap. You'd have to pay someone to take it." He moved toward a car. "Oh, just so you know, your boyfriend isn't here. Heard he's planting flowers today." He laughed too loud, ducked into the car, and slammed the door.

Evah fumed. She didn't like causing trouble, but she'd had enough.

She stormed into the building and followed signs down into the basement, unprepared for the sight that welcomed her. A stout lady in a brilliant floral dress sat behind the counter, her forehead wrinkled in concentration. And there, just behind her, lay Jonathan's daughter. A bright penguin blanket covered the child, who was sound asleep.

The lady's eyebrows narrowed when she looked up. In a split second, Evah felt unqualified for the task ahead of her.

"I'm Evah Rois, here at the request of Jonathan Green, about his daughter." She took a big breath and spoke fast, "And I also want to complain about a policeman."

"Okay," the receptionist's calm voice did little to sooth Evah's tension. "Which do you want to do first?"

"The cop. I want to report rude behavior."

The receptionist pursed her lips and raised her eyebrows. "All right, Miss Rois. Is it miss?"

"Yes."

"Here is a complaint form. Be sure to include the name of the policeman and what happened. There's a pen on the ledge there."

"I don't know his name."

"Fill it out as best you can. Depending on circumstances, we'll try to figure out his identity."

"He won't be hard to identify."

"Why is that?"

"Because he is . . ."

"Continue."

"He is very large. Not just tall, but big. With bushy eyebrows."

"Was he wearing a blue uniform or brown?"

"Brown."

"A brown uniform signifies county jurisdiction, not city."

"So, you can't help me?"

"On the contrary. Please fill out the form."

"I don't want to waste my time if—"

"Please fill it out. Our police chief will look into it. Without the form, he won't be able to do anything. Be sure to include your contact information."

Evah filled in the blanks, glancing at the child every few minutes. Precious. How could she have forgotten her name?

She finished the complaint and snapped the pen onto the clipboard. When she leaned on the counter to speak to the receptionist, the lady's smile appeared sincere.

Evah motioned to the child. "How long has she been sleeping?"

"Thirty or forty minutes. She wanted her daddy in the worst way. She almost brought the walls down before she crashed. Poor little sugar bug."

A short-lived smile tugged at the corner of Evah's mouth.

Now or never. She inhaled a deep breath and blurted, "I think it's absurd that Jonathan is in jail for this. He's been trying to find a job. I can attest to that because that's where I met him. In Livingston, job hunting. He had to take his daughter with him. This is so unfair, this community service thing. Isn't there some way—"

"Wait, wait, wait." The large woman sat straight. "Just hold on for one little minute. You think Mr. Green is in jail because of community service?"

"Well, yes. Isn't he?"

"I am not authorized to give details of Mr. Green's arrest. You'll have to speak to one of our officers. But I can tell you that he's in lots more trouble than community service."

A policeman came out of a side office. "Let me help you. I'm Patrolman Chuck Seamor.

She sat on a hard-backed chair while he filled her in.

Jonathan hadn't been arrested for avoiding community service. He allegedly shot a dog. She couldn't believe it. Had Princess been with him? Her head pounded and her stomach reeled.

Seamor led her through a maze of identification and rules, x–rayed her purse, and guided her through a scanner and metal detector. The lemon disinfectant didn't help her queasy stomach.

The place looked comfortable. In fact, she could've been sitting in a small living room. Two sofas lined the walls with an assortment of sitting chairs. The table where she sat almost divided the room in half.

Jonathan appeared in the far doorway. His dark curls were pulled back into a ponytail and he wore a bright orange jumpsuit with black numbers over his left pocket. His wrists were handcuffed together in front of him.

Just like on television.

To her surprise, a policeman guided him through a second doorway, where they disappeared. Moments later, he reappeared and asked her to follow him.

Jonathan sat behind a long glass window.

"Sit here," Seamor directed her.

She lowered herself into a simple chrome chair and nudged it closer to the counter. Wasn't this a bit much for small town security?

Jonathan looked apologetic. "Thanks for coming."

Seamor retreated behind Evah.

"Jonathan, I can't believe this. I thought you had been arrested for not finding community service. But, shooting a dog?"

"I didn't, I swear it. It wasn't me." He turned his face to the side, unable to control his watering eyes. "All I did was go to town with Precious. We stopped at the humane society."

"Why there?"

"Because she loves puppies and kittens." His sniffles turned into heartbreaking sobs.

"What happened?"

"A dog in the back room barked and growled. It sounded wild. Precious started to cry. I told the worker to shut him up or put him out of his misery. The guy gave me a dirty look and then turned his back to me. He ignored me, so I said, 'Give me a gun and I'll do it for you.'

"He gave me some guff. I grabbed his shirt sleeve. The next thing I knew, I was being fingerprinted and they took Precious from me." He cried.

~~~

Nolan rushed down the stairs leading to the police department. He had never seen Jane drive the truck, so Evah had to be here. Maybe she would answer some questions.

He stepped into the office. "Dawn, is Evah Rois here? I saw—"

Dawn held a finger to her lips. Hearing commotion at the back of the room, he looked up to see Evah emerge from the ladies' room.

She juggled a carry bag and blanket with a young girl snuggled in her arms.

Realization hit him like a train.

Evah Rois held Jonathan Green's daughter. He searched Dawn's face. She lowered herself back into her chair, her expression that of professional neutrality.

Nolan stepped toward Evah. "What are you doing?"

"I'm caring for Jonathan's daughter until you come to your senses and let him out of jail."

He looked at Dawn, who looked away.

He turned to Evah, his palms up. "You said you just met Green. And now you're watching his daughter? You also said that you couldn't wait to leave town."

"True on both counts."

"Then why?"

"Why not? Do you know what it's like to have no one to help?"

"Do you know who you're getting involved with? Green's arrest may lead to long-term incarceration."

"I know. Right now, I have to get this sweetie home. She's had a rough day. So have I."

~~~

Evah parked the truck near the house. Lights blazed from most windows. She lifted the toddler from the police department's loaner car seat.

At the door, she tightened her grip on Precious while she pushed it open. To her amazement, Cassie sat in a straight-back rocker. Jane sat in the recliner, reading.

"Cassie, you're downstairs." Evah's wide-eyed look was lost on the gaping faces of Jane and Cassie, staring at Precious.

Cassie's face transformed to instant excitement. "Gracious sakes alive! Who have we here?" She struggled to rise from her chair.

"No, no." Evah stepped forward. "Don't get up."

She neared Cassie, who caressed the toddler's dangling legs. "Hey, sweet thing."

Precious made a face and yawned, waking up.

Evah sat on the ottoman in front of Cassie's chair. "I know this is a surprise, but it's temporary. Her father is—"

"Of no concern." Jane glowered from her chair, with a magazine clenched in her fist. "Wherever you got her, you take her back. This is no day care center."

"Now, Jane," Cassie soothed. "Since when do you refuse to help anyone? I know better than that." She looked from Precious to Evah. "So, Evah, tell us."

Precious kicked with fervor.

Evah looked into Jane's sour expression.

She set Precious on the floor in front of her. The child clutched her blanket and Evah exhaled, relieved. A split second later, Precious grabbed Cassie's water bottle off the coffee table and shook it. Water slapped against the inside of the plastic bottle and flew onto Cassie and Evah.

Cassie's squeal turned to laughter.

"Get that water bottle." Jane barked. "I told you—"

Evah grabbed the plastic bottle and its cap off the table.

"Mine, mine!" Precious jumped up and down, her lip trembling.

Evah twisted the cap on the bottle and handed it back to Precious, who grinned as quick as she had complained. The child's dark eyes sparkled and Evah marveled at her transformation, and the transformation on the faces of everyone watching her.

Cassie laughed. "I see this place livening up real fast."

Evah looked at Cassie. They were sisters in Christ. How could they part ways?

CHAPTER SIXTEEN

Nolan read his notes. Cassie Ballard. Age thirty-one. No criminal record. Victim of a stabbing at The Cup in Mankato. He peered at the internet photos. It looked classy. He searched for Evah's history. There wasn't much. He reached for a binder and flipped pages. He dialed Sergeant John Alvarez. After the conversation, he placed the receiver back on its stand.

Evah Mae Rois. Foster child of Carl and Gina Barutska of St. Paul, both deceased.

Foster child?

Alvarez had reconfirmed it.

Nolan blew out a breath. Why would Evah have foster parents when her aunt and uncle had been alive?

He spun in his chair and studied the Quinn family crest above his credenza. As a kid, his dad often sprawled across Nolan's beanbag chair. Bedtime stories involving the crest had been common, whether it be the unicorn's courage or some heroic battle tale. The name Quinn meant a lot. To his dad then and to him now.

He missed his dad's camaraderie. Four years felt like forever. He thanked God that his mother, Alice June, still volunteered at church. When he visited last month, she reaffirmed that Alan Quinn had been the love of her life.

A queasiness like sour apples burned in the pit of his stomach. Professional curiosity had evolved into something personal. Could he get her to open up?

He headed out to run errands, knowing his first stop would be the McCormick ranch.

He parked in the driveway and movement drew his focus to the backyard. Evah leaned against a tree stump, blowing bubbles. Despite thirty yards distance, he noticed the sunlight glistening in her hair.

A toddler in bright yellow chased the bubbles. She flopped onto the grass, hands clapping.

He exited the SUV. The child's giggles wafted through the air, mingled with Evah's laughter. Accompanying yips filled the air and Nolan couldn't help but to smile. The herding dog was running circles around them.

The vision looked almost perfect. But the child was Jonathan Green's daughter and the picture was a sham.

Nolan felt like the big bad wolf, crashing the party.

Evah looked sideways, and then watched him approach. When he neared the back porch, no one else was in sight.

"Good morning, Evah."

Concern clouded her expression. "Morning, Chief." She pulled a fistful of grass from the girl's clutch and then stood up.

Not Nolan. Chief.

He took off his hat and lowered himself onto the stump. "How are you getting along with your little visitor?"

He hadn't needed to ask. Evah smiled at the toddler, who thrust a stuffed zebra at him. He petted it and read Evah's approval in his peripheral vision.

Evah brushed grass and leaves from her crumpled dress. "This is Precious, Jonathan's daughter."

"I remember. She's a cutie."

The child babbled. Nolan didn't understand a word of it.

"What's going on with Jonathan?" Evah spoke without moving her focus from Precious.

"His hearing is Monday morning."

"In front of a jury?"

"No, this is the first hearing. The court will decide if bail is applicable. He'll be appointed an attorney. After that, they'll schedule a prelim."

Evah stood tall. "I've been thinking about something and I want you to consider it. Jonathan was trying to find community service when I met him. I want you to recommend that he be remanded into my care, so he can work on the ranch."

"Out of the question. No way."

"Why?"

"You would be responsible for him. And he'd be here, where you live. I don't like it."

"But it makes sense and it's my request. If he works on the ranch, he won't be sitting in jail. He could see his daughter. I understand that he would need supervision."

"There's a lot involved." Nolan shook his head. "You would be responsible for making sure he stays put during the day and out of trouble. Would you be safe? I'm not sure if the judge would approve."

"The charges against him, they're serious, aren't they?"

"Battery with a deadly weapon, criminal recklessness. They're serious."

Evah lowered herself onto the grass next to where Precious sat building something from twigs. "I don't believe he did those things. Have you talked to him, heard his side of the story? Does he even own a gun?"

"We're checking everything."

Precious waved a twig.

Nolan rubbed his forehead. "So, you would let him work here for community service and still be around his daughter?"

Evah's warm expression made his heart thump. "Yes."

"I'll think about it. But even if I recommend it, that doesn't mean the judge will consent."

"I think it would be good for both of them and since I'm okay with it, that's what should matter." Evah moved her hand to her throat. A look of horror passed over her face. She scrambled onto her knees and ran her hands over the grass. "Oh no. It's gone."

"What is gone?"

Evah jumped up and stared at the ground. "Mama's necklace. It's gone."

Nolan glanced at the toddler whose hands were full of twigs. If it had been yanked from Evah's neck, it could be anywhere. They traipsed back and forth across the lawn.

"Uppie, uppie," Precious opened and closed outstretched hands.

Nolan scooped her into his arms. Evah looked more distraught than ever. He wanted to help find that necklace, but he had to be at the office in twenty minutes. He searched with diligence before walking to her.

"I'm sorry, but I have to get back. It may take you some time to find it, but keep looking. If you don't find it right away, I'll help you look, later. Here's your friend." He handed Precious back to her.

"I appreciate your help. Please see if the Judge will let me do this. Nothing should separate a child from their parents."

~~~

"That's a big commitment." Cassie tilted her head. "Are you sure you want to do this?"

"I am. We both know what it's like to be alone."

Cassie set her iPad on the dresser. "Yes, but you don't have a job. And you know my situation, somewhat."

Evah shot her a look.

"You know what I mean. And there's Jane. Things could get crazy."

"Aren't things already crazy? Remember what you said last night."

"I know." Cassie conducted the orchestra. "If God leads you to it, he'll lead you through it." She pushed the arm of the chair with her right hand and Evah helped her stand. Cassie continued. "If you believe that, then there's no need to belabor it. We'll be fine."

But Evah detected Cassie's apprehension. It was that unknown, the thing that Cassie could never tell, buried deep in the foundation of their friendship. When Evah quit prying, Cassie embraced her as a friend.

"You doing okay?" Evah led her to the hard-backed chair and supported her as she sat.

"Yes, thanks. Who knew that rocking could be considered exercise?"

"Your doctor, that's who."

"That's old lady stuff. Oh, I forgot to thank you for the fresh air earlier. It felt great."

"We'll sit outside again later, when we don't have company. Right now, you need to take advantage of Precious's nap time."

Why couldn't she heed her own advice? How could she stop living in fear when it had become second nature?

Precious fit into the household, although she kept everyone on their toes. Even Jane hadn't complained much. But then, she hadn't been around much either.

Jonathan's presence would create still another situation. How would he feel about being remanded to her custody? What would Jane say?

Lord, I need courage.

She reached for her mother's necklace, feeling more alone than ever in its absence. Even the memory of Nolan searching beside her did little to lift her spirits.

~~~

Nolan and Honey walked the sweet-smelling trail. He checked his watch. There was plenty of time to change for church.

"Hey there, Chief," voices called from behind.

He whirled to see Jess Paulson and his wife, Reena, walking their tiny dog. The leash looked like thin, red string. They waved and Nolan waited for them to catch up. Reena scooped the little dog into her arms and Nolan signaled Honey to sit. He didn't want an altercation with prominent trail supporters.

Nolan extended his hand to Jess. "Good to see you two. It's a quiet morning."

Jess shook his hand. "I hope this fiasco doesn't dampen the town's excitement for our trail. We've worked for so long."

"We need to keep positive, with the media and everyone else."

Reena petted her dog while she spoke. "It's a godsend that the culprit was captured right away, so the trail is safe again."

Nolan scanned the trees. He hoped they were right. But, the image of Jonathan Green and his little daughter gave him an unsettled feeling.

An hour later, he walked into Woodridge Community Church. He sat next to the Orton family and gave half-hearted answers to young Chaz's endless questions.

Commotion caught his attention on the far side of the right triangle of seats. Evah, wearing an attractive light blue dress, moved into the second row. In her arms, Precious beamed from under a pink sun hat that matched her dress. Nolan doubted that Jonathon Green's backpack had contained that outfit. Her chubby fist dangled off Evah's back. Nolan noticed the small stuffed zebra. A church bag of toddler toys hung from Evah's shoulder.

His view widened when Evah moved from behind a row of adults. Her right hand reached to adjust the bright shawl covering the shoulders of a slim lady who stood close. The lady's movements were slow and deliberate.

Cassie Ballard. It had to be her.

She turned toward Evah and spoke, smiling. Her right arm was strapped around her midsection. Most people would assume it to be broken.

Nolan struggled to concentrate on the day's message. The sacrifice of Jesus Christ's life cleansed us of our sins. Regardless of the severity of our wrongdoings, we are all made clean.

Nolan's mind whirled. What if Jonathan Green was innocent? That would mean the real shooter was still at large and Green was unjustly arrested.

Chaz squirmed next to him until his mother pulled him close.

When they stood and sang This Little Light of Mine, he glimpsed Evah's warm expression looking down at Precious. He wished he stood next to her, listening to her sing.

As the closing hymn ended, Evah gathered toys and stuffed them in the bag. He wasn't going to miss this opportunity. He waited for the aisle to clear.

Chaz Orton tugged on his sleeve. "Can I see your badge, Chief? Where's your gun? Are you going to arrest somebody?"

"I would never wear my gun in church, Chaz. This is God's house."

Maria Orton smiled at him. "Thank you for your patience, Chief."

"He might grow up to be a policeman," he laughed and tousled the boy's hair.

Chaz beamed and Nolan turned to his mother. "It's important to turn youngsters into friends of the police. The earlier the better."

He stepped into the still populated aisle and heard a voice blare above the congregation. He recognized the source in seconds.

Maura Price stood in front of Evah. "I've heard about you, Miss Rois. You live near our Sunrise Crik Trail and I heard you're a fan. And, well, I just knew that you would be eager to assist with our grand opening event. Oh, forgive me. I am Maura Price, chairperson of the Friends of Sunrise Crik Trail. Let me tell you about . . ."

Maura Price. He wasn't about to waste his time waiting. Now that he had seen the alleged Cassie Ballard, he would visit the ranch and get some answers.

CHAPTER SEVENTEEN

E vah tossed her work shoes by the back door and hurried into the kitchen. At the sink, she washed her hands and gulped cold water.

"Is that you, Evah?" Cassie called.

"Yes. You need anything?"

"Will you come up? It's urgent."

Evah sprinted up the steps. "What's wrong?"

"A man called. Simeon Pratt. You know him?"

"A little. He showed me some barn stuff. He's Uncle Regan's friend."

"He said you need to call him right away."

"Did he say what it was about?"

"No. Here's his number." She held out a slip of paper.

"When did he call?"

"An hour ago. He said you wouldn't be happy about it."

"Great."

"Will you call from here?" Cassie's brown eyes begged. "I want to hear. You can sit for a minute, can't you?"

"I'm grungy." Evah pulled the cell phone from her pocket, punched in the number, and hit speaker.

"Hello," Simeon bellowed.

"Hi Simeon. This is—"

"Evah. Hey, thanks for calling. I'm beside myself here."

She pictured Simeon's round face. She had never seen him frown. "What's going on?"

"I just got home from a short trip, visiting grandkids. Vince Stone, the shearer, left a message. You know that name?"

"No."

"He made arrangements with Regan seven or eight months ago. Didn't know Regan had passed. Said your ranch is scheduled for shearing if you still want him to do it. I told him of course you'd keep the date and that you, the new owner, would take care of the setup."

"But Simeon, I'm not the owner."

"I'm not talking legalities. You own at least the ten alpacas that Regan bought for you. All alpacas need to be sheared."

"So, who is Vince Stone?"

"He's the best alpaca shearer around here. Folks schedule a year out."

"Shearing. Shaving their hair?"

"He shears, cuts the fiber off the alpacas with clippers every spring. I told you. Remember?"

"Is it optional?"

"Nope. The animals will overheat in a month. You need to get established and get the fiber sorted so you can sell it."

Evah transferred the phone to her left hand and tossed a throw blanket onto Cassie's quilt. She sat on it and motioned for a piece of paper and pencil.

Cassie looked up from her self-hug position and handed them to her.

"So, he just shows up and takes care of everything? Is it expensive?"

"Not as expensive as those alpacas. It's worth every cent."

"What does he do?"

"He brings one helper with him. I would guess Jimmy Hoyer. It's a busy day, lots of work. Everything's got to be prepped. You'll need four or five people to help you." There was silence and then a tapping sound. "I can help. He'll be at your place Saturday. Eight o'clock."

"Saturday at eight. This Saturday?"

"Yup."

"What do I have to do?" Panic swept through Evah's veins.

"Can I come over tonight? I'll bring a list."

"Sure."

"Better yet, why don't you help me tomorrow? He'll be shearing at my place. You'll see firsthand and I'll give you the list. Then you'll know what to expect. Course, my operation's bigger, but you'll get the gist."

"How many alpacas do you have?"

"Thirty-two, not counting boarders."

"Okay. Where do you live and what time do you want me there?" Evah scribbled as Simeon recited the address.

"Be here at seven. Wear comfy shoes and working clothes. No fancy stuff."

Evah hit the end call button and stared at the phone.

Cassie shook her head. "What did you get yourself into?"

"You heard. We're shearing alpacas on Saturday. Tomorrow I'll be at Simeon's place, helping."

"You don't know anything about shearing alpacas."

"Don't you think I know that?"

Cassie drew back at Evah's harsh tone.

"Sorry. I'm getting a crash course tomorrow. I'll learn everything I can. What I don't learn, Simeon will help with."

"You're going to be a rancher yet, aren't you? You've gone from chef to alpaca owner." She laughed and slapped her thigh. "This is good. Real good."

A lot depended on her. Evah headed to the door.

"Where you going? I didn't—"

"It's okay, Cassie. I have lots to do and I need to talk to Jane."

Cassie leaned back in her chair and mouthed an O.

Evah found Jane in the backyard near the old shed, digging up a brittle bush. "Jane, I need to talk to you."

Kneeling on a green rubber mat, Jane leaned back. She peeled off a glove and ran her hand over the green paisley handkerchief holding her hair off her face.

"What's burning your britches?"

"I have to go to Simeon's ranch tomorrow. He needs help shearing."

"I doubt that Simeon needs your help. He's been tending alpacas for years."

"He's going to teach me what I need to do for our shearing."

"Our shearing? You think you're going to shear alpacas?" She laughed harder than Evah had ever seen.

"Yes. Vince Stone will be here Saturday. He had contracted with Uncle Regan. He's honoring that commitment. So am I."

"Well, do what you got to do."

"I need your help tomorrow, Jane. Cassie and Precious will need help if I'm not here."

"So now you need my help?"

"Yes, I do."

Jane looked toward the barn and pulled the glove back on her hand. "There was a time when people helped each other." She hesitated. "If the alpacas are to bring good money, they need to be sheared. We want top dollar, so I'll help."

We want top dollar? Ten alpacas are mine.

~~~

Evah dressed in old jeans and a long-sleeved tee shirt under the front-zip sweatshirt she found in a closet. The front read, "My ranch is my world." Covered with pink flowers, it would have belonged to Aunt Marilyn. She grabbed a granola bar from Cassie's stash and headed to the truck.

Her stomach fluttered with excitement. She drove toward Sunny Acres Alpaca Ranch. No wonder Simeon and Uncle Regan had been friends. They lived too close not to be.

She rounded the picturesque ranch house. A line of vehicles announced that help had arrived. Evah wondered where to find Simeon.

Moments later, he appeared in front of the enormous barn. "Miss Evah, come on over," he waved.

She took the left fork in the road. A ranch hand stood in the middle of a pen, running a wire wand over alpacas. Another worker approached a small herd in the back field.

"Morning," Simeon lifted his cap, exposing his bald head, and pulled the cap back on. "This setup will be similar to what you'll do. See the holding pens there?" He pointed. "I use portable fencing. It's easy to put up where it's needed. I can help you with that. Do you have enough panels?"

"I have no idea. There are some in the barn. I never noticed how many."

"The animals are sorted by gender. Males there, females there." He pointed. "For shearing, we sort by color. Shear white first, dark colors last.

"You're gonna' need four or five people. Some folks shear on the ground, on tarps, but Vince uses a folding table. He just pulled in, around back. You'll see him in a few minutes. He's dropping someone off to set up the second shearing station. Follow me."

Evah matched her stride to his shorter gait and paid attention as he pointed out one thing after another. "You'll need three of those thirty-gallon clear plastic bags for each animal."

"Three bags per animal." He pointed to a teenage girl, affixing stickers to bags. "Use a black marker. On each bag, write the animal's name. Then number each bag, so you have bags one, two, and three for each alpaca. Got that?"

"Uh huh." Evah hoped her eyes didn't have that glazed-over look.

"Bag one is for blanket fiber, bag two is neck and upper leg fiber—or seconds, and bag three is thirds—the ends and fiber that's not good for much else.

"If you want the fiber tested—and you should with new animals—then you need a small plastic zip bag for each alpaca, to hold a fiber sample, a histogram. They need to be labeled, too."

"I need to write this down." Evah panicked. "This is too much to remember."

"I printed notes for you. I did a workshop last year."

"Thanks."

His short, stout frame walked toward a tall, broad shouldered man who carried a portable table tipped sideways.

"Hey, Vince."

The large man set the table on the concrete floor. The two shook hands and greeted one another.

Simeon turned to Evah. "This is Miss Evah Rois. She's running Regan McCormick's ranch. He was her uncle."

"Yes ma'am." Vince set the table down and reached for her hand. "Sorry to hear about your uncle. Didn't see him often. Once or twice a year other than shearing. Don't know how I missed hearing that he passed."

"Thank you." Evah released her grip on the large, weathered hand. "I'm new to the world of alpacas. I appreciate Simeon's help. Yours, too."

Shrill squeals sounded behind them. All heads turned.

"Put those males in separate pens." Simeon called. "They're not used to being so close to one another." He turned to Evah. "Typical teenagers."

"This is Carla Kingsbury." Simeon introduced a young freckle-faced woman with wavy, red hair and shy, blue eyes. "She'll start bringing in the animals.

"Start with that pen over there." He pointed to five white alpacas. "You know the drill. The bags have ID's and are all lined up. Make sure we know which alpaca is next." He walked toward two men examining an alpaca.

Carla showed Evah how to position herself. "You're new at this, aren't you?"

"Pretty obvious, isn't it?" Evah's laugh sounded nervous.

"Do you want me to explain as I go?"

"Please do."

"This halter goes on pretty easy, but it's important that when the nose goes through the noseband, it should rest beneath the eyes, but above the nose. See what I mean?"

"Yes. Keep it above the nose so they can breathe?"

"Right. The halter has to be the right size. They're not one size fits all. Most halters adjust. See?"

Carla buckled the halter and held up the lead rope. "You never let go of this." She turned to the haltered alpaca wearing a collar with a pink name tag. "Come on, big girl." She coaxed the shaggy female to the table which remained sideways.

"Here we go. Hold her tight against the table," Simeon directed. Multiple gloved hands complied. A worker pushed a release clamp under the table. Its top flipped up, providing a solid surface for shearing.

The female thrashed her legs. Simeon hollered, "Grab her hind ankles, Evah."

Evah grabbed. Someone showed her how to insert the ankles, one at a time, into rope loops and pull them tight. The alpaca kicked against the binds.

"Tighten that rope," Simeon yelled and pointed.

She yanked it.

"Now's not the time to be gentle," Simeon commanded. "Hold her tight, for your safety and hers."

Evah had a vision of cattle branding operations.

Two people positioned themselves over the alpaca, one holding its head and the other holding the legs and midsection.

Clippers hummed. Evah watched Vincent's skilled strokes shear row after row of fiber while his free hand pushed fiber away from the shears. Workers' hands scooped the fluff once the shears moved out of harm's way, and deposited it into bags.

Simeon pointed. "He starts with the blanket fiber, the most valuable section. It's where a horse's saddle blanket would go. That's number one. Number two is the top of the legs. Then the thirds. Watch. Hold the animals. Get used to them. Then I'll have you roll the blankets to be bagged."

Vince finished the first side and stood straight. "Evah, loosen the ankle restraints a bit. Okay, Simeon?"

"Ready."

"One, two, three, flip."

They rolled the alpaca onto its other side, revealing shaggy fiber. Simeon hollered, "Tighten those ankle ropes." And the process repeated.

Vince checked each animal's teeth and sanded some with a tool, reminding Evah of the dentist office. Some alpacas screeched. Others drooled, a disgusting, stinky green spit.

Then Jimmy trimmed hooves with an instrument like a small shrub clipper. Evah brushed fiber and dirt from her jeans. Could she pull off this kind of organization on Saturday?

After all of these years, why would Uncle Reagan assume that she would want alpacas? His assumption confirmed that he knew nothing about her.

~~~

"Call for you, Chief," Dawn called from her desk.

"I'm in the middle of something. I'll call back." Nolan flipped through the top file on his desk.

"He said it's urgent. Something about an alert from Mankato."

Nolan reached for the phone. "Got it."

"It's Keith. Thanks for taking the call."

"What's up?"

"I've got eyes on the shop. Activity has escalated and something new has surfaced. They're using a decoy vehicle to cover for bigger scores."

"Good to know. Keep me in the loop."

"For some reason, Montana is the buzz word. It seems to be the hub for something."

"Okay. I'm calling a meeting. I'll call back in a couple of hours."

CHAPTER EIGHTEEN

E vah poured a second cup of coffee and studied her list.
The outside door opened and Jane stepped into the kitchen
dressed in green military attire. She looked ready to storm
enemy lines, except for the hot pink lipstick and a lime green
handkerchief in her hair.

She marched to the coffee pot, poured herself a cup, and glanced
at Evah. "You ready for shearing?"

"I am. Are you ready to help with Cassie and Precious? You look
dressed for battle."

"Could be. What are you dressed for?" Her eyes critiqued Evah's
attire.

Evah smoothed her pink long-sleeved tee-shirt and ran a hand
over her hair, pulled back with pink and green fabric. She reached
for her lightweight matching jacket. "Shearing doesn't require olive
drab."

"I live olive drab."

"I've noticed."

"You watch that crumb-catcher. Army is who I am. Not that you
care."

"You've been ordering me around with a heart of steel. I have
my doubts as to whether Cassie and Precious will be safe with you."

"What do you mean by that?"

"You heard me. I'm leaving them in your care while I'm committed to this event. I expect you to uphold your end of this agreement."

"And if I do, what's in it for me? What's your end of this agreement?"

What does she mean, if?

"Those alpacas are valuable. That keeps the ranch attractive and marketable."

"Marketable is good. But what about my vested interest? I've lived here all these years. You prance in, sell it all, make a bundle, and fly away home. What about me?" She pressed both thumbs onto her chest.

"In regard to what?"

"Everything." Jane spat the word like curdled milk.

"The estate is in probate. You know that limits what we can do. I think, though," Evah hoped she was right, "if we both agree and sign a blurb saying we agree, you could start the process by selling the original three alpacas. The three that were here before I arrived, Princess Peachy, Marcos, and Cocoa Lady. Sell them and I won't contest it."

"Just like that?"

"Sure. The Court shouldn't care as long as we agree. Sell them and take the money for yourself."

Jane eyed her like an undercover spy. "And you get the other ten?"

"I do. Uncle Regan bought them for me. It says so on the sales receipt."

"I'll take my three and half interest in the other ten."

"It's not going to happen."

"Then today's agreement is off."

"Oh, no it's not. Not today." Evah wagged her index finger at the petite bundle of dynamite. "Today, there's too much at stake. You watch Cassie and Precious as we planned."

"And if I don't?" Jane jutted her chin into the air.

"If you don't, you're going to be very, very sorry," Evah's voice escalated in anger. She clenched her fists. "You will regret—"

"Hey, you two, what's going on?" Cassie's high-pitched voice cut through the air.

Evah turned to see her standing in the living room doorway. She clutched her lavender bathrobe closed with her free hand. "I could hear you two all the way upstairs. I'm surprised Precious isn't awake."

Evah looked down before looking back into Jane's glare.

"Sorry. It was inconsiderate of us." Evah reached for her travel mug. "I'm heading to the barn. Wish me luck?"

"You've been working around the clock, getting ready for this. Everything will be fine."

Cassie and Evah exchanged a knowing look.

Evah stepped to the door and patted her back pocket. "Cassie, keep your cell phone with you today. If you need anything, call my number and I'll be here in a minute."

"Even with this broken wing, I can do what needs be with that child." Cassie shook her head. "Well, most of it, anyway."

Evah stepped toward her. "Not the lifting or—"

"Or anything else." Jane stepped forward, a determined look on her face. "And she won't need to be calling you. I'm here. I'll tend to what needs tending."

As she reached for the door, she called to Jane. "You need a camouflage-designed handkerchief."

Evah stepped outside. The way her knees were shaking, she hoped she wouldn't collapse. It wasn't her nature to argue. She had prayed for courage and wisdom. It seems that one didn't do much good without the other.

Please God, keep Cassie and Precious safe. And help me not to let everyone down.

~~~

By eleven-thirty, Evah's mind blurred between fiber, plastic bags, and more information than she would remember. Sweat rolled down her forehead.

"You doing okay?" Simeon thumped her on the back after she released the sixth alpaca into an outdoor pen.

"As good as everyone else. They look like skinny white deer with ostrich necks, wearing thermal underwear." She turned to Simeon. "Your operation moved faster with two shearing stations."

"Sure, but this is normal for a small herd. You don't want to spread yourself too thin. This is your first shearing."

Evah nodded. First and last.

"You need a break?"

"No." She was tired but energized at the same time. When had she felt so, what? Proud?

"If those sandwiches out yonder taste as good as they smell," Simeon continued, "well, I'm not used to such a spread."

"You peeked, did you?"

"You bet I did. Saw that van pull up. There's no food getting by without my noticing."

"I decided to serve lunch to the crew. It's the least I could do for the last-minute help." She turned to the interior of her barn and called out, "Come on, everyone. Lunch time out front."

Workers headed to the front of the barn, most of them brushing fiber from their clothes as they walked.

Shouts of joy greeted her ears. Simeon grabbed a sandwich in one hand and an individual bag of chips in the other. He wasted no time biting off a mouthful.

Workers surrounded the long, folding table heaped with plates of sandwiches, chips, cookies, sodas, and water.

She stepped forward and cleared her throat. Where had this sudden impulse come from?

"I'm going to say a quick prayer. Join me if you wish," she spoke loud enough for all to hear.

Surprised glances shot from one person to the next.

She bowed her head. "Dear Lord, thank you for providing help for this shearing event. Thank you for allowing me to meet people that knew my uncle and aunt, for skilled workers, good weather, new friends . . . and this food. Amen."

Muffled voiced echoed around her. Now she would be known as a religious nut. For whatever reason, she didn't mind.

Simeon looked at her, eyes glistening. "You downright surprised me there." He nodded and walked away.

Her smile felt like an extension of her thumping heart.

Crunching gravel made her turn. A familiar black SUV pull into the driveway. Her heart hammered when Nolan stepped out, wearing his uniform.

"Good morning," he looked from Evah to the assembly surrounding the food table. "This place is hopping."

"Sure is," Simeon walked toward her. "Evah, here, is raising the bar when it comes to alpaca shearing."

"And lunch," someone called.

"Hey, I had snacks and water at mine." Simeon faked irritation.

"But you've never had sandwiches," a worker teased. "Evah, you can invite me back next year."

~~~

Nolan couldn't take his eyes off Evah. Covered with alpaca fiber and dressed in hot pink, she glowed. Even with the dirt smudge on her right cheek.

"I need to talk to you," he lowered his voice. "In private."

She glanced at her watch and spoke to the crowd. "You all have thirty minutes." She turned to Simeon, "I'll be right back."

She followed Nolan to the edge of the crowd. "What do you need?"

"I wanted you to know that I'm making progress on your repo."

"Oh?"

"They have a short-stick policy. Unless an extra fee is paid, the rental is good for one day. They said you were aware of it. Do you remember anything about it?"

"No." Evah's posture stiffened.

Nolan recognized her armor. He pulled out his notebook and scanned the pages. "When a customer does not pay the—"

"Let me look. I'll check and—"

"Just listen. If you didn't pay the fee, you voided your right to retain the rental vehicle."

She leaned against a fence post. "I got a stub of a receipt. I didn't get a copy of any policy. What can I do?"

"I'm investigating. I think the company might be scamming customers."

"What? No, don't do that."

"I'm trying to get your car back. Or get you reimbursed. Isn't that what you want?" His tone cut and he knew it.

"You should've asked me. I don't want to be involved in another legal mess. I'm sorry but I can't handle anything more right now." Evah turned her back to him and walked toward the barn.

He watched her march away, acting like she preferred using Regan's old beater truck. Her quick temper puzzled him.

"Hey, Evah," Simeon's voice surpassed the din of worker conversations.

Nolan trudged behind her, heading to his car.

Evah veered toward the barn door. "What?"

"There's someone here who's interested in buying some hay. I didn't know if you'd be needing all of yours or selling some."

"I'm interested in selling it. Everything else, too."

CHAPTER NINETEEN

M emorial Day.
     He'd taken two calls before the parade ended.
     Mr. Lockhart rambled from his wheelchair near the picture window. "I saw him just like I said. Tall, he was. At least six feet. Dark hair and wearing one of those hooded gang shirts."

"Gang shirts?"

"Like the hoodlums on those crime shows. This guy was poking around the Murphy's mailbox two doors down." He pointed down the street. "I'm sure he took something."

"Mr. Murphy notified the department that they were to be gone for two weeks. I'll check with neighbors. Their empty mailbox may be from the post office holding their mail."

How could a neighborhood watch program become the seventy-five-year-old former teacher's pastime? Productivity had sunk to an all-time low this morning.

Nolan climbed into his SUV and headed toward the station. His radio crackled.

"Chief, are you there?"

"Just got back in the car. What's up?"

"Cliff called from Family Friendly Grocery on Hill Street. He requested you to come over. He's got a shoplifter."

"Again? I thought he'd be closed on Memorial Day. Okay, I'm heading there. I suppose a juvie ripped off his magazine rack again."

Nolan turned onto Division and made his way to Hill, where the battered grocery store marked the fringe of the city's impoverished section. He parked in front of a vacant barber shop's striped pole and crossed the street.

"Hey chief." Old Man Johnston pushed a shopping cart his direction.

"You found another stray cart." Nolan nodded to the grizzled man.

"Yup. Cliff owes me another dollar."

Nolan pushed open the paint-bare door and inhaled the smell of his mother's attic. Two young adults in faded smocks stood by the cash register.

"Over here chief," Cliff Appebee called from his small office.

Nolan strode past the register and into the dingy room shared by the veteran manager and his bookkeeper. He'd heard there was a new bookkeeper onboard. Cliff's desk was buried beneath piles of clutter. He did a second-take at the extra desk. Meticulous. The new part-time bookkeeper made a good impression.

Heart wrenching sobs came from Cliff's private restroom.

Nolan looked at Cliff. "What's going on?"

"Her name is Josie Decker."

"What did she lift?"

"Eggs."

"What?"

"I know, I know." He shook his head. "There was a half carton tucked in her sweater. I didn't know whether to call it in, but . . ." He pointed at the foam carton on his desk. "I feel kind of bad. She's pretty broke up."

"You made the call, Cliff, for a half dozen eggs. Seriously? You know the drill." Nolan couldn't abide law breaking, but everyone had a story. Some worse than others.

The bathroom door creaked open and a short, plump lady wearing a faded jogging suit stepped out. Her shoulder-length curls bobbing as she walked. She peeked at Cliff and Nolan. Then she looked down.

She hiccupped, not bothering to wipe the network of tears trailing down her face.

"I'm so ashamed." She pulled a tissue from her pocket and blew her nose. "In my whole life, I've never . . . my grandbabies haven't eaten since day before yesterday. I hoped I'd have enough, but I didn't. I told my neighbor I'd be right back. Ellen's watching them for me."

Nolan motioned to the empty chair. "Please, Miss Decker."

"Mrs. Decker." She raised her chin. "Mrs. Josephine Decker. My husband, God rest his soul, Bernard David, passed three years ago. What would he think? Oh, dear Lord." She burst into tears again.

Three tissues later, she continued. "They said my state check is lost. It's in the mail somewhere. Famous last words. How am I supposed to feed them? It's over a hundred dollars missing. Needed it a week ago. Everything's gone."

Nolan again pointed to the chair. "Mrs. Decker, please have a seat."

Thirty-five minutes later, he helped Josie Decker into his SUV. Paper grocery bags weighted with hot dogs, bread, eggs, peanut butter and jelly, macaroni and cheese, and bananas wouldn't last long. Her five-minute shopping spree hadn't been as lucrative as he hoped.

Way to go, Cliff. He seldom pressed charges. Mrs. Decker kept shaking her head and praising God. She promised to never steal again and offered Nolan the thirty-four cents in her pocket. It broke his heart.

As she directed, he drove three blocks and parked in front of a tired looking brick building. When she stepped out, two toddlers— a boy two or three, and a small girl in a dress so faded it had no color—raced forward. They hugged her legs and she gathered them into her arms.

She retrieved a banana from a bag, peeled it, and handed each child a half. They jumped up and down and squealed in delight.

He had never seen such excitement over a half banana.

~~~

Evah exited the bank feeling heavy hearted. She fanned the air with the envelope containing the notarized waiver. At the mailbox, she dropped it inside. If this enabled her to return to Mankato soon, it would be worthwhile.

She climbed in the truck and punched Nolan's number into her cell phone. Hopefully, she would be back soon to take Precious off Cassie's hands.

"Chief Quinn here," he sounded familiar, confident.

"You answered on the first ring. It's Evah."

"To what do I owe this pleasure?"

"I needed to call, to tell you something."

"And what is that?"

"I should've called sooner, but I'm heading out of town. I'll be back in a few hours."

"Where are you going?"

"To The Status. It's an alpaca fiber mill west of Bozeman."

"Oh?" He sounded surprised. "That's out of Park County. You're not driving Regan's old truck, are you?"

"I am and it's running okay."

"What's your business there?"

"I need to learn about the fiber-to-yarn process."

"You were advised not to leave the county, but I understand your rationale. I'll approve this trip. I saw your mountain of fiber bags."

"I'm not sure what I'm doing with it, but since I'm selling the ranch, I need the place to look productive."

"You're determined to leave, aren't you?" Nolan spoke sternly.

"You know I am. I don't belong here."

"Or maybe you don't want to?"

That is none of your business.

"I'm sorry, Evah. I wish you would give it more time. I wish you wouldn't rush your decision."

"I'm not rushing anything. That decision was made years ago."

"That's not true. This is your decision."

"And I've made it."

"And what about the friends you've made here? You would be missed."

"You're wrong. I'll be forgotten the minute I'm gone."

"You won't be. I promise you that."

She paused at his pleading his tone.

Thirty minutes later, she squealed to a halt in front of the large metal building she recognized from the website. Large white X's on the red doors and oversized flower pots gave it a cozy, country look. Flower pots like those would look inviting at home.

The thought stunned her. Not home. The ranch.

Wearing tan jeans and a designer tee-shirt, she walked into the huge building.

"Hello there." A lady wearing old chore clothes called. "Welcome to The Status."

"I'm Evah. I called about the tour and—"

"And the crash course in alpaca fiber." The lady flashed a brief smile and resumed her business tone. "I'm Karen. Hope you don't mind getting a little dirt and dust on you. Remember that I said it's a working ranch. Come on over and we'll get started."

For the next hour, Evah's head spun with trying to absorb information. The washer cleaned the fiber before it was laid out on drying racks. They went from one machine to another. She was fascinated but confused.

"Beautiful." Evah watched a rainbow of felt sheets evolve from the loom.

"This is a good way to use coarse fiber that's not good for much else." Karen motioned her forward.

Evah's brain felt like an ice cream freeze.

Tall red barrels filled with long rope-like fiber reminded her of the Mouse Trap game from years ago.

When she returned to the truck, she sat back and closed her eyes. It was too much to comprehend. Was a quick turnaround even possible?

I need help, God.

~~~

Nolan placed the stack of papers in Dawn's inbox. He was expected across town, but needed to check with the county. Keith wasn't a legitimate source to them. They were listening, but not hearing. Nolan understood. In police work, contacts had to be trustworthy. If he didn't respect Keith so much, he might not sit up and pay attention either.

Keith wouldn't have contacted him if this wasn't serious. The cross-country map they'd located highlighted multiple routes.

It was critical that he apprehend the mobile drug traffickers before their drugs passed into Woodridge. He needed to study the department's working map.

"Phone for you." Dawn called from her desk. "It's Sheriff Dettman."

"Chief Quinn here."

"Jonathan Green is now on your watch."

CHAPTER TWENTY

Evah awoke to sun streaming in her window. The thunderstorm had played havoc with her sleep. Her Bible lay open on her floral sheets. She rolled over and reread, "Cast your cares on the Lord and he will sustain you; he will never let the righteous be shaken." Her fingertips caressed the smooth leather.

"Evah, phone call." Jane interrupted her thoughts.

She raced downstairs and grabbed the receiver. "Hello?"

"Is this Evah Rois?"

Since when did the phone transmit into a speaker? Where was the speaker button?

"It is."

"This is Phyllis Jones. I'm sorry for phoning at this hour, but I wanted to catch you. I talked to Simeon Pratt yesterday. He said you're anxious to learn about alpaca fiber."

"Thanks for calling, but I'm on fiber overload right now."

"That's what Simeon said. This is last minute, but I have a lady coming to my studio this afternoon. I teach spinning and crafts a few miles east of town. Is it possible that you could come?"

"I don't know. I've already spent time . . ."

She turned to Jane, who brandished a metal spatula over a steaming skillet. She couldn't ask for help with Precious again.

"How about this?" Phyllis interjected. "Plan on an hour. I won't waste your time. I want to talk to you. Your fiber is worth money. Our alpaca industry needs it."

"I appreciate your offer, but I have a child to watch."

"Great! Bring her along. There's a playground next to my studio."

"But I can't leave her while—"

"I'll watch her." Cassie interrupted from behind. "Jonathan isn't supposed to be here today. Tell her you will meet her. I'll go with you and have a picnic with Precious. We could use the fresh air."

Jane spun around. "We'll all go."

All? Something like a frying egg hit the bottom of Evah's stomach.

Jane frowned at Cassie. "You'll run out of steam. I'll keep Precious busy."

This is getting weird. What's going on?

"All right," Evah answered Phyllis. "Give me your address and we'll meet you there. I can spare an hour, but no more." She couldn't handle another day like yesterday.

"Plan on one o'clock." Phyllis chimed. "You'll be glad you came."

Evah hung up the phone and turned to face Jane and Cassie. "Wouldn't it be easier if you two watched Precious here and—"

"No." They both answered in unison. They both looked at each other and laughed.

Cassie hugged her bathrobe. "Like it or not, you're going to have company."

"Well, that does present a problem." Evah looked from one to the other. "The truck isn't going to hold three adults and Precious's car seat."

"That's no problem," Jane put her hands on her hips, with a spatula still in one hand. "I'll drive my car." She turned to the smoking pancakes.

Evah read Cassie's expression. Should she face that unknown fear or face Jane?

Cassie blew out a breath and approached. "It'll be worth it, Evah. You'll attract alpaca owners through credibility."

A stream of toddler chatter floated down the stairway. Cassie nodded. "It'll be a fun outing. I'll go get our little visitor for breakfast."

"It's all you can do to lift her," Jane sprouted. "I'll get her. You finish the pancakes." She handed the metal spatula to Cassie and headed up the stairs.

Cassie leaned toward Evah and whispered, "It's too late to salvage anything. We'll need lots of syrup."

After breakfast, Evah sat on an overturned bucket in the middle of the pasture, with Precious on her lap. The more Precious giggled, laughed, and reached for the wide-eyed camelids, the further away they scurried.

Their large inquisitive eyes and fuzzy faces looked like balloons on top of long, sheered necks. Evah yearned to pet them, but even Marcos—the tamest alpaca on the ranch—skittered from Precious's squeals.

In Jane's sedan, Evah and Cassie listened to Jane's stories about the ranches they passed. Workers busied themselves, mostly with cattle, even though puddles and rivers scattered the low-lying areas.

Jane slowed to a stop. A traffic backup blocked the road.

"What's going on?" Evah peered at some kind of machinery tilting at a forty-five-degree angle. "I wouldn't have expected a traffic jam in the country."

"Looks like the front-end loader veered off the road," Jane announced. "The driver of that dump truck is trying to pull it upright."

A large red and white dump truck horizontal to the road blocked both lanes of traffic. With four or five vehicles between them, it was hard to tell what was happening.

"Look at the mud." Cassie made a face. "It looks like that big loader thing—"

"Front-end loader," Jane corrected.

"Yeah, front-end loader. It's sunk into mud near that clump of trees."

Men came and went. Cars didn't move.

"We're going to be late." Evah tapped her watch.

"No matter." Jane replied. "More important that the machine and its operator get moved safe. There's too many—"

An approaching siren muffled her voice.

"Neither of you would know," Jane continued after the ambulance passed, "but farming and ranching are the most dangerous jobs there are. Machinery, animals, weather. You can't be too careful."

They sat in silence until the ambulance screamed away.

"Could we help if we went over there?" Evah asked.

"No. Stay put," Jane barked. "They've got enough safety hazards."

Evah crossed her arms and pursed her lips. Jane and her snarky replies.

She punched Phyllis's phone number into her cell and left the message that they were running late. Good thing she brought the number.

Twenty-five minutes later, the front-end loader rested on the shoulder of the road. The diesel-puffing truck moved enough to make one lane passable. Cars wormed forward while everyone gawked.

"Jane," a male voice called from behind their car.

Jane pulled onto the shoulder and rolled down her window. A white-haired man wearing work grubs appeared at her window.

He tapped her car door. "If I'd have known you were in this car, Jane, I would've had you directing traffic."

"It's okay. Someone hurt bad?"

"Bad enough. Tried winching before towing. Bad idea. Got pinned between the bucket and truck tire."

"Gonna be okay?"

"Yeah. Raised the bucket quick enough."

"Good. I'd like to catch up, but we've gotta roll."

"Right. See you Wednesday." He gave her a broad smile and Jane pulled away from the scene.

He seemed to *like* her.

By the time they arrived, the other lady had come and gone, but Phyllis Jones's smile remained. Her cabin style home with a spinning and craft loft created a warm atmosphere that Evah found attractive and inviting. What a joy to work from home, doing something enjoyable. And making a living, of course.

The privileged elite.

The thought irritated her. Fairy tales seldom had happy endings.

She caught occasional glimpses of Cassie, Jane, and Precious from the second-floor window. After reassuring herself that they were all right, she focused on their discussion.

Phyllis didn't hold back. The alpaca industry needed to grow and it needed dedicated alpaca owners to make that happen. She provided options for Evah to create yarns and felted soap. "And best of all, alpaca organizations on all levels provide learning venues." Phyllis held out colorful yarns. "We're a close-knit group. We're here for each other. We would love you to join us."

Evah nodded. Nobody understood her sense of urgency and the fact that she had to leave.

At the sound of raised voices, she stood and looked out the window.

Precious sat on the ground between Cassie and Jane. The child's beet red face relayed the same message as the adults.

Cassie turned toward the house and her view locked on Evah. She shook her head.

Jane looked up and shook a pointed finger at Cassie.

Evah thanked her hostess, excused herself, and hurried toward the door. The outing was over.

~~~

Nolan pulled into the "Reserved for Chief" parking spot. Two television vehicles monopolized the lot. He hoped they were pestering the Recreation Department.

He yanked the heavy glass door and inhaled the old building smell. Balls thumped on the multi-purpose room floor. He crossed the lobby, his shoes clicking on the marble-looking floor.

"Hey chief, you've got visitors downstairs." Barry, the maintenance man, called out from where he knelt next to the drinking fountain. He looked up from his toolbox.

A young mother walked toward them, carrying a young girl with dark curly hair.

She resembles Jonathan Green's girl.

A quick vision of Evah under the tree with the toddler flitted through his mind. He needed to talk to her. She would get stranded driving that old wreck and what if it happened in a different county?

"Is the bubbler broken?" The lady tried to loosen the child's grip around her neck. "Cynthia, please. Let loose. Mommy can't breathe."

"Bubbler?" Nolan stepped forward to help.

"Yes, bubbler. The water—"

"The drinking fountain?" Nolan asked.

Barry nodded. "It's fixed now."

Nolan reached forward, but before he could regulate the water, the child turned the lever and a stream sprayed across her face. She wailed and buried her wet face in her mother's shoulder.

"Sorry. That backfired." He apologized.

"I'll get a towel." Barry scooted away.

"It's not your fault," the lady smiled. "I appreciate your help."

"Someone is very thirsty." Nolan offered a warm smile as he spoke to the child.

She nodded. "Thirty."

"Want more?" Nolan reached forward. "This time, I'll turn the water on. Look."

The girl frowned, watching water shoot out and flow into the drain.

"Go ahead. I'm holding it for you."

"Me do, me do." Her small hand covered his.

The touch of her warm fingers on his sent an electric feeling through him. Kids.

She gulped water, then looked up and gave him a big smile. Barry reappeared and handed a towel to the mother.

Nolan smiled. "What was that about the bubbler?"

"It's Midwest lingo for drinking fountain."

Commotion sounded from the basement. Nolan excused himself and headed downstairs, toward the lion's den.

CHAPTER TWENTY-ONE

N olan entered the Woodridge Police Department. Trey Kramer from the local paper and a handful of locals stood near two long tables that someone had pushed against the far wall. Piles of stuff on the tables made his pulse quicken. He didn't like messes.

The staff knew protocol. His face muscles tightened and he prepared for confrontation.

First impressions set the tone.

He blew out a breath and pushed the door open. Two men and an attractive brunette sat on the plaid sofa. Seeing him, they jumped to their feet and scrambled for writing tablets.

Reporters.

Trey lifted a box from the long table and shook it in front of Nolan. Cereal. "Look Chief!"

Nolan scanned the table. Paper bags, plastic bags, boxes. All full of groceries.

He gave Dawn a hard look. She looked back down at her steno pad.

Seated at the receptionist desk with the phone receiver in her left hand, she jotted notes. She shook her head, disagreeing with the caller.

When she hung up, she gave Nolan a distressed look. "Chief, I need to—"

"Chief Quinn, tell us about the video. What's your take on Josephine Decker?"

"Has she shoplifted before? Does she have a record?"

"What do you plan to—"

"Dawn." She met his gaze and stood up, squeezing her hefty frame between the reporters, and headed toward him.

Nolan turned to the expectant faces. "I'll be with you all in a few minutes."

Ignoring protests, he opened his office door, waited for Dawn to enter, and shut it behind them.

"You know what I'm going to say." He walked behind his desk and sat in the worn leather chair.

"I know, I know. You don't like surprises." She laid her steno pad on the corner of his desk. Then she gave him a hard look back. "I don't like them either and I didn't ask for this. It's not my doing."

"My department has turned into a thrift shop." He struggled to keep his voice down. "What is going on? And, I want the short version."

Dawn arched her eyebrows. "I'm sorry. It happened fast. I didn't get a chance to call." She glanced at the window. "Piranha."

"The short version." Nolan pushed work files to the side of the desk. He removed his hat, set it on the gray desktop, and ran his hands through his hair.

A quick smile came and went from the corner of Dawn's lips. "New style, short on the sides. A little longer on top. Nice."

"Don't change the subject."

The phone on her desk rang.

"Leave it. You can catch the voicemail later."

"It hasn't stopped—"

"Let's have it. Right now. The short version." Nolan smoothed his tie. Then he folded his hands and waited.

"One of the grocery clerks at that store recorded the last part of your interview with Josephine. Tears. Hungry grandchildren. And the missing check. He got it all. It went viral. The public is eating it up. Everyone is clambering for interviews and answers."

"Where's Cliff?"

"Won't talk to the press, sending everyone here. Making them mad as hornets. He says you decided that he shouldn't press charges, so it's your project."

"So, people are bringing groceries here?"

"Groceries. Some clothes. Companies calling to donate. Everyone wants in on it."

"What's your take?"

"It's a good cause." Dawn grabbed the steno pad and flipped through the pages, tapping her manicured nails on the paper. "Offers, donations. People are dropping off food by the cars full. Families, too. Here's a pledge for three boxes of cereal per week for six months. She shook the note like a dripping cloth.

"Look at this list." She picked it up in her other hand and handed it to him. "I haven't accomplished a single thing all morning." After scanning three pages, he returned it to her.

"Okay." He thought for a moment. "Get Millers on this. Have him contact Josephine so she knows what's going on. Get it organized. We need particulars from her . . . their current needs . . . food allergies, sizes of kids' clothes, all that."

"Got it."

Commotion sounded. In the reception area, a county deputy walked toward the tables carrying in a cardboard box. Reporters pushed toward him, all talking over each other.

"Tell Millers to get Josephine ready for an interview."

"What about her grandchildren?"

"They are welcome to be with her, but they need to be monitored. I won't stand for a free for all."

"You've already got a free for all."

Nolan pursed his lips and shook his head, putting it together in his mind.

Dawn leaned forward and spoke in a hushed voice. "She's a grandma. She'll want her grandkids to look nice."

"Of course." He reached in his pocket and retrieved his billfold. "That's why you will take them shopping for new outfits on their way here."

"Me?"

"You."

Dawn nodded.

"You okay with that?"

Her expression softened. "Very much so."

"This is snowballing. Have the guys coordinate deliveries. We'll use the office as headquarters. For now." He stood up and looked at the growing crowd.

"Call it the Josephine Decker Drive."

"Chief?"

He looked back.

"You know that someone's going to yell because she wasn't arrested?"

"I wouldn't be surprised, but let's try to keep the hype positive. It could do the department some good. The city. Take the focus off the shooter."

~~~

Evah sat in the passenger seat and leaned against the door. Jane's white-knuckled grip on the steering wheel matched her sharp driving.

Cassie wouldn't even look her way. She stared out her backseat window, her chin set in a way that never meant anything good.

Neither had said a word since Evah appeared in front of them at Phyllis Jones's place. They packed Precious and themselves into the car and headed home.

Evah glanced back at Precious, strapped into her car seat, playing with the stuffed zebra.

"I don't suppose either of you would care to tell me what this is about?"

Neither spoke.

When the wheels screeched around a sharp turn, Evah gripped the dash. "Could we please get there in one piece? The least you could do is think about your young passenger."

The vehicle slowed.

Evah looked at the spiral notebook on her lap. She had so many notes. Would they make sense? She needed to get rid of the alpaca fiber without taking a year to do it.

Jane clicked on the radio.

"Anyone can contribute to this fund drive." A man's voice filled the car. "Donations should be dropped at the police office, fifty-two north Rock Street. Primarily food. The list of suggested items is on our Police Department website. Direct questions to Patrolman Millers at the number I'll give at the end of the interview."

The voice sounded like Nolan.

"Thank you, Chief Quinn. Can you tell me—"

"Nolan." Evah squealed. "He's on the radio."

"A food drive?" Cassie leaned forward. "I didn't know police departments did things like that."

"I didn't either." Evah mused.

Nolan had provided an ice breaker. *Thank you, Nolan. Thank you, dear Lord.*

"It's not such a surprise," Jane piped in. "In small towns, people can do things easier than in big cities. And sometimes," she looked in her rearview mirror, "sometimes, people know what's best for one another.

"Must've been something happen to get this food drive going. Wonder what it's all about."

They passed through modest neighborhoods along the north edge of town, Evah turned to Jane. "Would you mind if I run into a grocery store? I would be in and out in no time. I need almond milk and cereal. It'll save a trip."

Jane scowled. "If you're buying milk, buy the real thing."

"I can get regular milk for you and almond milk for me. I'll be quick. I promise."

Jane turned into the local grocery store's parking lot. "Make it snappy. I need to get to my route."

Her route again.

Evah turned to Cassie. "Do you want to come in? Or do you need anything?"

Cassie shook her head, her chin still in that angry, determined pose.

Evah hurried into the store. She found milk and three aisles over, she located cereal. She grabbed two boxes and headed to the checkout counter. Maybe small stores could be convenient after all.

"Why it's just the saddest thing about those little kids." The lady in front of her conversed with the checker.

"I know what it's like. Used to live in the projects myself. Hard times."

"That chief." The lady gathered her items and started to walk away. "He's doing a good thing by this."

Evah wondered if Nolan knew what people were saying. She checked out, hoping for more information, but the cashier gave her a silent smile.

Ten minutes later, Jane pulled the car into the driveway. A black pickup truck sat parked in front of the barn. When Jane's car crunched across the parking lot, a tall, skinny man got out of the truck.

Evah's pulse quickened. "Jane, do you know who that is?"

"Nope. Can't say as I do."

"I'll see if I can help him. Just leave my things here. I'll get them later." She looked at Cassie, who glanced at her, eyes tight with concern. "Go on into the house. I'll be right there."

Evah exited the car and walked toward the man. His unkempt beard matched the battered cowboy hat on his head.

"Can I help you?" Remembering the alpaca delivery, Evah wondered if she should note his license number.

Don't be paranoid.

"Yes, ma'am." He tipped his hat. "Wondered if you would sell a bag of 'paca beans. For the missus' flowers."

At the blank look on her face, he offered a crooked smile. "'Paca beans. 'Paca poo. Whatever you call it."

"Oh, of course. Alpaca beans. Yes, all sales are welcome."

She hadn't thought of selling alpaca manure—beans. They were deposited along the east side of the property.

"I brought my own little garbage can to put it in, if that's okay."

"Sure, thanks."

At the sound of tires crunching on gravel behind them, they both turned. Nolan's SUV pulled up behind Jane's car.

The man grabbed his five-gallon can. "I'll just help myself. Is the price the same?"

"The same?"

"The same as what Regan charged?"

"Yes, I'll charge whatever he did."

She turned to see Nolan exit his SUV and stare at the man walking away from them.

"Do you know him?" his voice growled.

"No. He asked to buy alpaca beans for fertilizer. It seems that he used to buy them from Uncle Regan."

Nolan wore a long-sleeved black tee-shirt and jeans. She hoped her face wasn't pink. He looked good. Real good.

"Are you a civilian today?" She looked down at his black Sketchers.

He gave her a warm look. "I'm taking Honey to the trail. Want to walk Cash?"

"That's the best suggestion I've heard all day. Give me two minutes to get changed and I'll be right with you." She blushed. "Or I can meet you there. I didn't mean to presume. And I should wait for this man to finish his business."

"I'll keep an eye on him. Get ready."

Evah grabbed her items from Jane's car and hurried into the house. "I'm taking Cash for a short walk. Precious will be asleep for a while yet and I'll be back soon."

"That man gone?" Jane turned from the kitchen counter.

"He's finishing up. Nolan's outside with him."

"Cassie?" Evah hurried upstairs.

"I'm in my room," her voice had calmed. "I see that Nolan's here. That's good timing."

"Yes, the guy just wanted to buy alpaca poop."

"Yuck."

Evah changed into designer jeans and a striped blouse. Then she clicked Cash's leash onto his collar and dashed out the door. She scanned the yard for Nolan.

He stood at the far edge of the field, talking with the man. Nolan waved and crossed the field toward her, still frowning. When he closed the distance between them, he smiled. It looked forced.

"Your customer is leaving," he nodded toward the man. "He'll leave payment in the milk can by the barn door."

"Is something wrong?"

"No. He'll be gone in a minute. If we take our time, we'll see him leave." He motioned to his SUV. "Do you want to ride with me?"

"No, thanks. I wouldn't want to give people the wrong idea."

"Well, I do have friends."

"That's not what I meant. I'm not a criminal." She smiled. "Let's walk." She held up Cash's old, faded leash. "Do you have a leash for Honey?"

"I do." Nolan smiled. "And it's a bee-uty."

CHAPTER TWENTY-TWO

Evah watched the border collie's graceful, smooth gait. Nolan and his dog walked so nice together. He looked confident and handsome, yet he delighted in a leash covered with honey bees. When had she met a man confident enough to be in charge and soft enough to care?

"We'll veer off in a minute." Nolan turned toward a truck roaring past. "Get a good hold on his leash."

His muscular build and broad shoulders made her blush. Policemen must meet physical condition standards, even the chief.

He moved ahead to break trail. "Did you do anything special for Memorial Day?"

"No. Jane grilled." She couldn't help the disgusting tone of her voice. Overcooked hot dogs and blackened corn on the cob made for a disappointing holiday meal. Jonathan never arrived and, if she'd have known that Jane was going to leave before they ate, she would've gladly done the cooking. "How about you?"

"I worked."

"Get back here," she reined in Cash. Too bad they couldn't have spent the day together. "I hear there's a fundraiser going on. And the word around town is that you're the brains behind the operation."

"You're in on local scuttlebutt?" His light-hearted laugh made her pulse race. "I'm not sure about the brains of the operation. My department has turned into a food pantry."

Evah paused to untangle the leash. "Is it for a specific family?"

146

Nolan stopped. "If you bring up the slack in the leash, it won't tangle. Like this." He took the leash from her hand, looped the extra length, and returned it to her hand.

At his touch, his blue eyes met hers. Their gaze held until she crouched to pet the energetic corgi.

Nolan continued. "The food drive was initiated because of a particular need. At the rate it's growing, I'm not sure where it will end."

She shot up from her crouched position and moved past him.

Nolan fell into step. "Where did you hear about the food drive?"

"On the radio. The four of us, Jane and Jonathan's daughter, Precious, Cassie and I, were on our way home from Phyllis Jones's place."

"I'm not sure I know her."

"She's into alpaca yarn."

"Does she have a store?" Nolan moved up, crowding the right side of the path.

"Yes, it's just outside of town."

"Was it worthwhile?"

"It was interesting, until something happened between Jane and Cassie."

"That shouldn't come as a surprise."

"I know, but before we went there, they were laughing together."

"That *is* a surprise."

Cash swung his head and pulled on the leash. Evah pulled him into place. "You're not a donkey. Get over here."

"He's trying to reach Honey."

"But he needs to mind."

The dogs, nose to nose, wagged tails and bounded with excitement. Evah stepped between them and turned in a circle, pulling Cash away from the collie. She stepped forward, but he darted in front of her. Evah sidestepped to avoid being tangled.

"Hold him close on your left."

She pulled him in tighter. "He's strong for his size." She resumed walking and Cash strained to the right. "How about if you walk on my left?"

"Good idea."

She hugged the right side of the path. Nolan pushed left.

"That's better. Thanks. I don't know who needs training more, Cash or me." She laughed and looked at Nolan. The corners of his mouth lifted and she noticed the gleam in his eyes.

"The more you walk together, the easier it gets. So, about Phyllis Jones. How did that go?"

"Not good, really."

"What happened?"

"It's a lot to figure out. I would have to pay for fiber processing, and then what and how to have a product made. Once I'm back in the city, how would I sell the stuff and where would I store it?

"I understand Phyllis's determination to grow the alpaca industry, but I'm getting inundated with information. I don't know how to sort through it all to make sense of it."

"Which appointment went better, the one with Phyllis or the fiber mill?"

"It's a toss-up. Either way, there's a gap between processing fiber and having products to sell. And keeping Jane off my back is no small task."

"Is she being difficult?"

"She, Cassie, and Precious came to the meeting. Not to attend it, but to entertain Precious. It ended in disaster."

"With Precious?"

"No. The adults."

"It's a lot to contend with, especially when your heart isn't in it."

His comment stung. Could she sell a business and keep herself from caring about it?

Nolan stopped near a sign displaying the trail system. Their shoes swooshed over the grassy single-file path. "This is my shortcut. We're heading to the wooden bridge over there."

Moments later, they stood in front of the arched bridge. He pointed to a sign. "This is Knowles Bridge. It was donated to the trail. It crosses the little crik we've been walking parallel to."

Nolan stopped. Evah almost collided with him, but stepped backward. Too late. She had inhaled his spicy scent.

"I hadn't even noticed that little bit of water. The ridge is just high enough to block it."

"The bed is dry most of the time. It's part of Sunrise Crik. Across the bridge starts the Green Loop. You can take that full circle back to where we are now, or," he pointed ahead to the left and then to the right, "you can take it to the Yellow Loop that joins back to the main trail."

His finger traced the map. "The Green Loop is .3 mile. If we walk to the Yellow Loop and then this section, that's another .6 mile. Are you up for it?"

"Oh, yes. Come on Cash, let's go." Her brisk steps moved forward, her shoes echoing on the wooden bridge. Rows of empty flower pots lined the sides. Would they display colorful varieties for the grand opening?

"Hey there," a man and woman's voices called out. "Look, it's Chief Quinn."

Evah and Nolan looked toward the voices. A petite gray-haired lady walked a small dog on a leash. At her side, a slouched man in a motorized scooter moved with her.

"Well, if it isn't Roger Z speeding over the trail." Nolan stepped forward and gave the gray-haired man a hefty handshake.

"And look at you." The lady scooped up the small dog. "It's not very often that we see you out of uniform."

Nolan turned. "Evah, this is Roger Zimmerman and his beautiful wife, Aggie." He turned back to the Zimmermans. "And this is Evah Rois. She's new here."

Evah smiled and shook Roger's frail hand. "It's nice to meet you." She turned toward Aggie. "And who is this?" She patted the dog's head. Aggie's eyes glistened.

"This is Astro, our pride and joy." A gust of air ruffled her short haircut and Evah noticed dark circles under her eyes. "I needed help to keep this husband of mine in line. We've had Astro for four months now. We just love him. Don't we, Roger?"

Roger's shaky hand reached forward to stroke the dog's neck. "Oh, he's a pistol, he is."

"Chief, what's this about a food drive? Can we help?" She petted the dog as she leaned against Roger's scooter.

"News gets around fast." Nolan squatted down and petted Honey. "I received a shoplifting call that turned out to be a grandmother heisting eggs for her grandkids. A bad situation. The whole thing went viral—online for the world to see. Before I knew it, my office turned into headquarters for a food drive."

Aggie placed the dog on Roger's lap. She kept a tight grip on the leash. "It's great that you're supporting this. We saw the lady being interviewed. I think at her home."

"Yes, it was her home." Roger chimed in.

"Any help you can give them will be a godsend, chief."

"Thank you." Nolan stepped back. "It's great to see you two. Enjoy your walk. And no hot rodding, Roger."

"So, have you heard about a food drive going on?" Roger looked at Nolan.

Aggie patted his hand. "Yes, dear, he's heard. Come now, let's continue our walk."

Nolan and Aggie exchanged a knowing look and Aggie set the dog back on the grass. The threesome moved away.

"No hot rodding?" Evah teased.

Nolan's pink ears contrasted his dark hair. "Roger used to drive truck. He had a bit of a heavy foot, so we've been acquainted for years." He moved forward and motioned for Evah to move beside him. "He loves trucks, tractors. Used to compete in truck pulls at the fair. She was always there to watch him. On the flip side, he always bragged about her cooking and projects."

"It sounds like they've been through a lot together."

"Not many couples live like that anymore."

Evah squirmed. "Is the scooter permanent?"

"Yes, but he doesn't know it. His legs are bad and he has early dementia. Aggie is determined that they enjoy being together as long as possible."

A rabbit scooted across the path. Evah's arm jerked forward as Cash pulled his leash from her grip. *Oh, no!* The small dog darted off the footpath, racing around pines and hardwoods. His leash flapped and dragged.

"I lost the leash! Come back, Cash."

The corgi barked and Evah rushed forward. She heard Nolan's breath and footsteps behind her.

"I think I see him." She pushed through tangled tree limbs. "How can he run so fast with those short legs?"

"Be careful," Nolan warned. "This is prime territory to turn an ankle."

Honey whined. Evah glanced back to see Nolan tighten the slack on her leash.

"Oh no you don't," Nolan scolded Honey. "I'm not spending an hour pulling burs from your hair."

"If you let her loose, would she lead us to him?"

"At first. Then she would join him for a romp." They moved deeper into the pines.

"Am I getting us lost?"

"No. We'll come out near the Yellow Trail. We're taking a shortcut."

"Some shortcut." She pulled dried leaves from her hair.

"Stay to the right. It gets rocky."

"I'm glad you know the way. I came here once before, but never saw the trail.

"You were here and didn't see the trail?"

Evah whirled so fast that she almost collided with Nolan. Her muscles tensed. "You don't really want to discuss this, do you?"

"Why not? What's wrong?"

"You're asking as if you don't know. You were the one who invited me here."

"But I didn't think you came."

"I know you were caught up in that shooter mess, so I asked the other cop to tell you that I came to see you. But he didn't have the right to treat me like that."

"Who treated you like what?"

"That pompous friend of yours. The guy in the brown uniform."

"Brown uniform? Who and what did he do?"

Recalling the humiliating conversation, she turned and walked fast. "Just forget it. We've got to find Cash."

They crunched forward without speaking. Moments later, excited barks filled the air. Evah stepped into a clearing.

"There he is!" She rushed to capture his leash. Cash bounced at the base of a large tree. A cloth bag hung from its lowest tree branch. "What's that?"

"I'm not sure. A bag with something hanging out of a pocket." Nolan side-stepped and took a closer look. "Don't touch it." Using a small-but-sturdy branch, he lifted the bag from the tree. "It's an ammo bag with a stick of unwrapped beef jerky sticking out. No wonder Cash treed it."

Evah rubbed her forehead. "It's military green."

Nolan reached into the bag. "Here's a box of ammo cartridges."

"What? Live ammo?"

He tucked the ammo bag under his arm. "Let's go. We have a distance to cover yet."

~~~

Nolan's mind raced. This could be a lead to the shooter. Or, it could be kids playing. He'd have it checked for fingerprints. And just in case, he'd order a substitute to replace it as soon as possible.

"It's a clue, isn't it?" Evah sounded excited.

He didn't want to alarm her. There were too many factors that needed to be sorted out. "It could be something or nothing."

She looked disappointed. "If someone left it here, they might not have been able to find it. But, why would it be here at all?"

"That's a good question."

"Dispatch to Chief." Siemor's voice interrupted.

He pushed his mic button. "Chief here."

"Sheriff Dettman returned your call. He wants to meet."

Priorities were overlapping.

I need to make wise decisions, Lord. Please direct my path.

"What do you think? You're a million miles away." Evah gazed at him.

"Sorry. I've got a lot on my mind."

"Care to share?"

"Not right now, but thanks. I prayed for guidance."

"Does it help?" Evah crunched forward. "I plan, but God always has something else in mind."

CHAPTER TWENTY-THREE

Nolan entered the Park County Sheriff's Department in Livingston.

"Morning chief," the receptionist smiled. "Haven't seen you in a while."

"I try to keep my distance. Is he ready?"

"Yes, go ahead." She buzzed him in.

"Nolan, come in." County Sheriff Cecil Dettman shook his hand. "It's been too long."

"Good to see you, Cec."

The stout sheriff removed his glasses and set them on his cluttered desk. "You, too. I'm hearing good things about your team."

"Thanks. It's an uphill climb." Nolan sat in the hard-backed chair in front of the desk.

"If I were a betting man, I'd wager this isn't a social call. What's up?"

"You know I hate this trivial stuff."

"I do, too."

"I've got an unpopular topic, Cec. Protocol."

"Something in particular?"

"Someone."

"Fill me in."

"Jonathan Green."

"Not popular around here."

"I figured. But I have some light to shed. And I have some questions."

"I'm all ears."

"Your department made the collar. Grease."

"Yeah, Bob. Not a bad cop overall, but a thorn."

"I know, but this was over the top. I was uninformed about the arrest, on purpose, and abandoned at the site. There's no excuse for that and I won't tolerate it."

"I'll set a meeting. You, Grease, Human Resources, and myself." Dettman straightened the tie clip securing the light brown tie to his dark brown shirt. "As far as Green goes, there are politics involved. He ticked off folks that want him to pay."

"At whose expense? Do you know about his child?"

"Yes. It's unfortunate."

"You revoked his community service."

"Judge Hacker did. I feel bad about it."

"Then make it right. We had community service arranged. It wasn't to code, but you've made exceptions. Come on, Cec. You would do more for a drug thug."

"The ranch you offered isn't non-profit and we're talking about a sniper. A danger to the community."

"Charged and found guilty?"

"That's how it looks."

"Can't you minimize it, for the girl."

"I can't."

"You can. He doesn't need to sit in jail." Nolan laid an outstretched palm on the table. "You don't want to upset the powers that be. I get that."

"Don't you tell me what I want." Dettman pointed his index finger at Nolan.

"You know what I mean. Green is arrogant, but he's a misdemeanor at best."

"You're assuming. And you're asking a lot."

"It isn't for me. And there's one more thing."

"The moon?"

"Grease again. He's been shooting his mouth off. It's personal."

Dettman raised an eyebrow. "And you're bringing that to me?"

"I'll take it up with him myself. But I want you to know if he persists, I'll do more than have him written up."

"Fair enough."

Dettman picked up a letter opener and fingered the blade. "You're bulldogging this mobile drug operation."

"It's firsthand information. Reliable. And if it ties into Young's death as I think it will—"

"Maybe, but we don't have hours to spend on unknowns. They could be picked up anywhere." Dettman set the letter opener down. "It's low priority. Drug arrests along 90 East are constant."

"No matter which way they come, they'll drive through here."

"We don't know the vehicle, drivers, nothing. We need more. I'm not spending manpower on a failing venture. We all want Young's killer."

"Woodridge and Livingston were circled on the map, along with Bozeman. They're going to meet someone or make drops. We have to stay on it."

~~~

At the sound of her ringtone, Evah grabbed her phone. "Hello?"

"It's Carolyn."

"It's great to hear you." She lowered herself onto the bench next to her blue dresser.

"I wanted to update you. The contractors are stalling. They want this place tied up so I can't reopen. Word is getting around."

"Oh no. Is it—"

"Listen. I'm having major second thoughts about reopening."

"What do you mean?" An alarm sounded in Evah's head.

"I don't know if this is worth it. They're willing to pay me a decent amount."

"Wouldn't you regret it?"

"I can find another location, a different town. It's the staff that I'm thinking about. I don't want to hurt feelings. They're counting on me for their livelihoods."

Mine, too.

"I understand, Carolyn. But this isn't about everyone else. I know you don't want to suffer hardships for the next decade because you foiled their plans. You shouldn't be bullied."

"I don't think I can be happy here anymore. I just wanted to voice my thoughts to you."

"I appreciate that." Evah searched for words. "Know that I'll go along with whatever you decide."

"That means a lot," her friend's voice broke and they ended the conversation.

Evah scribbled a note to Jane and Cassie. They could take Precious to Frank's Furry Friends today. She wasn't up to it.

She needed to get away for a few hours, to think. And meeting Nolan for dinner? She wouldn't be good company. Better to phone and cancel after her drive.

She walked downstairs and pinned the note under a ceramic apple on the kitchen counter. Outside, she pulled keys from her back pocket and slid across the truck's worn seat.

The engine sputtered. She moved the truck alongside the barn door and dashed inside.

"You're waiting for me, aren't you?" She dragged the alpaca's pellet bag forward, filled the bins, and returned to the truck.

She rummaged in her duffle bag until her fingers latched onto hard plastic. There. Her old orienteering compass from college. She stuck it in her pocket and slid behind the wheel.

The road bordered the backside of Uncle Regan's acreage, which changed from sunlit hardwoods to dense evergreens. She parked, walked into the pines, and paused while her eyesight adjusted to the sun-deprived forest.

Each step echoed brush crunching underfoot. She inhaled the fragrance of trees, fresh air, and whatever else smelled so good.

She moved forward, pushing face-height branches away from her. After a dozen or so steps, she felt uncertain and pulled out the compass. The needle didn't move. She tapped it and tried again. She stuffed it back in her pocket. Useless.

She and Nolan had been somewhere in this area. She hopped a tiny creek—or maybe it was a crik—and kept walking, ducking under protruding branches and sidestepping rocks. The ground became slippery and she remembered Nolan's cautions.

Her heart leapt at the thought of his warm blue eyes and the lips that she yearned to kiss. But it could never work between them. Her past imprisoned her.

She pushed through thick brush. Barbs cut through her tee-shirt and scratched. Terrain closed in, thick and tangled on every side. She pushed on, exploring the unknown. Her breathing became labored.

Her life echoed the forest, tangled and dark. She'd been a schmuck kid, lashing out at anyone who would dare come close. When she finally turned things around, God sent her Carolyn and Cassie. If the bakery closed, would she lose them?

Woody debris dotted the terrain. She picked up a broken branch and hurled it into the brush. She kicked at undergrowth, anger pulsing through her veins.

The angrier she felt, the faster she walked. She had tried so hard.

Her toe sideswiped a rock. She steadied her footing and scrambled sideways to avoid a hidden stump.

The compass didn't work and she had already walked a good distance. She slowed and eyed a slight rise ahead. Maybe she could see something from there. She moved forward.

Her left foot slid backwards. Her neck jerked. She landed flat on her back. "Ow. That hurt!" Something hard and uneven jutted against her back.

She rolled to the side and brushed dirt off the top of a rusty, gray barrel lid. "What's this doing in the middle of the woods?" She clambered to her feet and kicked at it.

"What's that?" A deep voice thundered through the bramble. "Listen."

Evah stood still. Who had she come upon?

"Is it a deer?" A softer male voice asked.

"Not unless it talks."

She had found help. "Hello!" Hope surged through her being.

Men shouted. Metal banged. A dozen footsteps later, Evah stepped into a clearing and squinted in non-filtered sunlight.

Two men sat on rusty half-barrels in front of a dilapidated shed. "It's a girl!"

They gawked at her like Big Foot had appeared.

CHAPTER TWENTY-FOUR

A long-haired man wearing a beat-up Aussie hat chewed a mouthful of something. She could barely make out his face under overgrown whiskers and beard.

The other man was slighter in build, twentyish, and wore a cap with netting draped from its sides. He crushed an empty can between his hands.

"Hi guys. I'm a little off course." She brushed off dirt and brambles.

"A little?" The Capped Man pointed to where she had just emerged. "Lady, you walked out of a patch that I avoid."

Evah recalled the alpaca delivery men. She stood tall and placed her hands on her hips. *Be with me, Lord.*

"I'm glad to see you two. You're my knights in shining armor."

"How do you figure?" Aussie sneered.

"You must know the area. You can help me get out of here."

"We should know the area." Aussie narrowed his thick eyebrows. "But you? What are you doing here?"

"I was out walking, getting fresh air. But I don't know the area."

"You're off your rocker, lady." Aussie shook his head.

The other man stared. "You're lost?"

"I am." She smiled, despite her shaking knees. *Don't let them think I'm afraid. Help me, God.*

"I am," Aussie mimicked.

The Capped Man squinted.

158

Evah's pulse quickened. "I'm not from around here. I couldn't find my way back any more than my way here." Evah knelt on one knee and tightened her shoelace. "When they come looking for me, they'll laugh at how turned around I am."

"Who's coming looking?" Aussie looked skeptical. "And how did you expect to get back?"

Evah dug in her pocket. "Take a look. It's broken." She placed her orienteering compass in his thick fingers yellowed by foul-smelling gasoline or something. She stepped back.

"I've never seen a compass like this." He held it out for Cap Man to see. "Look at this rig. How can you tell it's broke?"

Evah pointed. "See that magnetic needle in the middle?"

"Yeah."

"Turn the compass around. It doesn't even—"

"Yep, I see." He stood and turned back and forth. Snags and rips covered the back of his jacket. "It ain't movin'."

"Can you help me?" Evah looked from one to the other. "You can have my compass as a souvenir. Maybe you can get it working."

"How much is it worth?" Aussie looked interested.

"At least fifty dollars."

The man wearing the tan cap nodded. "If anyone can fix it, Daimon here can."

Evah forced a smile. "I don't know about compasses, other than how to use them. If it can be fixed, keep it or sell it."

"I dunno." Aussie shook it.

"Sounds like a plan," the Cap Man said.

"Listen, I don't want my friends to traipse through this mess, looking for me. Will either of you point me in the direction out of here?"

Aussie scowled and Cap Man stared.

Cap Man removed his faded tan cap and stuffed the netting up under it. Then he pulled it back over his dark curls. "So, where are you supposed to be?"

"Don't you be helping her," the long-haired Aussie frowned. "You don't know what she's doing out here. She could be—"

"Come on, Daimon. Let me do this." The younger man smiled and turned red. "I can help. Sides, you don't want her friends—"

"You watch yourself—" Aussie pointed a finger at Cap Man. He turned to Evah. "You say a word about this to anyone, you're dead. And the person you tell, too."

Evah froze. What were they doing back here? She eyed the rickety cabin and inhaled the odd smell.

"I know what I'm doing." The young man faced Evah. "Come on. I'll show you the way out."

A trail of mumbles followed them. Evah followed the young man who circled around Aussie, giving him a wide berth. They headed through dense scrub and hardwood.

Would the brute come after them?

The young man's shoulders relaxed. "You aren't from here?" He dropped back to match Evah's gait. She side-stepped to keep a distance.

"No." She tried to sound calm.

"But you live here now?"

"I'm visiting."

"We have a lot in common, you and me."

"We do?"

"Yeah. I'm not from here either. My name's Pierce."

The foul smell had disappeared.

"I'm Evah. Where are you from?" She scanned the terrain.

"Minneapolis. I'm visiting, too, paying back—" He shot Evah a sharp look. "Forget I said that. Anyway, I'll be heading home soon."

They walked another hundred yards, dodging face-level branches and side-stepping uneven footing. She hoped that he knew where he was going. Her throat ached for a drink.

He turned sharply. She followed through brittle underbrush.

They emerged onto an open field and her heartbeat quickened. She could see the wooded perimeter. They were west of the trail.

"I remember this area. Thanks, I can take it from here."

"Are you sure? Where do you need to be?"

Evah scanned the area to confirm her bearings. They were around the corner from the truck. She didn't want him to see it.

"Back to the trail. The south side." She pointed left, away from the farm.

"Stay in this clearing 'til you round that border of trees over there." He pointed. "You'll come onto the trail entrance around the corner."

Evah felt relief. She recognized familiar terrain. The ranch would be to her right, west. But she headed to the trail entrance. She wasn't about to risk being followed.

A dog barked somewhere. Cash? No, too deep and too close.

He stopped walking. "I'll say good-bye." He stuck his thumbs in his belt loops. "You can find your way from here."

"Thanks for your help. I hope you don't get much flak."

"If you know what's good for you, stay away from there. Way away. You got lucky this time."

"I couldn't find it again even if I wanted to." She turned and took two hesitant steps.

Was he watching her? She turned, relieved to see that he had vanished into the forest.

She walked as fast as her legs would go.

~~~

Nolan sat at his desk, scanning the printout of veterans registered with the local post.

He'd distributed the list to his staff, requesting specific individuals be checked. He didn't want
to create a stir. One name on the page bothered him.

Mary Jane Martin.

Personal feelings didn't belong in a professional investigation. He still hadn't heard back on any veterans missing an ammo bag. He glanced at the duplicate bag propped on his file cabinet. He needed to return it before someone missed the original.

The thought of Evah and him hiking made him smile. And after two "thank you but no's", she consented to dinner tonight. He had the perfect place in mind.

Patty's opened two weeks ago. A few friends touted the place as top-notch. If his inclination was right about her appreciation for baking, she would enjoy it. He wanted her to have fun. To smile. The few time she'd let her guard down, she took his breath away.

"9-1-1 call." Dawn's voice escalated. "Shooter at Sunrise Crik Trail."

Nolan grabbed the ammo bag and rushed out the door. The County would have to listen now. He hit the siren and sped across town.

"Dawn to chief. Are you there?"

"Yes, I'm two minutes out."

"I have news on the false teeth. I—"

Glass exploded into the car. Nolan ducked and hit the brakes, screeching to a halt on the shoulder of the road.

"Chief, are you there? Chief?" Dawn's voice escalated into a near yell.

"Someone just shot out my back window. Get me backup!"

Ducking, Nolan looked out his windows. He saw no movement. A large abandoned brick building, a shed, and some rusty iron barrels. The timing of the 9-1-1 call and someone shooting at him couldn't be a coincidence.

His back seat glistened with shards of glass.

Thank you, God, that Honey isn't with me.

Pistol in hand, Nolan exited his vehicle and scanned windows in the long-abandoned apartment building. With the 9-1-1 call, his route could have been predetermined by anyone who knew his whereabouts.

Despite the broken glass throughout his car, he turned the car to face the brick structure and hit the gas. He screeched to a stop just as Captain Bosco's patrol car arrived.

His officer hurried from his vehicle, gun in hand. "You okay, Chief? What's the situation?"

"Someone blasted out my back window. Scared the sox off me."

"You and your sox."

"I was in route to the 9-1-1 call at Sunrise Crik Trail." Nolan brushed the sweat from his upper lip.

"Did you see anyone?"

"No."

"Long range rifle?"

"Sounded like it."

"That might tie in with the trail."

"Let's move. We'll work up to the third floor."

They took opposite sides of the hallway, kicking open doors and checking for inhabitants. At the end of the hallway, they headed upstairs to the second floor. After another fruitless search, they scoured the third floor and then headed downstairs to the first floor.

"This entrance needs to be barricaded." Nolan closed the door to the last room. The hairs on the back of his neck prickled. "Bosco, we've got to get to the park. Our delayed arrival may be intentional."

~~~

Nolan leaned against the picnic table and wiped his brow. He stifled the urge to stretch his back since tiny glass fragments were interwoven in his shirt's fabric. He'd brushed it off as gently as he dared.

The park provided thick cover, perfect for hiding. Searching wasn't easy, pushing through brush and tangled vines. He grabbed a water bottle and gulped.

The two rifle shots scared the Barretts, but they couldn't agree on their point of origin. First on the scene, Moss commenced the search at Knowles Bridge. Bosco headed east, Nolan west. Bosco should've returned by now.

"Chief, this is Siemor."

He pushed the mic button. "Chief here."

"What's your status?"

"Unable to locate. Estimate thirty minutes to clear out."

"Can you stop at the McCormick ranch when you're done there? 2901 Straight Street. A lady asked for you. Her name was—"

"Evah?"

"Yeah. I told her you'd stop."

"As soon as I finish here." He sensed motion to his left. "Ten-four."

"I'm glad to be out of that mess. My dogs are barking." Bosco's tall frame sank onto the picnic table and he stomped his black leather shoes. "Jennine will be polishing all night. Why would anyone walk that far of their own free will?"

"Exercise. A nature hike."

"Not me."

"See anything?"

"Quiet as a tomb."

"I'm going back in to replace the bag. I put a new jerky stick in the bag and stones in a cartridge box. There was a half-full box in the bottom of the bag so it weighs the same. Hope nobody notices the switch before we spot it."

"Why didn't you give it to me? I covered that area."

"It has to be placed on the same tree, same branch. The area's clear, I'll run it in."

"I'll wait."

"No. Call it in. Check with Dawn. Food deliveries need to be made."

"Okay. I need to clean up first. I'm giving disgusting a whole new meaning."

"I hear you."

Bosco headed to his car.

Nolan scanned the area. Who shot out his back window? Was it a warning shot or a miss? Did it connect to the trail?

His shoes clicked across the bridge. He didn't have time to waste if he was to catch a shower before dinner. He walked until the tree came into view, its low hanging branch just as he remembered. He scanned the area and lifted the bag into place.

His Thin Blue Line watch showed five ten.

Adrenaline pumping, he waded through tangled vines. His mind drifted to tonight's dinner date. Would he settle down enough to have his long-awaited heart to heart talk?

"Ouch." His shoe banged into a rock. He looked down. Something jutted out of a crevice. He scooped up a red pen and stuffed it in his pocket.

Fifty yards later, his footsteps echoed across the bridge. He squinted at the parking lot—and the person leaning against his SUV. As he neared, he zeroed in on Evah's stern expression.

"Is it time for dinner? I'm a mess." He gingerly peeled off his soggy, glass-laden shirt and pulled his WPD jacket over his tee-shirt.

"What happened to your car?" Her voice quavered with worry. "The back window is broken. And look at you." Alarm sifted into her voice.

"It's all in a day's work." Nolan opened the trunk and deposited his shirt. "It will be fixed tomorrow."

"I need to talk to you. I guess we can't sit in your car." She bent to see inside.

Nolan's senses hit alert status. "No, it's filled with broken glass."

She looked around, obviously nervous. "I kind of wanted to be sheltered."

Nolan detected her trembling hands and quick breaths. "You're safe here, with me. What's wrong?"

"I heard that there were shots fired here. I was afraid. I thought you were walking Honey. It's been a nerve-racking day."

"We conducted a 9-1-1 search. Either there's a copycat shooter or the same person as before, which would confirm Jonathan's innocence. Of this shooting, anyway."

"Did you see anyone?"

"No. Why?"

"I went for a walk this morning. I drove way back around the property and hiked in from there." She unfolded the events of the day.

Nolan embraced her, wishing he could control her shivers. "I can't believe you were in there, Evah. What if those thugs had something to do with the shooting? You could've been hurt." His throat went dry. He needed to search the rear of the property as soon as he could get there.

If he declared the trail off limits, the City Manager would fire him.

"If it hadn't been for Pierce, I don't know how, or if—"

Nolan kissed her forehead. His heart pounded. He couldn't let harm come to her.

"I'm sorry if I messed up your search." Evah laid her head on his shoulder.

"You didn't mess up anything. You're okay and that's all that matters. Whatever those guys were doing, they were trespassing. Up to no good. I'm thankful you got out of there when you did."

"Don't search in there, Nolan. Not alone."

"I'll get backup. For now, let's get you home."

"The truck is where I left it. I couldn't risk them watching me or following me home."

"You were smart. I'll have one of the guys drop it off. You have something else to do right now."

"What?"

"My mom's choices would be between a bubble bath, hot tea, or soup."

Evah smiled. "Right now, I'll go for hot tea and a warm blanket. About dinner—"

"Don't give it a thought. There will be others."

He slid an arm around her shoulders and pulled her tight as they crossed the crunchy driveway and headed to the ranch.

When it came into view, Cassie stood waiting on the front porch. Jane walked past her, followed by Cash.

"Wait here." He settled Evah on a stump outside of the main yard. "Jane. I want to know what your beef is with Evah."

Jane shook her head and put her hands on her hips. "You keep replaying the same record. I've told you. She's trouble."

"To who, you?"

"What do you think? She's got no business here, a spoiled twit who doesn't care a lick about this place. I want her gone. There, I said it. Is that what you wanted to hear?"

"That's harsh. She didn't come here of her own accord."

"That's what I mean!" Jane hit a high pitch. "She would never have come here. Why now?"

"You know why."

"You bet I do. She wants everything Regan left, everything that's mine." She stuck her hands in her pockets. "She's got no right to it. None at all."

"You sure of that?"

"I am sure. What would you know?"

"I know she doesn't want the place. She told me when I first met her."

"So?"

"So, I have a question for you. If she doesn't want anything to do with the place, why is she doing chores and mowing and painting—like that mailbox post over there—and fixing things up? She doesn't have to do what you tell her to do."

"She wants to sell the place out from under me."

"So, you want to scare her off. And you aren't concerned about what happened to her today?"

"No. I hope she leaves and never comes back." Jane's frown lines deepened across her forehead and between her eyebrows.

Evah walked toward him, but looking at Jane. He steadied her steady, careful not to embrace her.

"Jane, did you know where Evah walked today? Did you tell anyone?" Nolan's voice escalated.

Jane whirled to face him. "If you knew anything about me, you'd know I'm military. Military is honor. You wouldn't have to ask."

"But I am asking."

Her hostile look all but shot darts. "As I recall, her note said she went for a walk. I wasn't about to go looking."

What made her so bitter? He rested his hand on the small of Evah's back and guided her to Cassie. He watched the two ladies embrace.

Would he ever have all the answers?

He retreated down the porch steps and squeezed his mic. "Chief to dispatch."

"Chief here. I'm initiating a search. Have Moss and Bosco in my office in fifteen. And, two more things."

"Chief?"

"Get a message to Patty's. Cancel my reservations for tonight. I'll reschedule."

"What else?"

"I need a tow truck and a ride from the new trail. ASAP."

Nolan watched Cassie and Evah walk into the house. Jane remained on the porch, looking into the distance.

He headed toward the park, feeling a weight as heavy as the mountains on his shoulders.

CHAPTER TWENTY-FIVE

Nolan paced the confined space within his office. Thanks to Evah's tip, his men located the shed. Unfortunately, someone—probably the men Evah had encountered—had already emptied it. A barrel lid discovered near the vacated shack was being tested. Its odor suggested meth being transported in a gasoline mixture.

By the scrapes in the dirt, it was evident that things had been moved. Deep circles in the ground confirmed the barrels that Evah mentioned. If they were full of meth, the stakes were climbing. The team would resume the investigation at 0900 hours.

He reached for his hat and walked through the reception area. Dawn stood at the back table inventorying a shopping cart stacked with groceries. A shopping cart in his department.

She looked at him over her shoulder. "I know, I know. There are two complaints waiting to be typed." She set her clipboard on the groceries. "I'm almost done with this. Do you want me to have it delivered?"

"Yes. I'll be at the McCormick ranch." He headed toward the door. "And please keep my calendar clear this afternoon and tomorrow morning. Would you reschedule my ten o'clock?"

Dawn's expression evoked questions, but she nodded. He appreciated that about her.

After two brief stops, he parked in the McCormick driveway and climbed the steps.

168

"Hi, Chief." Cassie stood in the doorway.

"Miss Ballard." He removed his hat, "Is Jane here?'

"Yes, she has some kind of project going in the kitchen. Come in."

He followed Cassie through the living room. The kitchen counter appeared covered by every utensil in the house. Jane leaned on the counter, scribbling on a tablet.

"Wow." He whistled. "Looks like full-scale warfare."

Jane snapped, "What are you doing here again?"

"Good morning to you, too." He ignored her remark.

Jane continued writing.

"Cassie, when I called earlier, I relayed the message that Evah should stay home."

"Yes. She's laying down. She woke up with a migraine. I don't think she slept much."

"I wanted to let you know that we haven't found the men yet. It would be a good idea for all of you to stick close to the house. Keep an eye on each other."

Jane's disrespectful behavior irked him. "You hear that Jane?"

Silence.

"Jane, I'm talking to you. Those guys could be lurking around the area, up to no good. You could be in danger as well."

"You talk to Cassie about herself and Evah. I can take care of myself and I'm not a babysitter."

Cassie looked disappointed. "Please help us, Jane. We don't have military training or the keen eyes that you do."

Jane straightened. "You've got that right."

Nolan hadn't expected that from Cassie. Reverse psychology? "I'll be leaving now. Please give Evah my regards and tell her I was here. If you see or hear anything unusual, call the number that I gave you."

"We appreciate it." Cassie looked into Nolan's eyes.

"Hmph." Jane didn't look up.

He looked back at Cassie. "You haven't seen anyone suspicious, anything that didn't seem quite right?"

"No. All I found was her note yesterday." Cassie's shoulders sagged. "If what you said is true . . ."

"Don't beat yourself up. She'll be fine. She had quite a scare and needs rest. We'll have answers to everyone's questions soon."

Nolan looked at Jane, who continued to ignore him. "Jane?"

"No, I haven't seen anything. But if she's lured those no-goods onto my ranch, she's responsible for whatever happens."

Cassie straightened and faced Jane. "You take that back. How can you be so mean?"

"It comes natural." Jane snarled beneath her green paisley scarf and lipstick. "Nobody's going to throw me off this property or scare me." She gave Nolan a daring look "This place is mine. Regan wouldn't give it to anyone else. Especially not some outsider. She doesn't belong here. She'll be gone, one way or the other."

Nolan raised his eyebrows. "That's not a threat is it, Jane?"

"No. That's a promise."

"Tread with care." Nolan walked to the counter and laid his hand over her tablet. "You wouldn't want to end up in jail as an assault suspect, would you?"

"You speak one bad word against me and," Jane yanked the tablet out from under his hand, "the City Manager will hear from me."

Nolan's voice rose. "You're treading on thin ice. If Regan was alive, don't you think he would want his niece shown a bit of compassion?"

Jane's eyebrows shot up. "If Regan was alive, his niece would never have set foot on this ranch." She spat the words, whirled around, and stomped out of the room.

Nolan reached in his pocket. He produced a business card and handed it to Cassie. "If you need a ride anywhere, for any reason, you call that number." He met her look. "You won't have to explain a thing. Just ask. Don't go anywhere alone."

She took the card and nodded, her lips quivering. He wanted to reassure her, but this wasn't the time. He stepped toward the door. "I'll be out of town until tomorrow evening. I'll talk to you then."

"You're not going up to see Evah now?"

"No. I'll be back tomorrow."

"Well, I'm sure you know what's best." Her statement sounded more like a question.

He did know what's best. And it involved a plan that he couldn't share. He turned to leave. His shoe bumped Cash's food dish.

He reached for the door handle. Cash hadn't barked. In fact, he'd not seen him at all. Unusual.

He drove toward the interstate. He'd catch his flight to Mankato as Keith requested. It was time to put his plans into action.

~~~

The door creaked and Evah opened her eyes.

"Hey, girl," Cassie made a face at the cloth spanning Evah's forehead. "I've never had a headache like that. It looks painful." She gave Evah's hand a squeeze. "Promise me that you'll never do that again."

Evah pulled her friend into a one-armed hug. "What, leave a note that I'm going for a walk?"

"That, too. I mean leaving me with that fruitcake, Jane." They giggled. After releasing their embrace, Cassie stepped back and looked at her. "Are you all right? Be honest."

"I'm okay. And yes, I promise not to leave you." Evah looked at the door expectantly. "I thought I heard voices."

"You did. Nolan didn't want to disturb you but said to tell you he'll talk to you tomorrow, when he gets back in town."

"He's not here? He didn't even come up to see me." Disappointment clutched her heart.

"He had urgent business."

Evah's eyes burned. Wasn't she urgent business? She had confided in him yesterday and today he left town.

"I think I'll sleep a while longer," she told Cassie.

Now, my heart hurts as much as my head.

CHAPTER TWENTY-SIX

N olan shook Sergeant John Alvarez's hand. His friend wore jeans, a button-down shirt, and leather-look sneakers.

"I wondered if I would recognize you out of uniform, John. There were no expectations when I called. I appreciated you driving me during the funeral."

"You said that. But any way I can help, I'm here. I'm getting pretty good at this chauffeuring stuff." He nodded. "Are you anxious to be going?"

"Can we grab some fast food before we hit the highway?"

"Sure. Any preference?"

"Good burgers, fries, hot coffee."

"Good." John grinned. "You can't leave here without a burger from Minnesota Wild. You ever had wild rice?"

"Not that I remember."

"You'll remember it after today. Theirs is the best."

Nolan grabbed his overnight bag and matched John's step.

His friend chuckled. "Good thing you travel light."

~~~

Nolan recognized a few landmarks as they drove to Mankato. Funeral memories emitted a blur of faces and exhausting details, but his thoughts warmed at the memory of meeting Evah for the first time.

Small talk wasn't his thing and he was glad that John seemed comfortable with silence.

"First stop?" John broke the stillness as they entered Mankato.

"Carolyn's Bakery."

"Don't tell me you're still hungry."

"No. The owner of the place is being pressured to sell. Evah works there."

"Got it." John redirected his phone. "We're just a few minutes out. Is anyone expecting you?"

"No. I prefer to keep it that way."

John slowed in front of a building with pink- and purple-striped awnings. Cardboard covered the large front window. A sheet of paper had been taped to the front door. Black lettering read, "Closed for Repairs."

Nolan scanned the building. "I know there was a fire. Let's park around back."

"A couple cars over there." John parked by the dumpster at the far end of the lot. "Do you want a stakeout placed here?"

"No. I just wanted to see the place for myself."

"No problem. Shall I stay here?"

"Sure. Take a breather."

Nolan approached the building's rear door just as it opened. Two uniformed security guards stepped out.

"Hi fellas," Nolan greeted them. Both men wore black jeans and white shirts that bore a Bemka Enterprises logo. One wore black sneakers, the other hiking boots. The guy nearest him was built like a truck. The other bore tattoos with long hair pulled into a ponytail.

The tattooed guy looked straight ahead, but his fingers massaged the straight stick hanging at his side. The bigger guy flexed his fingers.

"Is there a problem?" Nolan asked. "We are officers from—"

The big guy swung. Nolan blocked it and redirected the swing. Nolan punched fast and hard, slamming him back into the bakery's interior. It appeared to be some kind of storage area. The big guy straightened up and pulled back, ready to swing again.

The tattooed guy followed the other guy into the bakery. He yanked out his straight stick and pulled back to strike. Nolan landed a blow, smashing the tattooed guy's nose and careening him into the other guy. The tattooed guy screamed and cupped his bloody face.

Nolan's peripheral vision noticed John's approach. The big guy lunged at John, getting him in a grappling hold. They struggled.

Nolan jumped sideways to avoid the tattooed guy's straight stick. The swing caught him on the shoulder, pushing him back into the other guy, who hollered and lunged, thrusting Nolan against the wall. Nolan pushed clear and ducked.

The big guy broke loose from John and his stick caught the edge of Nolan's chin.

"Ah." Nolan staggered and the world spun.

The big guy lunged. Nolan sidestepped and pushed him into the wall.

John thrust the tattooed guy forward, into a counter.

The guys looked at each other, yelled, and charged the officers. Nolan and John were thrust backwards, toppling shelves of cans and plastic bags that exploded into white clouds.

"Ugh!" John crashed into the wall. Metal utensils clattered onto the cement floor.

The two assailants raced out of the bakery.

"You okay, John?"

"Yeah. Just give me a second." John looked dazed.

Nolan ran out of the bakery. The assailants exchanged words as they neared a car bearing the initials JDE. They both looked toward Nolan, surprise in their expressions.

Hurrying forward, Nolan jumped and snapped a kick. Both men fell backward into the car, and onto the ground. They lay still.

Nolan handcuffed them. John helped get them into the police car.

Wiping his sleeve across his bloody chin, Nolan groaned. "I need stitches."

He grabbed his hat off the floor and walked to John. "Are you okay?"

He had yet to talk to Carolyn.

~~~

Evah rolled over and caressed Aunt Marilyn's hand-stitched quilt. She couldn't get Uncle Regan out of her mind. What if she hadn't come to the ranch? She had so many questions.

A light knock sounded. Cassie stepped in. "How are you feeling? Is that headache better?"

"Yes. I need to be out of bed." She shot Cassie a daring look.

"You sure are. This afternoon." She made a face, patted her styled hair, and sat in the rocking chair.

"It's quiet. Where's Precious?"

Cassie's forehead wrinkled when she opened her eyes wide. "You won't believe it. She's outside playing—with Jane!"

"What?" Evah struggled to sit upright.

"Relax, relax."

"Is she safe? I don't trust—"

"I can see them from the window and I've checked every little while. They're fine as long as . . ."

"What?"

"As long as you don't mind Precious wearing Army green."

"Tell me you're kidding. Are you serious?"

They both laughed. Cassie wiped at tears. "She is a sight."

"This can't be good."

Cassie shook her head. "I've never seen anything like it. Once Jane got it in her head. Well, she's obsessed."

"She's obsessed with everything. That's no surprise."

"There is something weird, though." Cassie's eyebrows arched. "Cash hasn't been around at all. Jane put his food dish in the living room again today. When I asked her about it, she about bit my head off."

"Do you think he's lost?"

Cassie's cell phone buzzed. She answered it and bit her bottom lip.

Evah mouthed a silent "who?"

Cassie shot Evah a stern look.

"You were where?" Cassie's one-sided conversation intrigued Evah. "You got that right." She licked her lips. "Yes, she's doing better. I'll tell her. I promise."

Evah turned her palms upward and whispered, "Put it on speaker."

Cassie shook her head. "I'll see you tomorrow. Don't worry so much."

She punched the end button, puckered her lips, and squeezed her cheeks in.

"You look like a fish. Who was that?"

Cassie gripped the wooden arm rests. She looked out the window and then back at Evah.

"That was Nolan."

Evah ran her fingers over the colorful stitching. "What did he want?"

"He won't be back until tomorrow. He wanted to know how you were doing."

"How good of him to make time for a phone call. He apparently didn't want to talk to me."

"Don't you be like that, Evah Rois." Cassie scolded. "He asked me not to worry you. Just know that he's detained out of town."

"Detained?"

"Yes. He's meeting with someone, but he got in a fight."

"What?" Evah's heart threatened to burst.

"He's okay, but he's staying overnight with a friend. He'll be back in the morning."

Questions assaulted Evah's heart. He's a cop. It's inevitable that he would be hurt now and then.

Don't care. But, she did.

"He said he'll be home tomorrow. You are not to worry." Cassie crossed her arms. "He is worried enough for both of you."

"About what?"

"About you."

~~~

Nolan acknowledged the many-earringed waitress who delivered his coffee, but kept his main focus the front door. He shifted his weight. He hadn't been this sore since chasing two men into an alley where two more waited.

A young woman entered, wearing a pink baseball-style cap and matching smock. She settled her gaze on Nolan and walked his way.

Nolan smiled. "Please excuse me for not standing. You're Carolyn?"

"Yes. And you caught a pair of intruders at my bakery?"

"Yes."

"I understood there were two of you." She sat across from him.

"Yes, my driver was involved, too."

"I'm sorry. I wish you hadn't gone there."

"I wanted to talk to you. Evah told me you are fighting to keep your bakery."

"Evah told you that?" Her already-pale face tensed.

"Yes. Can you give me any details?"

He could almost see her defense barrier.

"Evah knows the details. If you know her, she would've given them to you."

"I will talk to her again. She is a friend. I wondered if I could help, that's all."

Carolyn pushed back her curls and Nolan looked into her eyes, very stressed and sleepless.

"I've had plenty of opposition to keeping my bakery here. I don't mean to be rude, but it's hard for me to know who to trust—regardless of your uniform. I have a proposition. When you talk to Evah, give her a message. She'll have a response. Then I will give you all the information you want. Here's my card, with my cell number." She handed it to Nolan.

"What is the message?"

"Tell her that I miss her photography."

"I didn't know she was into that."

"She'll know what I mean."

"I will. Since I'm here in town, it would be nice if you could tell me—."

"It's a no-go. Sorry."

"Do you mind if I look around the place? You did have intruders."

"I'll give you the five-cent tour."

CHAPTER TWENTY-SEVEN

P recious waved a butterfly net and teetered around the picnic table where Cassie worked on her laptop. Evah soaked it all in from her seat opposite Cassie.

"You underestimate marketing." Cassie insisted. "To get top dollar for an alpaca ranch, you need to prove it's a thriving operation. You need to promote the business."

"I would buy into that if it was going to be marketed exclusively as an alpaca ranch." Evah waved at Precious as she toddled by. "But it's an ordinary ranch."

"You're a glass half empty girl, aren't you?"

"It's called reality. Glitter falls off."

"That's sad." Cassie lifted her face to the sunshine. "You could sell the place with no mention of alpacas, a hobby ranch like others. But what is going to catch a buyer's eye? Don't underestimate the power of suggestion. If buyers see a successful business, they'll presume their business will succeed here, too."

Jane stepped onto the back porch. "The only business going to succeed here is mine."

"And what business is that, Jane?" Evah teased. "Are your three alpacas going to be the deal breaker? Are you selling them with the ranch, sweetening the pot?"

"My alpaca is gonna' be worth way more than all yours combined." She patted her styled hair, jingled the keys in her hand,

and walked toward her car. She tossed a backpack-type of bag onto the passenger seat, climbed in, and drove away.

Evah untangled Precious's net from a thin branch. "What do you think she meant by that?"

"I have no idea. There's no reason why one of her alpacas would be more valuable than the others."

"She is acting funny."

"Funnier than normal?"

Car tires crunched. Nolan's SUV pulled in the driveway.

Evah jumped up. "I'm going to freshen up. Would you—"

"I see how it is."

"No, you don't." Evah rushed into the house.

Inside the house, the answering machine clicked on. "Jane, this is Arlene calling from the vet's office. I'm checking in about Princess Peachy. Call me back."

Evah's muscles ached, from stress or her ordeal in the woods. She wasn't sure which. She changed her blouse and ran a comb through her long hair. Was something wrong with Princess Peachy?

She hurried down the stairs and out the kitchen door. Her heart raced at the site of Nolan crouching next to Precious. The left side of his chin boasted an enormous black and blue bruise next to a band of stitches.

Her forehead had brushed against his warm, smooth skin. Now that same skin looked painful, a reminder of his human vulnerabilities. Most of the time, she felt like he was indestructible, her superhero.

He smiled. "The sun is doing you a world of good."

Evah lowered herself onto the picnic bench. Nolan sat near her. She put her hands on the warm table, next to his.

"I feel better. Thanks." She looked at his chin. "Maybe you're the one that needs sunshine. What happened?"

She touched the bottom stitch. Electricity sparked through her hand and she jerked it away.

She glanced at Cassie, bent forward over paperwork. Nice try.

Nolan produced a sheepish smile. "If you think I look bad, you should see the other guys."

"Guys? More than one?"

"They weren't a problem."

"Tell that to your face. I didn't think a police chief would be involved in fights."

Nolan ran his fingers through his hair and stretched his arms. It happened more than he cared to admit. He didn't want to scare her.

"Now and then. I can't use sparring as my only way of keeping in shape. I've got to stay on top of my game."

"Do you spar with guys from your department?" She tapped her fingers on the table.

"At least every other week. Unused skills disappear fast. When I was in college, I belonged to a gym. We sparred twice a week. I was in top shape those days. It was great fun."

"Getting beat up was fun?"

"No." Nolan tilted his head back and laughed.

Evah wished she could capture its sound.

"Physical conditioning is exhilarating. When you're in the habit of sparring, you don't feel beat up. Your adrenaline takes over."

"Where did you go to college?"

"Campbellsville University, Kentucky."

"That's a long way from Montana. Are you from there?"

"No. Dubuque, Iowa, the home of Betty Jane Candies." He raised his eyebrows and grinned.

"Sounds yummy, but that's still miles from Kentucky."

"The place has a great criminal justice program."

"Nothing closer?"

"I was blessed to win a scholarship. But even with it, I worked very hard to get the degree."

His gaze met hers. "Tell me what happened. This time, in detail." He touched the back of her hand.

She blew out a breath, but kept her hand in place.

"It's like a bad dream. I try not to think about it. But there are parts," she swallowed and turned away, "there are parts that I can't forget. Like the evil glare in Aussie's eyes."

"Aussie?"

"The guy with the Australian-style hat. That's what I call him."

"So, tell me."

Cassie stood up and disappeared into the house.

Evah watched Nolan's black SUV until it was out of sight. He would never know what she felt for him. His patience and compassion were unlike any man she had met. He made her feel safe, even when she knew there was danger.

Cassie reappeared on the back porch.

"You disappeared."

"I'm not in the habit of eavesdropping." Her hitch-hiking thumb pointed toward the house. "You have a phone call."

"On the house phone?"

"Yes."

Evah headed to the house.

Cassie held her nose. "Be prepared."

"For what?"

"Jane burnt whatever she was making. The whole mess went into the trash. The good blue pan, too."

Evah wrinkled her nose. "After I take the call, I'll start dinner myself. I found a great recipe for chicken cordon bleu." She reached for the doorknob. "I've never seen Jane hang around the kitchen. Do you think she's worried about Cash?"

Cassie threw her head back. "Who knows? I ask and she either ignores me or says it's none of my business. If it was me and I knew he was missing, I would be scouring the countryside." Cassie followed her into the house and sat at the kitchen table.

"Of course, it's our business." Evah walked to the phone on the nearby counter.

Jane's metal spatula clinked over and over on the countertop. Evah turned her back to her.

"Hello?"

"Evah?" A soft female voice questioned.

"Yes. Who is this?"

"Carolyn."

"You sound so far away! I didn't recognize your voice. Why are you calling this landline? How did you even find it?"

"I've left three messages on your cell. They go into your voice mail."

"Oh, I didn't know. I'm sorry."

"Can you talk? Do you have ears listening?"

"Well, kind of. But it's okay." She leaned against the counter and looked toward Cassie.

"I have to be careful, Evah. You, too. Does the name Sid Elmer mean anything to you?"

"No. Should it?"

"I don't know. A real estate agent left an advertisement on my door, so I called."

"You what?"

"It was curiosity, that's all. I called her. She came over and met with me. "I didn't say anything about the damage in the bakery, just that we were renovating. I mentioned that I was entertaining the idea of relocating."

"Are you really considering—"

"She acted like my best friend," Carolyn cut her off, "until I mentioned that I wanted to talk with you and you were in Woodridge, Montana.

"Her eyes widened like pizza pans. Said her uncle lived there, named Sid Elmer. I told her you were on a ranch outside of Woodridge. She said he was, too. Then, all of a sudden, the conversation ended. She stood, straight as a tree, and left.

"She was half way to her car when she stopped and turned. She called out that she wasn't interested in selling the bakery. She didn't say why or anything."

Evah's brows knit together. "That is odd. And her uncle lives near here?" She didn't want to say much in front of Jane. "I don't know what to think of that."

"She looked guilty or something after she mentioned his name."

"Maybe it was personal."

"And there's something else, too."

What else? Evah tugged at a tangle in her hair.

"You should know that a cop was here, asking about the bakery. I didn't know you talked to the police."

Evah sat, stunned. "I don't remember. Maybe a friend—"

A scream pierced through the phone receiver.

Evah gripped it with both hands. "Carolyn? What's wrong? Are you there?"

Cassie hurried to Evah. "What's wrong?"

"I don't know. She screamed. Now she's not answering." She gripped the receiver. "Carolyn?"

Jane stepped toward her, spatula in hand. "Check the wire from the receiver to the phone."

The line crackled. Someone whispered.

A gravelly voice ordered, "Get that phone number."

Evah slammed the receiver onto its cradle.

~~~

Nolan parked in front of the police building. Three boys shot hoops next to the building. Three boys. Friends. What would their futures hold? Would he be able to positively influence their lives in any way?

No time like the present.

He dug in his back pocket and approached the boys, who stopped their game and eyed him tentatively.

"Hey guys. Having fun?"

They shrugged and mumbled.

"Good. Here are three tickets to Saturday's "High Hoops Fundraiser." He held them up. "Interested?"

The boys exchanged glances.

"You can have all three tickets, if any of you can beat me in a quick game of twenty-one.

One boy crossed his arms. "You wearing your uniform to play?"

"I am. I can beat you all in a matter of minutes."

They shouted, clapped, and laughed.

"Game on!"

CHAPTER TWENTY-EIGHT

The man looked like an old-time prospector from the Grasshopper Creek gold rush. Worn denim overalls and flannel shirts were common, but the shirt desperately needed patches to cover both frayed elbows, and a jagged whole declared where a collar button used to be. Two off-color patches, sewn with large, uneven stitches, covered his right knee, and the sole flapped loose on the toe of his right boot.

Nolan cringed inwardly when the long, tangled beard almost touched his paperwork. He slid the stack across the table from where he'd been working.

"So, I was sittin' on that fallen tree," the man said. "It looked to had been struck by lightning. Full of holes, the trunk was, like it had been shot at a hundred times. I was pure tired and snuggled in, used my hood as my pillow. The sun shone down like a blanket."

One of the man's unsteady hands clenched a coffee mug and the other held half of Nolan's roast beef sandwich.

Nolan leaned back in his chair. "So that was before—"

"Like I was saying, I was just nodding off and I heard the most awful screech. I looked up and there was a mountain lion! I don't know what was upsetting it and I wasn't going to stick around to find out. I ran for my life. A nice young man picked me up not far down the road. Said he was heading west. He dropped me off in Bozeman.

"I was pretty rattled." He sat the mug down, ran his fingers over his unkempt beard, and then pulled one and then the other ear flap hanging from his weathered trapper's hat. "I didn't want a mountain lion trailing me. It was too late when I remembered my teeth laying by that tree. I never thought I'd get them back. I sure thank you. They cleaned up like new."

"The cleaning was courtesy of Dr. Birch."

"Please thank him for me."

Nolan wondered how he afforded them in the first place, but wasn't about to ask. "We packaged the false teeth and sent them from dentist to dentist, hoping to find their owner. Once you were identified, it was a challenge to find you, Jed."

"Yup, yup." He laughed. "I stay in a general area, but get itchy feet. I like to move around. The woods is my favorite place to be."

Nolan smiled. "The man that picked you up. Was there anything unusual about him? Do you know if he lived in the area?"

"I don't know. He was looking to meet up with some friends he hadn't seen in a while. That's about it. He was a nice fellow with a purty blue truck. Said it was good I didn't have baggage since a big ol' plastic-wrapped gift took up his whole back seat. He said it was somebody's birthday present."

~~~

Evah's words tumbled over each other. "I was talking to her and she screamed. I heard whispering and someone said 'get the phone number.' Right then, I hung up."

"Slow down," Nolan sputtered. "I'm trying to write this down." Evah sat on the kitchen chair, a pitcher of lemon water on the table. "This is the second time I've told you. I could type faster."

"I'm almost finished. How long ago did she call?"

"How long did it take you to get here? Fifteen or twenty minutes. I wanted to call the Mankato police. Cassie didn't think I should, so I waited."

"I'm glad you didn't call. She's right."

"She is?"

"You said Carolyn called the land line?"

"Yes. I don't know how she have found this number. The phone is listed under McCormick. She wouldn't know that."

"Did you leave a forwarding address with anyone?"

"No."

"Personal information is easier to obtain than we think."

Evah noticed the flash of panic cross Cassie's face.

"You're suspicious. It comes with your job." She twisted the corner of the placemat. "Even if that's true, I don't know where she could have found it."

"Until I get some answers about your friend, I want you to stay here on the ranch. Don't leave the property. Understand?"

Evah's face warmed.

"Do you hear what I'm saying?"

"Don't yell at me. Yes, I understand." Evah drummed her fingers.

"I'm sorry, but this is important. You are close to Carolyn. I can't risk anything happening to you."

She pressed her lips together and looked at Nolan. He didn't hide emotions well. His expression was all business, but the wrinkle across his brow showed concern.

He glanced toward the door. "I have calls to make. I'll be back soon. And, I'm assuming that the girl is here?"

Evah gave him a sharp look. "Yes. And she's staying."

"That's fine but keep a close watch on her."

Cassie walked to the stairs. "She's napping, for now."

"Just be safe. Both of you. I'm saying this because I care."

He cared. Wasn't that good?

"I'll be back soon," he repeated.

Cassie lowered herself onto the boot bench near the door. "I know you're doing your job."

He nodded, turned, and walked out.

Evah frowned. "I can't believe this. I think Carolyn put herself in danger by calling. She was telling me about a realtor that had a relative here in Woodridge. The realtor freaked out about it."

"Why didn't you tell Nolan that?"

"I just remembered. And besides, I can't remember her uncle's name. When I do, I'll tell him. I can't think right now."

"You have to remember. It's time for us to take action." Cassie's tone stung.

"What do you mean?"

Cassie stood up and placed her free hand on her hip. Her jaw clenched and unclenched. "We're not getting run off this ranch by Jane or anyone else. She thinks she has grit. Well, we do, too." She marched into the living room and a moment later, the front door slammed.

Evah followed her friend outside. Cassie's hand formed a fist. Evah covered it with her own hand. "I detest feeling like a victim. What can we do?"

"Look." Cassie pointed to a black and white squad car turning into the driveway.

"That isn't Nolan—"

A tall, lanky patrolman got out. His eyes lingered on Cassie.

"Morning, ladies. I'm Patrolman Aiden Bosco. The Chief said you needed help."

Evah tensed. "We don't need help. My friend does, in Minnesota." An invisible rope threatened to choke her. "The Chief knows all about it."

Bosco nodded. "He filled me in."

"I need to know if she's okay. She is in Mankato and owns a bakery at—"

"He's making calls to the Mankato Police Department and some security people."

"Have I met you?" Evah studied him.

"Not sure. You might know my wife, Jennine. Shall we go inside?" he looked at Cassie. "The chief will call when he has something to report."

"Come in, yes." Cassie motioned.

Evah watched Bosco cross the living room. His leather belt squeaked from the multitude of gadgets hanging from it.

Evah crossed her arms, trying to stop shaking. "I need to remind Nolan where she works."

"He has everything he needs. He said to 'sit tight.'"

Jane sauntered through the kitchen door, clutching a camouflage vest and cradling a cardboard box in the crook of her arm. She looked from the gathering to the box and slapped the top shut. She turned, and headed back to the outside door. She hesitated and her harsh voice cut the air, "Looks like a tactical meeting. What are you doing on my ranch, Aiden Bosco?"

"Come in and I'll tell you."

"I'll be back in a minute." She walked back outside. Moments later, she reappeared without the box. Wearing faded green fatigues and matching shirt, she sat on the overstuffed chair.

Bosco met her gaze. "I'm here about security. You should be part of the conversation."

"Security? Here? I know all I need to know." Her face bore an expression of contempt.

"In light of recent developments—"

Jane stood up. "You can talk to these two."

Bosco stepped forward. "This includes you, Jane. Have a seat."

"Are you trying to tell me what to do?" Jane all but stood on her tiptoes.

"No ma'am. I'm not trying. I'm ordering."

Evah fought an uncontrollable urge to giggle. Until she looked at Cassie. She faked a cough to conceal her laugh.

Jane glared. "Nobody talks to me like that."

"Have a seat. It'll be quick and painless."

"Hmph." She sat down.

Cassie, having regained her composure, looked at Jane. "We need your help, Jane."

"You need my help?" Jane's voice crackled.

"You know we do. You know everything about this place. We don't."

Bosco nodded. "We can use your expertise."

"Why didn't you say so?" Jane pointed her nose in the air and crossed her arms.

"It's standard operating procedure." Bosco continued. "Evah's friend in Mankato was relaying a message to her when the conversation ended. That in itself is not cause for our alarm. The fact that Evah overheard a directive to identify your phone number gives us probable cause. A land line can be tracked. It is our job to make sure—"

"Siemor to Bosco. Siemor to Bosco."

He pinched the radio attached to his shoulder clip. "Bosco here."

"Update from Chief. Ten-fifty-seven from Mankato. Multiple addresses being secured. Proceed with caution. Repeat. Proceed with caution."

"Wilco."

Evah looked from Cassie to Jane and then to Bosco. "What is ten-fifty-seven?"

"The person, the subject, is missing."

Evah bolted from the room and up the stairs. She made it to the bathroom just in time to lose her breakfast.

She heard a car. Someone came or went.

Thirty minutes of sitting in her bedroom wrapped in Aunt Marilyn's quilt didn't shed light on anything. She'd been over the facts until her brain felt weary. She had come to Montana as requested. Uncle Regan—who she hadn't seen in twenty-one years and never expected to see—had purchased alpacas for her.

Her rental car had been reclaimed. The men she'd encountered in the woods were up to something. Even if Nolan couldn't find them, she felt that they were still in the area.

She heard Carolyn's scream over and over in her mind.

Did any of the pieces connect?

She pondered Sid Elmer—that was his name! She jumped up from the bed.

Sid Elmer. He was that realtor's uncle. Was he well known or a recluse? Jane might know, but asking her would complicate things.

Evah opened her bedroom door. Silence. She walked downstairs and through the patio door.

Cassie and Patrolman Bosco sat in porch chairs, talking. Precious played in a playpen they'd placed next to them. Bosco pointed toward the barn.

Jane wasn't in sight.

Evah stepped out of the front door and walked to Jane's cottage, some fifty yards from the house. Holding her breath, she rapped on the door.

"Jane?"

She turned the doorknob and stepped inside. She crossed the cozy sitting area and scanned military paraphernalia, the primary décor.

Interspersed were framed photographs, large and small, families and soldiers. Jane knew a great number of people.

A wooden stairway off to the right led to a small loft or storage area.

Off the sitting area, she peered into the apartment-size bedroom. Where had she seen a quarter bounce off a taut blanket?

On the floor next to the headboard, sat the cardboard box that Jane had carried into the house.

Evah lifted the top flap.

Little black components. Electronics of some kind. She glanced around the room. Meticulous.

The front gate creaked. Evah jolted, sped across the bedroom, and headed to the back door. She softly closed the door behind her.

Jane spoke aloud. "I don't care what you think. I know what I'm doing."

Tires crunched on the gravel.

Evah breathed heavy. She was about to be seen. A magazine with tattered pages lay on the garden bench leaning against the backside of the cottage. It flipped in the light breeze. In one move, she grabbed it and sat down.

The side door opened and Jane stepped out. "What are you doing, looking through my recipe magazine?"

"Yes. I hope you don't mind. I saw the magazine here on the bench. Did I hear you talking to someone? Cassie and the policeman are out back."

"A young man from the post borrowed my car for an hour or so. Hope I don't regret it."

"Oh, Jane, I'll be starting dinner in a few minutes. It's a little late, but this has been a crazy day."

"You don't know the half of it."

Evah walked to the ranch house, her heart pounding.

~~~

Sheriff Dettman waved Nolan into a county deposition room. "You said you were heading my way. I hoped to see you. I have good news."

"I could use some."

"Jonathan Green."

Dettman lowered himself into a straight-backed chair. Nolan did the same.

"The Judge has allowed community service at Municipal Pantry. There's been a big brouhaha since grandma's egg theft and fundraiser. The pantry received a sizeable donation for construction of a storage area."

"I hadn't heard. Why the change of heart?"

"I don't know and I'm not asking. You said the child is receiving day care at that lady's ranch?"

Nolan's heart quickened. "Yes."

"Green will now be allowed to keep his daughter evenings and overnight. Your friend won't be tied down any longer. Maybe a few days where the girl can't be with him."

"He's been released?"

"Conditional bond. Never question authority." The Sheriff stood up and opened the door. "Anyway, your friend will hear from them about his girl's status."

"Thanks. She'll be glad."

Would she? He remembered blowing bubbles and giggles.

There were too many unanswered questions floating around in his mind. Even with Keith Strickland's connections and insight, it was difficult to predict the drug runners' next steps.

And what about Carolyn's disappearance? Was it a coincidence that she had been talking to Evah when something happened to her?

It was time to start cleaning up the messes. That meant telling Evah about Mankato. And no matter how he put it, it was going to be nasty.

CHAPTER TWENTY-NINE

Nolan parked near the barn. He'd wrestled this all night. He couldn't avoid it any longer.

Evah appeared through the open barn door. Her downcast expression increased his guilt. After his confession, things would be even worse.

While walking toward him, she pulled off her gloves. "Any news?"

"Can we talk?" He removed his hat and held it out toward the house.

"Sure. Over coffee? I made some."

He nodded and their shoes crunched across the gravel. "Are you out here by yourself?"

"Yes, but before I did anything else, I walked around the barn with this whistle in my mouth." She held up the silver whistle on her neck chain.

"I'm glad Bosco suggested it." Nolan scanned the terrain.

"I felt like an idiot, but safer when I knew that no one was around." She brushed off her clothes. "Not to change the subject, but does Woodridge have a dog pound?"

"They have an animal shelter. Why?"

"We think Cash is missing. Jane won't answer our questions. Says, 'It's none of your business.' But we haven't seen him in days."

Cassie sat at the kitchen table with a cup in her hand.

"I'm glad you told me." He placed a hand on Evah's shoulder and, like lightning, removed it. "Give them a call and I'll check around."

Evah leaned forward and peered into Cassie's cup. "Latte?"

"Homemade and unsuccessful." Cassie made a face.

"Have a seat." Evah gestured to Nolan. She lifted a pot from the counter, filled two cups, and set one in front of him. "Nothing new?"

"Mankato police and private security are still searching."

"Private security?" Evah walked to the opposite side of the table, facing him.

"A good friend is a private subcontractor in St. Paul. He's a security expert."

Evah set her cup down. "What can he do from there?"

"He was my mentor in college and a good friend after that. He works security and has plenty of connections."

"But what is he doing?" Evah lowered herself into a chair while watching him.

"Running checks on Mankato area contractors, hired help, that kind of thing. If anyone can turn up leads, he will."

"It's hard to wait."

"Chief, you look exhausted." Cassie chimed in. "Don't forget that Jesus said, 'Come to me, all you who are weary . . . and I will give you rest.'"

"Jesus did say that." Nolan nodded. "But I don't have time to be weary. Right now, I need to share something with you both."

Evah glanced at Cassie.

"I couldn't tell you sooner," he rubbed his chin. "I want you to know that I talked to Carolyn on Monday."

Evah bristled. "You called her?"

"No. I talked to her in person."

Evah leaned forward, her face animated. "In person? In Minnesota? On Monday?"

"Yes, to all three questions."

"We've been so worried since Carolyn's phone call." Evah put her hands on her hips. "How could you not tell us? You flew half way across the country!"

Cassie waggled a finger. "Let him explain."

"You were hurt, Evah, and you've been through a lot. I didn't want to worry you. I had other business in Minnesota, so I made time to speak with her. She was very tentative. That's my own fault, because she didn't know that I was arriving. She asked me to give you a message."

Evah shook her head. "She told me that a policeman came to the bakery. It was you!" She stood and walked to the kitchen window. "You say you didn't want me to worry, but Cassie told me you were in a fight. But I wouldn't have worried about that either, would I?"

"Don't blow this out of proportion." Nolan pulled the notebook from his pocket. "Her message to you was, 'Tell Evah that I miss her photography.' She said you'd know what it meant."

Evah's eyes opened wide. "Photography? She said that? Are you sure?"

"I'm sure. What does it mean?"

"You didn't tell me you talked to her and she told you *that*?"

"I'm sorry. What does it mean?"

Evah fidgeted with a potholder. "Carolyn and I couldn't talk much in front of the other employees. A couple of years ago, we watched a spy series together and we made up a code. It sounds dorky, but we used it once in a while when we needed a laugh. Photography meant someone was being framed or set up."

Nolan saw the fear in her eyes. "They are backing her into a corner, aren't they? So, they can take her bakery?"

"They're trying, but I have an idea or two."

Evah's fingers worked to untangle a knot in her hair. "You snuck behind my back."

Skreek. Nolan pushed his chair aside and stood.

"I believe your friend is a victim of big business. How can you not want me to help her? You aren't thinking straight. And what about you and this ranch? And your uncle's death? You're not thinking straight about that, either."

194

"Who made you my guardian?" Evah blinked. "I thought you cared." Palms up, she held an invisible globe. "Well, Police Chief Quinn, I've got to do what I've got to do. That means sell this ranch and go home."

She ran outside. The door slammed behind her.

Nolan picked up his half-full coffee cup and placed it on the counter.

Cassie's large eyes studied him. "You may be trying to clear her name, but you're in deep water. You know that, don't you?"

He nodded and picked up his hat.

"So, what are you going to do?"

"Swim upstream." He strode outside and spotted her standing near an alpaca pen. He walked forward, his feet crunching on gravel.

Evah whirled. "Can't you leave me alone?"

"No. I can't."

"What is your problem?"

"You." He pulled her to him in a warm embrace. His lips fell upon hers. Shock and revelation pulsed through him when she hesitated just a bit and then responded with warmth and compassion.

"I'm out of line and I know it. But I love you." He looked into her sky-blue eyes. Then he released her and walked to his SUV.

His lips tingled. For that kiss, a letter of reprimand would be well deserved.

~~~

Evah felt the heat from her lips. His touch had been tender and when he held her, she could think of nothing else.

But even with her feelings for him—maybe even love—it wouldn't work. He was a policeman from Montana. Cowgirl clothes wouldn't make her a cowgirl.

Could she trust him after he went all the way to Minnesota without letting her know?

She needed to refocus, to get a job, one that meant something. She didn't want to disappoint . . . who, herself?

CHAPTER THIRTY

Evah held her side and slowed to a walk. The quiet morning and warm sunshine soothed her soul, but not her lacking self-discipline. She had ignored her morning workout regimen for too long.

And what about self-discipline toward Nolan? She smiled, remembering his kiss.

She picked up her pace again and jogged along Straight Street toward the trail.

She loved him. She knew it. His faith and compassion spoke volumes. But his secrecy with Carolyn pricked her ego. Being a policeman, he probably had boundaries for sharing information. But this involved her friend.

Evah passed the entrance to Sunrise Crik Trail. Maybe she could check it out later, but first she had business to complete.

Rat-a-tat! Rat-a-tat!

She jumped and spun around, wide-eyed. Gunfire. How far away was it?

P-taff! P-taff!

Rat-a-tat!

She raced ahead. Target practice was one thing. This was something else.

She crossed the road and headed toward a two-story ranch house a way off. Broken sticks covered the field, along with decayed fruit, or berries maybe, from the trees along the fence line.

Evah slowed to a walk and brushed off her tan tee-shirt and green khakis. A dog yipped ahead. She could make out its blond profile straining against a chain. The house faced Stone Road, perpendicular to Straight Street.

A second dog joined in the barking. Were they both chained?

She stepped out from a line of fruit trees to avoid crushing rotten berries underfoot.

A detached two-car garage stood a few feet away with a rusty pole barn in the background. Rickety trash cans blocked the side of the garage. She maneuvered the loose steps and pushed the doorbell.

A petite man with a near-bald head and wire-rim glasses peered through the storm door. His gaze held steady.

"Hi. Are you Mr. Elmer?" Evah peered inside, trying not to look nervous.

"Yes. Do I know you?"

"No. I'm a neighbor."

"I'm taking a break from my work." He stepped outside, his crumpled work clothes and ratty slippers read like a lie detector.

"I'm Evah Rois. Regan McCormick's niece."

"Oh," he studied her. "I just heard something about Regan having kin. I didn't know."

"I thought I'd stop to say hello. It's perfect walking weather."

"You walked all the way from the ranch?"

"It wasn't far." A green tarp next to the pole barn covered a large object. Its shape suggested a vehicle. The blond dog woofed repeatedly. So did another dog.

You're visiting. Act like a friend.

"Did you know my Uncle Regan?"

He removed a handkerchief from his pocket and patted his forehead. A nervous reaction since he didn't appear to be sweating.

"Our dealings were business. I leased some of his land for a few years to plant crops. That's about it."

"I didn't know if you were friends."

"No ma'am. Not at all."

He looked at his watch, fingered the band, and looked uncertain. That was her queue.

"I'll be heading back. I'm glad to have met you."

"Glad you dropped by." He didn't sound convincing.

"Do you live here alone?"

"Yes, but my niece, Mariah, visits. She comes every few weekends. She says it's boring here, but she makes the trips to see me.

"She really drives cars here for her boss. He has business associates around here, for sure in Great Falls. Anyhow, it's a good way for us to keep in touch."

Evah smiled. "I like the name Mariah. It's unusual."

"Yes, I do, too. Mariah Tierney."

~~~

Nolan followed the receptionist into the doctor's plain white office that smelled of lemon and bleach.

She motioned to a chair. "Have a seat. The doctor will be right in."

Nolan scrolled through office messages.

Where can we store a pallet of toilet paper?
Also, an anonymous donor delivered four banana boxes
full of assorted perishable food items. They need
refrigeration. Dawn.

This food drive was out of hand.

The door opened and a man with tight gray curls walked in. He dropped a phone into his shirt pocket. "Good to see you, Nolan."

"You, too, Doc. It's been too long . . . for coffee, not medical." They laughed and shook hands.

The doctor set a clipboard on his desk and lowered himself onto a squeaky chair. "So, what's this all about? You're here about a former patient?"

"Regan McCormick."

The doctor sighed. "That again? You know I'm still bound."

"I know. But circumstances have changed, Griff. A family member is in the mix and the City Manager wants all bases covered."

"What?" The doctor removed the stethoscope from his neck. "I wasn't aware that Regan had any kin."

"I wasn't either. What can you tell me?"

"His health was generally as expected. Meds looked fine. Some prescriptions were from Bozeman. Want a list? The death certificate said natural causes."

"Yes, thanks. I know it said that, but an autopsy is underway. For some reason, it had been put on hold. Not anymore."

The doctor sat back in his chair. "Regan had a Power of Attorney. It calmed him to know arrangements were made, that someone would oversee it all."

"Who's the attorney-in-fact?"

"An attorney in Livingston. Angeli." He buzzed the receptionist and asked for a printout of Regan's prescriptions.

Back in his SUV, Nolan patched through to Dawn. "Requesting the phone number for Gallatin County Medical in Bozeman. I'm on my way."

"You okay?"

"Yes, it's business."

"A family is waiting here for you. I told them you'd be back soon."

He paused at her assumption. "I'll stop in for a minute and then head out."

He drove to the office, parked, and hurried inside. His shoes echoed across the empty lobby and down the stairs.

Dawn stood. "These are the Smiths. Gerald and Isabella. And their son, Daniel."

A young couple sat on the sofa. A five-or-six-year-old boy sat between them, staring at the ball that he shifted from one hand to the other repeatedly. The adults rose. The boy didn't move.

Nolan cupped his hat under his arm and shook their hands. "I'm Chief Quinn. How can I help you?"

"We were robbed two days ago," the father said.

"I'm sorry to hear that. Did you report it?"

"Yes. Most of what was stolen was Isabella's necklaces. But that's not why we're here. Daniel's puppy was stolen, too."

"They stole his puppy?" Nolan glanced at the boy, who remained focused on moving the ball from hand to hand.

"Yes. One of your men took the report." He looked at his wife. "Daniel has medical issues. His puppy is special."

"Have you checked with neighbors? Maybe he got out during the robbery. Have you called the Humane Society?"

"We've checked everywhere. We wouldn't have come, but Daniel needs him. Desperately."

"Please excuse me." The boy's mother sat on the sofa where her son hugged himself and rocked back and forth, still gripping the blue ball. She wiped tears off his cheeks.

The father lowered his voice. "Daniel has surgery scheduled two weeks from tomorrow. We've waited for months. The puppy was a gift, so he would focus on getting well. The dog helps him focus. In case you can help," he dug in his pocket, "here's a picture of Daniel with Mozart."

Nolan gazed at picture of the dark-haired boy laying on a Superman bedspread, hugging a furry young dog. The boy wore medical bands on one wrist.

"Mozart?"

"Yes, the dog. In the beginning, classical music calmed Daniel. The dog's much better."

"Golden retriever?"

"Yes. Five months old. Forty pounds. A bundle of energy." The father blew out a breath. "The dog is valuable. Would someone try to sell him?"

"It's possible. But with the robbery so recent, I doubt they would have unloaded him yet."

CHAPTER THIRTY-ONE

E vah sat on an upside-down bucket in the holding pen. A chocolate brown alpaca nuzzled pellets from her hand. There was no way to keep them. Any of them. Not unless she boarded them. And who in their right mind would move alpacas nine hundred miles?

She had no answers.

Nolan said he loved her. Was he kicking himself over that impulsive blurt? The one person that ever loved her was mama. And God.

Did Carolyn know God? She was upbeat, but had never mentioned her beliefs. At least not that Evah recalled.

Jane's car backed to the barn.

Evah yelled, "Where are you going?"

Jane stuck a thumbs-up through her open window. "Reconnaissance."

Reconnaissance?

Evah entered the back door. The house was quiet, thanks to Jonathan taking Precious for the day.

Cassie sat at the kitchen table, a downcast expression on her face.

Evah hesitated before approaching. "I've messed this up. You were
supposed to be recuperating and I've had you helping with—"

"It's not that." Cassie ran her fingers around the cup's rim. "There are things I can't tell anyone."

"I love it here, Evah. Montana is one calendar picture after another. And the people are sincere. Some even want to know me. But I can't let them."

~~~

Sitting at his desk, Nolan pushed his knuckles against the small of his back. Stiffness diminished and he relaxed, satisfied at the sight of his almost empty out-basket.

"Another puppy lead," Dawn called. "Moss is checking it out."

"Have the guys check the Lakeview Drive and Johnson Street areas north of 90. Someone reported seeing a dog running loose."

His stomach rumbled. He didn't want to miss lunch, again. He lifted
his hat off the coat rack and headed through the door

"Got a minute, Chief?" Bosco burst in, almost colliding with him. "I need to talk to you about that Cassie lady."

~~~

Evah reached into the canister, retrieved a handful of flour, and sprinkled it across the elasticized dough. Her palms continued to knead, working bubbles from the yeasty mixture. She lifted the dough off the floured board, formed a ball shape, and placed it in the large ceramic bowl. Then she rubbed butter on her palms and caressed the dough's smooth top.

She placed the checkered hand towel on top of the bowl and wiped her hands across Aunt Marilyn's floral apron. Wrapped twice around her waist, it made her feel closer to her aunt.

"Oh!" She jerked to attention. Nolan stood outside the glass door, a silly smile on his face. Wearing jeans and a maroon Griz tee-shirt, he looked great.

Her face heated. "How long have you been standing there?"

He pushed the door open and stepped inside. "Long enough to see you doing what you love."

She moved to the sink and scrubbed dried flour from her hands. "You're right. I love to bake."

"What are you making?"

"Cinnamon rolls. The dough will rise for a about an hour. Then I'll punch it down, roll it out, and add my top-secret cinnamon and sugar mixture."

"That's it?" He smiled.

"No," she grinned. "Then I cut the rolled dough into strips and put them in a pan. When the cinnamon rolls raise, they go in the oven."

"That's a lot of steps."

She laughed, "And I enjoy each one. I'm very passionate in the kitchen."

"I see that. I could be passionate in other rooms, too."

Evah grabbed a hand towel and turned to face him.

He rested his hands on her shoulders. "I'm passionate about eating, too. Especially cinnamon rolls." His eyes teased. "And what's top-secret about cinnamon and sugar mixed together?"

"I can't tell you," she teased back. "It's a secret."

"Well, I hope you save me one." He ran a finger along her nose. "Did you know that you're covered with flour?"

"I must be a sight."

He pulled her into his arms. "You are. Beautiful. Can you guess what I'm thinking?"

"No."

"How wonderful it would be if you could keep doing what you love. Because, when you're happy, so am I." He tipped her face upward. "God has a plan for you. And whatever it is, I hope it includes me."

He kissed her with gentle compassion. Evah responded. She felt the electricity between them. But she couldn't lead him on. He pulled back and looked into her eyes.

She put her hands on her hips. "What I'm thinking is very different than what you're thinking."

"What's that?"

"I do have feelings, very strong ones, for you." She felt her cheeks warm. "But I must return to Mankato when the ranch sells. Carolyn has talked to several realtors about selling her bakery. In fact, one realtor has an uncle that lives here. His name is Sid Elmer. Do you know him?"

Nolan's eyes widened.

"Anyway, if she does sell, she may have to relocate. She'll need my help. And Jane told Cassie that there have already been inquiries about the ranch."

"It isn't listed to the public yet, is it?"

"Word gets around. It's in the works. I think Jane met with someone."

His eyebrows arched. "I don't want to move on without you. Why do you want to stay in Minnesota when we can be together, here? Give me a chance. I see a future for us."

Evah's eyes teared. She turned away and heard Nolan walk out.

She wanted to run after him and tell him she would stay. She had lost her heart to him. But she couldn't stay. She and Carolyn had a business plan, a promise made years ago.

Carolyn. Are you okay? Where are you?

She leaned her forehead against the wall. She couldn't desert her friend. She knew firsthand what it felt like. She wouldn't do that to anyone.

But, was she doing that to Nolan?

She tried to push the thought aside by grabbing a writing tablet and pen. Facing the bookcase, she recorded book titles, authors, and publication dates. Her brain felt like rising bread dough, ready to overflow its boundaries.

Cassie walked in. "I need a change of scenery."

"I'm making cinnamon rolls, so I'm taking inventory to stay close."

"I never knew books to get you revved up. You're slamming them like gym weights."

"Sorry."

They exchanged an understanding look.

"Look at this." Evah held a book open to its inside cover. "There are so many inscriptions. Uncle Regan's handwriting is large and bold. Aunt Marilyn's is light," she pointed, "with curlicues. This says, 'for your birthday with love'."

They loved each other, but not her.

Evah placed a few books in a stack on the end table.

"You in the mood to read?" Cassie glanced at the titles.

"Maybe."

"Be careful. Jane will knock them off of there."

Evah knelt and moved them to the bottom shelf. When she straightened up, her head bumped its underside.

"Ouch." She ran her hands through her hair. "What was that?" She picked a small black object off the carpet and balanced it on two fingertips.

"I have an idea." She set the object in Cassie's palm and headed to the door.

"Where are you going?"

"Have you seen Jane, lately?" Evah hesitated at the door.

"She was talking to a man near the barn." Cassie peered at the object.

"I'll be right back." Evah hurried to Jane's cottage and burst inside. In the bedroom, she reached into the box near the bed, grabbed a clear bag of black components, ear pieces, and small black boxes. She carried them to Cassie. Evah read off a box, "Wireless Voice Transmission".

"Are you kidding me?" Cassie cried out. "That was under the end table. Has she been eavesdropping on us?"

"How many more might be planted around the house?"

Cassie headed to the stairs. "I'm going to find out right now. If she's bugged our rooms, I'm going to—"

"Going to what?" Standing in the doorway wearing military fatigues, Jane's eyes bulged.

"Jane, why?" Evah whirled toward her and held out a component. "We're supposed to be, kind of, a family. If you want to know something, ask. This is, among other things, illegal."

"You two come in here. Invade my home. Undermine my plans. I can't trust anyone. Even Regan lied to me."

"Regan? What are you talking about?" Evah looked from Cassie to Jane.

Jane scooped up the electronics parts. "He told me many years ago that he'd take care of me and mine. He didn't."

"But you're here in this house. What didn't he do?"

It was me he abandoned.

She looked down. "It's my business. Jimmy . . ."

"Your business? Why the secrecy? Who is Jimmy?"

"These bugs were for experimenting. New equipment. I meant to take them out for recon. I haven't used them until a few days ago." She broke into a lopsided grin. "You two live dull lives. Boring as trees." She cast a sideways look at Evah, "except maybe for that Police Chief or the Minnesota folks."

Cassie snapped. "How dare you eavesdrop. And what do you mean 'for recon'?"

"That's need to know. Classified."

"Well, we need to know." Cassie squeezed the chair arm.

Jane walked toward the doorway, holding her items. "Stay out of my house. Both of you." She looked at Cassie and then Evah. "Or you'll put yourselves in harm's way. I won't be responsible." She slammed the door.

Jane cared about Jimmy, whoever he was. And Regan, for some reason, had done wrong toward him.

"Cassie, Jane's holding a grudge against Regan."

"I've never seen such a mess. Oh," Cassie pointed to the kitchen. "You're going to have bread dough all over the counter."

Evah steepled her fingers. "If Jane wants us out of harm's way, I'm sure of one thing."

"What's that?"

"She is already in it."

CHAPTER THIRTY-TWO

Woodridge couldn't compete with Mankato. It wasn't supposed to. Nolan wanted to love someone who loved him, here in Woodridge, Montana. Was that so much to ask?

"Hey, Chief?" Siemor called from Dawn's desk.

"What?" He growled.

"Does Dawn log phone calls on white or yellow sheets? Someone complained about loud music north of Sunrise Crik Trail."

"When?"

"This morning."

Nolan rolled the red pen in his fingers. The one he'd found by the ammo bag. He rolled it over. *Milt's.*

"Chief," Siemor said. "We've got another dog lead. I'm spending so much time—"

"Don't complain. Find that boy's puppy."

~~~

Evah stood in line, waiting for her latte. She couldn't help but to hear the conversation between two patrons as to whether or not hot dogs should be categorized in the sandwich column or listed by itself. Café customers laughed and cheered when the conversation ended.

The enthusiastic debater turned to Evah. "I didn't intend to talk so long. But I love all things culinary. I'm Emmie."

They chatted while waiting in line to pick up their beverages.

"I'm anxious to get my bakery built," Emmie offered. "And I'll be looking for help, too." Emmie glanced at her watch and Evah felt a tug at her heart.

They received their beverages.

"I enjoyed meeting you. It's so exciting that you're going to build a bakery." Evah took a sip of her caramel macchiato. "You've got great energy. Culinary energy."

"But it sounds to me like you do, too, with your classes in Minnesota and working at the bakery." Emmie grasped Evah's hand. "It's not often that I meet a kindred spirit. Lots of people bake. Not many are passionate about it. I wish you were staying—"

"Me, too. It's a dream of mine."

Where did that come from?

"If you change your mind, I would love to talk to you again. It will be a few months before construction is complete. I won't hire for weeks. Here is my card." She handed it to Evah. "Maybe it's a God thing that you were here."

A God thing?

Evah grabbed her ringing cell phone. "Hello?"

"Evah, this is Nolan. Are you still at the Café?"

"Yes." She tossed her napkin into the trash receptacle.

How does he know where I am?

"How long will you be there?"

"I'm leaving now."

"Will you stop at my office? I have news."

~~~

Nolan looked up when Evah crossed the reception area toward his office. Her expression appeared pensive, contrasting her floral top and pink leggings. He stood and waited.

"You can go in." Dawn directed.

Nolan opened his arms. "It's okay, Evah. Carolyn is all right."

Evah flew toward him, unable to contain tears of relief.

"She's okay?"

"Yes. She's being checked out at a clinic. The PI said she's exhausted and severely stressed."

"Where was she? How did they find her? What's a PI?"

"A private investigator got a lead from neighborhood watch. She was in a small house west of North Mankato. A lady was observed coming and going from the house, dressed to kill and carrying food trays. Every visit, she would stay for about twenty minutes and then leave. That's the importance of a neighborhood watch."

"Have they arrested the kidnappers?"

"Yes, two men employed by Bemka Enterprises were supposed to scare Carolyn into selling."

Evah tensed. "Bemka is named on documents that Carolyn sent me."

Nolan nodded. "She told police that a couple guys took her from her office. Covered her eyes until she was in an empty utility room. We're still getting details. Doctors will make sure she's fine before releasing her. Then the police will need statements. It'll be a few days before she goes home, but she's safe."

Evah brushed away a tear and silently thanked God. She faced Nolan, "I am so grateful."

Nolan wondered how long it had been since she felt thankful for anything. He stood holding her, taking in the scent of her shampoo and the overwhelming feeling that all was right with the world. He wanted to protect her and love her. Forever. If she would only listen to her heart.

But she had other plans.

He released her from his embrace. Even if she wouldn't admit her feelings, he couldn't stop loving her. It hurt. Again.

He left the office with her at his side. "Will you come this way?"

"Sure." She followed him through the building and outside, along a sidewalk that wrapped around to the back of the building.

They stepped onto the parking lot and Nolan reached in his pocket. A beep sounded. He took hold of Evah's hand and dropped a key into it.

"What's this?"

"That truck isn't safe. Someone owed me a favor. Drive this for the next few days."

She gaped at a copper colored car. "It's like a shiny penny."

"And a penny is good luck. It's a Ford Escape. Let me know what you think."

"Just like that, I drive away with a different car?"

"I'm borrowing it. I have connections. And I'll feel better with you driving something reliable."

"But—"

"If you leave the truck keys, I'll make sure it's dropped off at the ranch."

CHAPTER THIRTY-THREE

E vah and Cassie dug through boxes. Stacks of photographs lined the table in front of them.

Cassie pointed. "Is that your uncle, standing beside this pony?"

"There's Pepper, the pony I used to ride!" Until now, the image had been in her memory. "And yes, Uncle Regan."

"Is this your aunt?" A stout woman held a birthday cake while Uncle Regan tipped his hat.

"Yes, and look. She's wearing the apron that I've been wearing." Evah laughed and Cassie joined in.

"Now I see why it circles you twice. And look, a little girl is peeking around the corner."

Evah stared at the cowgirl with curls. "That's me," she whispered. The memory was no longer a lofty dream.

"And tell me this isn't Jane," Cassie hooted.

"It is, isn't it? She's wearing Army stuff. And smiling." Evah flipped the picture over and read, "Mary Jane and Jimmy. That's the little guy."

"Who is he?" Cassie murmured. "We've got to ask Jane."

"Ask me what?" Jane stared at the boxes. "You shouldn't be into that."

Evah held up the picture. "Who is Jimmy?"

"None of your business." She turned and walked out the back door.

Moments later, the doorbell buzzed. Evah greeted a silver-haired man.

"Good afternoon. I'm Henry A. Leeland. Hal. I'm here to see Jane about her alpacas."

"Is she expecting you?"

"I told her I'd stop by."

Cassie stood. "Evah, I'll get your brownies from the oven. They're almost done."

She yelled out the back door for Jane.

"What do you want?" Jane appeared in the doorway and looked at Hal, who had stepped into the living room. "Who are you?"

"I'm Hal, Henry Leeland. We spoke about the alpaca."

"Oh, yes." She looked from Evah to Cassie, who emerged from the kitchen. "Let's talk in the—"

"Talk here, Jane." Evah dropped into a chair. "I told you to sell the three alpacas. They are yours to do with as you please. I can learn from you. I have alpacas to sell, too."

"Great idea," Hal beamed. "That would be fine, wouldn't it? She can learn about these dealings and perhaps I'll work with her to sell her alpacas."

Jane motioned Hal to the sofa. She sat at the opposite end. He placed his briefcase across his lap and smoothed his light blue suit.

His smile widened. Evah recognized the sales pitch in progress.

"As you requested, Jane, I'll be brief. My business partner and I agreed that our original offer of five thousand dollars was a bit low. We've upped the price to seven thousand dollars." He grinned.

Jane showed no emotion. "Is that your final offer, the best you can do?"

"Yes, dear Jane. This is very generous."

Jane chewed her bottom lip.

Hal gazed at Evah. "And may I ask, Miss, what you think of this offer?"

Jane's expression threatened.

Evah sat up, unsure of whether to respond. "Seven thousand dollars for what alpaca?"

"Princess Peachy is what Jane calls her. A catchy name."

Jane pursed her lips.

Evah sat back. "Sorry, I'm just observing."

"But you have an opinion," Hal insisted.

Jane glared. "This is my decision. Mine alone."

Hal fidgeted. "Jane, if the young lady has an idea of value, it might be a good idea—"

"Oh, hazelnuts," Jane spat. "Get on with it then."

Evah leaned forward. "I've done research, too, Mr. Leeland. But my figures differ from yours."

"So, you acknowledge my generosity?" He fake-laughed.

"On the contrary." Evah shook her head. "Princess Peachy is worth no less than twenty thousand dollars."

"What?" Jane jumped to her feet and faced Evah. "How dare you say such a thing? You would begrudge me even this?"

"Jane, this man is trying to practically steal Princess Peachy from you. I mean it."

"What do you say to that, Mr. Leeland?"

"Hal, please." He forced a smile. "My friends call me Hal."

"I'm not your friend."

Evah tapped her index finger on her other palm. "I can back up my figures, Jane. Princess Peachy's blood lines are impeccable. You can do much better."

Jane's eyes narrowed. "You swear to it?"

"I swear. I can verify it."

"It isn't necessary." She stared at Evah. "Your word is good enough."

It is?

Hal's forehead glistened. "But, Jane, you have my offer."

"I can do better."

"But Jane—"

Jane grabbed Hal's collar and ushered him outside. When she turned around, an amused look crossed her face.

"You mean that, don't you? About the worth of Princess Peachy?"

"I wouldn't lie to you. She's worth at least twenty thousand dollars."

Jane clapped her hands. "And suppose I tell you that she's going to have a baby? Any day now." She rocked with laughter.

"That makes her even more valuable."

"Well, hot dog." Jane dropped to the sofa and bounced.

The phone rang. Cassie popped up. "I'll get it." Moments later, she reappeared.

Evah turned. Cassie looked ready to cry. "What's wrong?"

"I should be happy for you, but . . . there's an offer. Someone's buying the ranch."

"It's not on the market yet." Jane puckered.

Cassie hung her head. "It's a preliminary offer. But it's in writing, in the possession of the realtor. She'll make an appointment with you to discuss it. She wanted you to know."

Evah slumped. "It's my fault. I signed the waiver, allowing the sale of our home."

Our home.

~~~

Nolan, Bosco, and Moss exited vehicles to the sound of yips, barks, and a baying hound. He recognized the house and the tarped vehicle from Evah's description.

Nolan directed, "Bosco, secure the back. Moss, perimeter check. Garage, too."

A man opened the front door. "What's going on here?"

"Mr. Sid Elmer?"

"Yes. What's this about?"

Nolan climbed the steps. "I am Police Chief Nolan Quinn. Would you step outside, sir?"

He did.

"Is there anyone else here with you?"

"No."

"Is your niece here? Mariah Tierney?"

"Not until Friday."

"Is that her car under the tarp?"

"One of her boss's. She drives them here, they get a maintenance once-over, and she drives them back to Minnesota. What's this all about?"

"Mind if I look around?"

"You got a search warrant?" Wrinkles appeared across his forehead.

"Yes. The Judge is sending it over."

Barks sounded from the garage.

"There must be twenty dogs here." Moss yelled from near the garage. "One has a fancy collar with the name Mozart on it."

Nolan followed Elmer into the small home. Aiden approached from the rear hall.

"Chief, the back is—"

A large man with long hair lunged at Bosco, who fell back and crashed on the kitchen floor.

Nolan charged forward, grabbed the guy's shoulders, and pulled him off Bosco. Nolan punched and the man lay silent.

An enormous man with a round face and thick eyebrows leapt in front of Nolan and punched him in the chest. Nolan flew backward but regained his balance. He landed a punch on the assailant's nose.

The man screamed and flung his hands to his face. Then he threw his entire body against Nolan. They toppled backward.

Something rammed Nolan's back. He groped and found a walking stick. He thrust it at the man's head. The man ducked, turned, and dashed toward Sid Elmer. A table lamp toppled and crashed.

Elmer cowered in a corner. "I told you, just a few dogs, but you wouldn't listen!"

The man grabbed Elmer by the collar and drew back to punch. "Why, you—"

Nolan shoved him away from Elmer and grabbed a cast iron skillet off the counter. The man screamed and lunged forward. Nolan smacked the man's head and he fell to the floor.

Moss raced into the house. "You okay, Chief?"

"Read him his rights." Nolan, trying to catch his breath, motioned to Elmer.

"Cuff them both. They'll hear the same thing. This one has to wake up first."

Bosco tried to sit up. He winced.

Nolan knelt next to him. "Stay still. Help's coming. You got trampled by a Mack truck."

Voices and commotion sounded outside. Nolan pulled his firearm and moved to the door.

Three cars were parked behind the police vehicles. Men swarmed into the garage, following someone wearing military green.

Jane.

Barking escalated.

Nolan felt his arms for bruises as he marched across the yard. "Jane,
I need to talk to you."

She knelt on the ground. Cash raced toward her, whining and licking her chin. "Found my Cash. Found him, I did." She grinned, rocking him back and forth. "I knew it. There's lots of dogs."

Nolan rubbed his forehead and looked at the dogs being walked from the garage. He spotted the golden retriever.

"I had to get him back. My plan worked." She continued to pet Cash.

"What are you doing here, Jane? How did you know about the dogs?"

Cash squirmed from her arms and raced in circles.

Jane walked to Nolan's SUV. She reached for the door handle and yanked it open.

"Jane! Stop right there." Nolan tensed.

She bent low and reached inside, then turned back to Nolan and dropped a small black component into his palm. An audio surveillance device.

"Jane, what have you done?"

~~~

Two hours later, Nolan pulled into Ellen's Café parking lot. His mic crackled.

"Dispatch to Chief, come in."

"Chief here."

"It's going down. Drug runners." Siemor's voice boomed. "Scenario four, Sunrise Crik bridge. County called it in."

Nolan ignored his rumbling stomach, hit the siren, and sped to the bridge. Flashing lights announced two squad cars on the scene, both County.

He parked near them and exited his vehicle.

Dressed in dark brown pants and light brown shirt, a County cop leaned against a man, cuffing him. From the back, Nolan couldn't identify the officer.

"What do you have?" Nolan approached the second officer, Deputy Sheriff Grease.

"Suspected drug runner."

Grease stood in front of the second secured suspect. "Two nine-millimeter semiautomatics. As always, you're a day late and a dollar short." The thin man squirmed against a car. He looked fresh out of high school.

Nolan tapped the hood. "Stolen?"

"You guessed it." Grease shoved the young man into the car.

"You gave the car a once-over?"

"Found a brown lunch bag half full of individual portions of cocaine. I'll open the trunk."

Grease shoved the prisoner onto the back seat and slammed the door shut. He sauntered to the rear of the car, inserted the key, and popped it open. He pushed aside a partially shredded green cloth.

Nolan stepped behind him.

"One kilo?" Grease rocked on his heels.

"Did you arrive first?"

"I beat Redding by thirty seconds." He smiled. "You were nowhere to be found. Maybe with that chick, hey?"

"What?"

"The chick from the trail. Eye candy. I—"

Thunk. Nolan's fist caught the side of Grease's jaw. Grease fell to the ground. He rolled over and struggled to regain his balance. Once upright, he pulled back to punch.

Nolan caught him with a left hook. Grease landed on his knees. "Why, I—"

"It's time you learned some manners." Nolan glared. "We're supposed to be on the same team. And you owe Miss Rois an apology." He pulled Grease to his feet. "And if you care to complain about me to Dettman, please do so. He's well informed about your unprofessional behavior."

Redding guided his prisoner to the car's back seat. Then he walked toward Nolan.

Nolan met him half way. "Deputy Sheriff Brian Redding. I remember you from the truck recovery."

"Yes, sir. Um, I have to ask, was that necessary?"

"How long have you known Grease?" Nolan smoothed his shirt.

"Long enough to despise his rude and crude methods." The young officer walked to the front of the car. "By the way, I didn't see a thing."

"But I got the bust," Grease sneered.

"You did," Nolan agreed. "And as planned, you bought into their decoy."

CHAPTER THIRTY-FOUR

E vah stood on the back porch and gazed across the fields. It hadn't taken long for her to fall in love with this place.

Had she fallen in love with this place or with Nolan? Or both?

The kitchen phone rang. She hurried to answer it.

"Hello?"

"Evah, it's Carolyn."

Evah's hands trembled. "Carolyn! I was sick with worry. How are you? Are you okay?"

"I am. Or, I will be. That's partly why I called. I've decided to sell, Evah. The developer's associate is facing harassment charges but the project will continue. They've offered me a fair price. I had to tell you, but I feel bad—"

"Don't worry." Evah's eyes stung. "We'll find something else."

~~~

Nolan examined the prescription label through the clear bag. "This is Regan McCormick's prescription?"

Bosco sipped from a paper cup and leaned against a file cabinet. "Yes, it was in Elmer's closet. The name's rubbed off, but it has the out-of-town doctor and prescription number. The pharmacy identified the prescription as Regan's, but not the pills in the container. Why would Elmer keep evidence incriminating himself?"

"Maybe he planned to sell the pills." Nolan squinted at the label. "They confirmed the contents?"

"They did. It's meth."

"You did good, Bosco."

"Sorry to interrupt, Chief." Dawn approached his desk. "Mr. Green is here."

"Bosco, give me thirty. Then we'll wrap it up."

Bosco stepped out as Green entered.

Nolan motioned. "Have a seat, Jonathan. What can I do for you?"

Jonathan lowered himself onto a chair. Shadows underlined his eyes. "I wanted to thank you."

"Glad to help. You're out now?"

"Yes, and I have Precious back. Whatever you did . . ."

"I did my job."

"You did more than that." His voice waivered. "It's been a long time."

"Mind if I ask something personal?"

"Ask."

"How'd you get into this? You have a daughter. I can see that you're an attentive father."

Jonathan sighed. "After my wife died from cancer, I don't know what happened. I couldn't concentrate. Couldn't hold a job. I focused on Precious, but not like I should have."

"Did you have a house?"

"Had a nice one, before. Hospital bills piled up and I lost it. We wandered and, after a while, came here. I got us a little place on the northeast side. A glorified shack. It'll be in shambles now."

Nolan listened. Sadness had consumed Jonathan's life for too long. Bad break after bad break.

"There's one thing I want you to do." Nolan stood. "Leave your address with Dawn."

Precious giggled from the lobby.

"I want you there, at your place, at eight a.m. sharp on Monday. We're going to do some fixing up."

"But—"

"That's an order from the Chief. You don't want more trouble with the law, do you?"

"No, I sure don't." He smiled through teary eyes.

~~~

Nolan dropped a handful of zoning requests into his out file, but studied the last application. Someone had submitted plans to build a bakery. He didn't recognize the name.

"Bosco is on the line," Dawn called. "Says it's urgent."

"Put him through."

"Chief, a gas station west of Livingston was just robbed. Two men in a pickup truck. They pulled out fast, heading west on 90. They had a large box or something on the back seat."

"Could be our runners. Get everyone to the pressure points. What are they driving?"

"Ford F-150, blue with black grill. Minnesota plates. The station owner is checking the security camera for license plate numbers."

"This could be the one, Bosco. Weapons?"

"A tall black-haired guy flashed a pistol at the Truck Stop. Shot up the place for no reason. The owner didn't know the make of the handgun. The driver waited in the truck."

"Exercise caution, but be aggressive, alert. I'm on the way."

The old guy, Jed, had ridden in a blue truck with something large on the back seat. This could be it.

Nolan hit his siren and sped to his check point. He looked at Luke's photo, taped to his glove box. "We're going to catch them and they're going to pay."

"Deputy Clark to Chief Quinn."

"Quinn here."

"They're heading toward you, Chief, screaming fast."

". . . screaming west on I-91" Nolan recalled Young's voice, saturated with adrenaline.

"Is the highway secure?"

"Yes."

"I'll be set." Nolan screeched to a halt across both lanes of traffic. He opened the door and exited. At the sound of approaching tires, Nolan turned. A County Sheriff squad car burnt rubber, skidded to a halt, and faced him bumper to bumper.

Nolan drew his weapon and stood beside and behind his vehicle.

Deputy Sheriff Bob Grease exited his vehicle. He pulled his gun and faced east. "I'll get this bust, just like I did the last one."

"Stay out of my way," Nolan growled. "Young was my officer."

A fast-approaching vehicle captured Nolan's attention.

"They flew through our blockade," Bosco called over the mic. "He dented up that truck pretty good. Stay back. He'll run you over!"

Perspiration covered Grease's oversized uniform shirt. He gripped his handgun and waved it. "I'm ready for them."

"Grease, move back! They crashed the barricade."

"You move back. You want me out of the way so you can get the collar."

"Move back, I'm telling you." Nolan looked down the road. The blue truck came into view, speeding toward them. The left side of the front grill was bashed in and the hood crumpled.

Grease opened fire, propelling one shot after another toward the truck.

Nolan raced across both lanes, toward Grease. "Get out of the way! They're going to crash it!"

Grease continued to shoot.

Nolan threw his body onto him just as the truck rammed their vehicles, flinging both vehicles apart and back.

The blue truck flew into and over the police barricade, bounced on two wheels, and skidded sideways, off the shoulder of the highway and toward the evergreens.

Momentum thrust Nolan sideways into Grease, then backwards onto something hard. When he caught his breath, Nolan scrambled to his feet. Sliding metal, blue and shiny, twisted and crunched like a slow-motion movie. Metal parts scraped, bounced, and clanged, ringing in his ears.

Nolan turned to the hefty officer thrust against the trunk of a fir tree.

"Grease!"

He didn't respond. Blood trickled below his left ear.

The truck, turned on its side, slid toward a line of tall evergreens. A shattering crash deafened his senses. The air rang with grinding metal and—after what seemed like a slow-motion time warp— deafening silence.

The putrid smell of hot chemicals filled the air, maybe from under the hood.

Nolan raced to the smashed-out windshield.

Two men. Late twenty's or early thirties. Bloody. Not moving.

Nolan hit his mic, "Chief here. Send an ambulance. Deputy down. Two suspects unconscious."

He thumped his baton on the remaining windshield and broke out the glass. Trying to avoid jagged edges, he pulled the men onto the ground, about ten yards from the wreck.

Nolan returned to the truck. On its side, the cab door sat some five and a half feet in the air. He scrambled up onto the side panel and reached for the door handle. He yanked with all his might, pulling against its weight.

Sirens blared and an ambulance crew rushed toward the injured men.

"Grease is behind the car over there!" Nolan yelled and pointed.

"Let me help, Chief." A man wearing recovery gear climbed beside Nolan. Together they tugged until the door creaked open.

"The mother lode," Nolan whispered.

Cocaine. Shrink wrapped. Stacked so tight that it hadn't moved during the crash. A gaping hole in the bottom corner displayed the white powder.

The recovery helper whistled. "There must be a pallet's worth here, Chief. Congratulations."

"Start taking pictures," Nolan ordered a camera-toting deputy.

He walked to his battered SUV and leaned against it. A medic approached.

"The one guy is DOA. The other is just hanging on. You want to talk to him?"

"Is he coherent?"

"You can try."

Nolan walked toward the man lying on the ambulance stretcher. Blood smeared across his forehead and a turban-style scalp bandage covered his head. The man opened his eyes at the sound of Nolan's approach.

"Faint pulse, shock, confused. Sometimes non responsive," a young EMT updated Nolan. "He's lost a lot of blood. Doesn't look good."

Nolan nodded and knelt by the stretcher. "You're in a lot of trouble. You know that, don't you?"

"What's new?" He scowled and coughed. "You couldn't catch us. Road runners mostly head east from California. Not us."

"Did you shoot my patrolman? South of the highway on Elk Ridge Road?" Nolan's heart pounded. "Did you?"

"Not me, man."

"Who then?"

"You can't touch him. He's free." He grimaced and held his stomach.

Nolan fought the urge to shake him senseless. "Where is he?"

"Right there, going home in a box."

CHAPTER THIRTY-FIVE

D riving to the McCormick ranch, Nolan sensed Bosco's uneasiness.

"You're not the silent type. What's up?"

"Can I ask you a question?" Bosco glanced at Nolan.

"You can ask."

"You and Evah. I heard the whole household is packing. Is that true?"

Nolan's throat tightened. He nodded.

"It's a shame. I thought you two . . . you know."

"Yeah."

"Hate to see it end like this."

~~~

Cash twirled and yipped behind the front door. Evah greeted Nolan and Bosco. One glance at their faces made her breath catch.

"This looks serious."

"May we come in?" Nolan appeared solemn.

"Please." She held the door open. His demeanor weighed on her heart. Even the whiff of after shave didn't lightened her spirits.

"Are Jane and Cassie here?"

"Yes. Everyone is packing and sorting."

"Would you gather everyone?"

Evah turned toward the kitchen. "Jane and Cassie, will you come here?"

They appeared, Jane grasping a roll of packing tape and Cassie holding a dish towel. They walked into the living room with somber looks on their faces.

Evah's glance met Cassie's.

Bosco stepped forward. "I'm glad you're all here." He approached Cassie. "You in particular, Cassie. Or should I say, Camille? Camille Genreau."

Cassie gasped and her mouth fell open.

Jane stepped away from Cassie and sat in a chair.

Evah gasped and stepped closer to Cassie. "What are you talking about? This is Cassie Ballard!"

Cassie trembled. "This can't be happening."

Bosco pushed downward with open palms. "Easy, it's not what you think. Relax, please."

Nolan remained at Bosco's side.

Evah hugged Cassie, staring at Bosco. "What's this all about?"

Bosco planted his hands on his hips. "Camille has been part of the witness protection program for years. I doubt that she's told any of you."

Evah's breath seemed to catch in her throat. "I knew she had a past that she couldn't talk about. But the witness protection program?" She stared at her friend, wide-eyed.

Bosco nodded. "I served on a special team a couple of years ago, when I was in Chicago. We hunted high and low for her."

"You weren't supposed to find me." Cassie's voice shook. "I moved and moved. Kept changing names. I didn't want anyone to know where I was, even the police. Now, I'm . . . I'm going to have to move again." Tears filled her eyes and her chin quivered.

"No," Bosco continued. "We were trying to notify you that there was an imminent risk, about the guys who tracked and eventually assaulted you in Minnesota. The last survivor is now behind bars. You've been released from the program."

"No." Fear shone in Cassie's eyes.

"The organization that killed your parents is gone. The last one has been incarcerated. You are free. Free to live wherever, however, you want, Camille—or Cassie."

"I'm free, after being stabbed?"

Bosco continued. "Those guys were friends of the one that is now out of the picture. You have no more worries."

Evah wiped her tears. "I know you couldn't discuss your past, but this is so awful. Your parents were killed? I can't imagine, Cassie."

Her friend gave her a sharp look.

Evah ignored it. "Oh no, you're not Cassie. You're Camille!"

"My past is out in the open. What about yours?"

Evah's eyes watered. "My past is behind me. That's where I intend to leave it."

"But you said—"

"What I said was wrong. Bad things happened. I've learned that I can't do everything by myself. And if nobody else loves me, God does."

Cassie nodded.

Jane squirmed. "I knew there was something, Camille."

"I haven't been called that in years." Cassie laughed.

"And there's more news." Nolan gripped the visor of his hat. "Evah, your tip paid off. Pierce returned to the shed and we picked him up."

His appreciative gaze warmed her soul.

"He and Mast, the guy you called Aussie, planted drugs in cars that Mariah Tierney drove from Mankato. They've picked her up and—get this—she's the lady who took food to Carolyn. As a realtor, she knew where to hide Carolyn, in what vacant building. Community Watch neighbors identified her right away."

The room echoed with comments.

"On another note, Aussie had a red pen with *Milt's* on it, identical to the one I found. It's a resale shop in Great Falls, where they picked up the Silverado. The truck and shop were a few blocks apart."

"But why so far away to steal a car?" Evah asked.

"It's three hours," Nolan replied. "But in a city of sixty-seven thousand, they figured we wouldn't notice. According to the Great Falls Police Chief, it turns out their mobile drug haven has evaded them for some time. You helped break the case, Evah."

"Aussie was so mean," she whispered. "It's too bad that Pierce got mixed up with him."

Nolan added. "Mast was apprehended trying to hock the .22 rifle, the one he used at the trail. He bragged about being the shooter. Lucky for us, he wasn't a good shot."

Bosco stooped down to pet Cash.

Nolan cleared his throat and stood tall, looking from one person to the next. "So, you're all packing and sorting, according to—sorry, you're still Cassie to me."

She giggled and grinned under watery eyes.

Evah's stomach quivered. "Yes, we're packing. And I'm glad you're here because I need to ask you about the legalities with my uncle. Am I, officially, clear to leave?"

Nolan nodded. "Yes, you are, as far as the police are concerned. The investigation is no longer pending. Bosco found meds at Sid Elmer's place that matched the container left in Regan's medicine cabinet. Sid Elmer will be tried for Regan's murder. On the other hand, you will need to check with the attorney about probate."

"I don't understand." Evah's voice tightened. "Why would he hurt Uncle Regan?"

"According to Sid's niece, Mariah—Mariah Tierney—Regan owed him a huge gambling debt. Sid wanted Regan to sell, but he wouldn't. Regan vowed the ranch would go to his niece. You."

"But now . . ." Evah clutched her throat, where mama's necklace used to be.

Nolan nodded. "Elmer heard that Regan purchased alpacas for you. He went ballistic and planned a way to kill him."

He turned to Jane. "Attorney Angeli planned to fulfill his own debt with this place."

Jane's mouth fell open. "What? You can't mean that! We had plans."

"He had plans," Nolan corrected.

Evah sighed. "I'm sorry that Uncle Regan's wish didn't come true."

"Are you?" Nolan stepped closer and looked down at her.

"I am. But I can't undo what I've done."

Jane picked up a picture. "If you all can spare a minute, I'd like to explain something, since we'll be parting ways." She looked at Evah. "Marilyn McCormick's maiden name was Martin. She was my sister."

"What?" Evah whirled. "You're saying that you're Uncle Regan's sister-in-law?" She jumped to her feet. "Why didn't you say so? The ranch will be yours!"

Bosco shook his head. "How could no one know that?"

"It's not like you think." Jane hung her head. "It's been so long. I was in the Women's Air Corps—a WAC. Proud of it, too."

Her eyes watered. "Regan disinherited me. Even legally. I shamed him. Had a baby boy after being discharged. My . . . he had a distinguished career. So, I made a life for Jimmy and me."

"Jimmy, the boy in the picture is your son?" Evah blurted. "Does the father know?"

"I couldn't tell him."

Jane is crying.

Evah stared, dumbfounded.

"Jimmy has a mental disability." Jane blinked away tears. "It costs me everything I make, but he's in a fine home. Stoneybrook, ten miles from here." She fingered the camouflage scarf tied around her neck. "You see, he's full grown but has a child's ability to reason. I visit him every day—my rounds."

Jane had a son. Jimmy. The boy from the picture.

"Regan said I was nuts. He never let me forget it. He promised that if anyone found out I was his sister-in-law, he'd give me the boot. Said the boy was nuts because I was, too."

"How could he say such a thing? Did Aunt Marilyn know?"

"Of course, she was my sister. But there was something else. Regan drank, heavy at times before the cancer. Gambled, too." She licked her lips. "He wouldn't let my boy on his property."

She gave Evah a hard look. "In everything he did, he pined for you. He called you his little *buttercup*." She whispered the last word.

Evah stood. "Jane, Uncle Regan *disowned* me. He left me in group homes and foster care. He wanted nothing to do with me, even after mama died."

"You're wrong. When your mama was dying, he and Marilyn begged for your custody. But your mother knew about Regan's habits. She forbade either of them to contact you. Forbade. She got some fancy court paper to say so. It all but killed Regan."

Tears coursed down her wrinkled face. "For years, I hated you. And then you showed up on my doorstep." She lowered her gaze. "I hope you can someday forgive me."

"Forgive you?" Evah ran to Jane.

Jane ducked.

"Jane, I'm not going to hit you. I'm going to hug you." Evah embraced Jane, who sat as still as a statue. "You're my aunt! My family. And I have a cousin, Jimmy. I can't wait to meet him."

Nolan stepped close to Evah. "You said you didn't have a family. But you do, in Jane, Jimmy, and Cassie."

Cassie gave him a quick look.

"You don't have to be blood relatives to be sisters," he said in a soft tone. "You two are sisters in Christ."

Evah pulled Cassie close and hugged her. "That's what I've heard."

She looked at Nolan. "You're right. And look what I've done. I signed a waiver and someone is buying the ranch. Our home."

Nolan stepped to within inches of her. "Where is your faith, Evah? God has been here with you, every step of the way."

"If that's true, why have I lost the ranch . . . and you?"

"Why would you think that? I'm right here and I still love you."

"I love you, too." Evah released Cassie and rushed into his open arms.

But Nolan released his grip. "You don't need to rush to pack. The sale won't be finalized until after probate. In fact, you don't have to pack at all. It's up to you." He gave her a sheepish look.

"What do you mean?" An idea hit. "Do you think the buyer would rent it out?"

"No. He intends to get married and live in this house. With his family."

"How would you know that?"

"Because I am the buyer." He took Evah's hands in his. "Would you marry me and live here in Big Sky Country? I always say that stars shine the brightest here."

Evah recalled Abraham's star-filled sky. "Big Sky County. I would like that."

Jane and Cassie bumped elbows. They giggled and laughed, their faces radiating joy.

Bosco doubled over in laughter. He slapped Nolan on the back.

Nolan looked from one face to another. His eyes watered and he grinned. "We may need to put an addition on this house."

CHAPTER THIRTY-SIX

Two and one-half years later . . .
Evah grasped the cumbersome plastic carrier and slid it into the back of her creamy yellow SUV.

"Emmie will dock your pay if you're late for work." Cassie stood on the cobblestone walk leading to the barn addition.

"She wouldn't. We're partners. And besides, that's not fair. You're already at work." Evah stood back from her car.

Cassie pointed to the container. "She and Carolyn will love those samples. Just like your husband did."

"I hope so. But Nolan prefers chocolate to almond."

"That's your man." Key in hand, Cassie unlocked the deep red door. The sign overhead read Cassie's Fine Things. "Will you help address postcards tonight? The grand opening is three weeks away and I'm having a bit of a panic about it all."

"You panic? You're the master marketer. You've covered everything."

"That may be true, but I'm also the storeowner, sales clerk, bookkeeper, shelf stocker, designer, and every other thing."

"I understand. I'll be here. Aunt Jane, too."

"Did she leave for work yet?"

"Yes. She left early. Her car is going in for repairs later this morning, so I'm picking her up on my way home. She was pumped to teach Exercise Warfare at the senior center today."

Cassie looked up. "Mercy. I hope they know what they've gotten themselves into."

"Me too. We'll visit Jimmy on the way home." Evah fingered mama's necklace. Her heart warmed at the memory of Nolan's first anniversary gift. He had searched until he found her mother's lost necklace. Then he had it repaired, cleaned, and added a diamond to the front.

"Jane is so excited to bring Jimmy home." Cassie ran her fingers over the white door trim. "They'll finally live together, after all this time."

"It sounds like he'll still spend time at Stoneybrook, too." Evah closed the SUV's back door. "Aunt Jane is working out some arrangement with them. Nolan said their guest house will be ready next week. How are you managing in her cottage?"

"Great. I don't think she appreciated me painting over her camouflage wall, but I like turquoise."

"I'm so happy you're here. I couldn't imagine you not being part of my life."

"Me too. This place is home. I've got privacy, everything I need. And we're all here. Woohoo!" Cassie stood with her hands extended upward. "All in God's time, right?"

"Yes." God had been with her always and look what he'd planned. "I have to pinch myself."

"I'll leave that for Nolan." Cassie called. "Speak of him and here he is."

The black SUV turned in to the driveway. He left the motor running and exited the vehicle. "I hoped to catch you before you left."

"And why is that?"

They shared a warm embrace before he turned to his SUV. "That was reason enough, but I wanted to give you this."

He opened the back door and pulled out a large metal sign. Red wording on white background read, Shooting Star Alpacas. Mountains above water brightened the upper left-hand corner and a shooting star left its trail overhead.

"You remembered." Evah ran her fingers over the lettering and the shooting star. "How did I ever get so lucky?"

She embraced him again.

"Careful now, don't mess up my uniform." Nolan's eyes teased. "The Chief of Police is supposed to set a good example."

She released her grip and he brushed his shirt.

"You'll get used to being crumpled." She reached in her blazer pocket and handed him a palm-sized package.

Nolan looked at his watch. "You're going to be late."

"I'm already late."

Nolan unwrapped a baby rattle fashioned into an alpaca face on one end and a smiling star on the other.

Suddenly, she was off her feet, being twirled in his embrace. She squealed.

Nolan beamed with joy. "I am so blessed. Your star is brighter than ever. How do you like the name Abraham?"

"It's a wonderful name," she giggled, "but then, so is Sarah."

"It will be fun to choose the perfect name."

"There's a problem with that thought."

"What do you mean?"

"We need two names."

THE END
(Watch for Sunrise Crik Series Book Two.)

QUESTIONS FOR DISCUSSION GROUPS OR PERSONAL REFLECTION

1. Why do you think the author opened Intentional Heirs in Minnesota rather than Montana?

2. Rebecca's background as an alpaca owner inspired her to incorporate alpacas into Intentional Heirs. She gave the story a twist by making Evah unfamiliar with animals. Can you name books or movies in which the heroine is out of her element? How would this story have differed had Evah been from a country setting? How did you feel about Evah's adaptation to ranch life?

3. Evah felt abandoned and unloved after the death of her mother. How do you compare her feelings to your own feelings about your parents or guardians and their siblings?

4. The loss of her mother dramatically affected Evah's life. How has the death or absence of a family member or friend affected you?

5. The theme of Intentional Heirs is forgiving past hurts. Evah can't let herself want the ranch because she wasn't welcome there after her mother died. She is afraid to love for fear of being abandoned

again. Nolan needs to get past his former fiancé's departure. Can you think of a time when forgiving someone was difficult for you? Did your faith help you to overcome this obstacle?

6. Although eccentric, Jane harbors forgiveness issues, too. Do you know what they are?

7. Evah trained to be a bakery chef. Could you relate to her aspirations? How do they resonate with lifestyles of today's young adults?

8. Nolan's father died when he was young, leaving him feeling responsible for protecting his mother. How does this protective personality change between a police chief protecting his community to that of a personal family or friends?

9. Nolan has a soft spot for helping people in need. Can you remember a time when you helped with a feed-the-hungry type of campaign? If so, how did it make you feel to be involved in such a project?

10. Jane is overbearing and eccentric. How much of her behavior was meant to be intimidating? Do you know anyone whose behavior borders eccentricity versus a disability?

11. Rebecca loves when the heroine overcomes dangerous or daunting situations. How did you feel about Nolan's reaction to those situations?

12. Many children are raised within foster care or orphanage systems. As children grow, outcomes vary, depending on compassionate and effective caregivers. Could you relate to Evah's feelings or experiences?

13. Cassie's past weighed on her heart. Did you suspect that she was in the Witness Protection Program? Do you know anyone who won't talk about their pasts? Do you know why?

EVAH'S ANGEL-FOOD FRENCH TOAST

(Regular Recipe OR Gluten Free Recipe)
Note: For gluten free version, make sure all ingredients are gluten free, in addition to those specifically stated below.

Crispy-fried angel food cake bites, topped with Evah's honey butter and real maple syrup.

INGREDIENTS

PREPARED ANGEL FOOD CAKE (regular OR gluten free)
1 angel food cake, cut into cubes, approximately 1" square
(If homemade instead of purchased, use well cooled cake to ensure clean-cut cubes/minimal breakage.)

FRENCH TOAST MIX
6 eggs
1 ¼ c. milk (use your preferred brand and type – whole, 1 or 2%, or Evah's choice of almond milk)
1 ½ tsp. vanilla
Half pinch of nutmeg (small amount pinched between your fingers)
1 tsp. ground cinnamon

Butter for frying.
(Ingredients for Evah's honey butter – optional but preferred – recipe below)

Maple syrup – Prefer real syrup

Preparation:
Cut angel food cake into 1" cubes.
In a bowl, beat eggs, milk, vanilla, nutmeg, and cinnamon.
Add cubes, a handful at a time. Let them soak up the mixture, but not too much.
Note: Don't let the angel food cake get mushy.

Frying: In your skillet (cast-iron preferred), melt a small amount of butter, a little extra for cast iron.

When the butter is sizzling, add cubes. Cook, flipping as necessary, until golden brown, about 5 minutes. Repeat until all cubes have been fried to golden brown.

If necessary, keep warm in oven until served.

EVAH'S HONEY BUTTER – OPTIONAL BUT OH, SO GOOD!
Butter – Use amount preferred, unsalted. For example, ½ c. (1 stick)
⅓ c. honey
¼ tsp. ground cinnamon
Vanilla – dash
Salt – pinch (optional – cuts down the sweetness)
Using your preferred mixer of choice, beat until smooth. Serve or refrigerate until served. Keeps 2-3 weeks in refrigerator.

Recipe by Rebecca M. McLafferty 7-5-2019

EVAH'S BLUEBERRY COFFEE CAKE

(Regular Recipe OR Gluten Free Recipe)
Note: For gluten free version, make sure all ingredients are gluten free, in addition to those specifically stated below.

Crunch-and-melt cinnamon sugar topping with drizzled vanilla icing.

INGREDIENTS

CRUNCH AND MELT CINNAMON SUGAR TOPPING
½ tsp. ground cinnamon
⅓ c. all-purpose flour OR gluten free flour
½ c. granulated sugar OR ¼ c. sugar substitute (i.e. Truvia® or Splenda®)
¼ c butter, softened

COFFEE CAKE
¾ c granulated sugar OR 6 Tbsp. sugar substitute
2 c. all-purpose flour OR gluten free flour
¾ c. milk
1 egg
3 tsp. baking powder
¼ tsp. salt

2 c. frozen blueberries (thawed and drained) OR fresh

DRIPPING VANILLA DRIZZLE
½ c. powdered sugar
¼ tsp. vanilla
(Approximately) 1 ½ tsp. HOT water

Preparation:
Preheat oven to 375°. Grease bottom and sides of 9-inch square
pan. Bake time 45 minutes.

Crunch and Melt Cinnamon Sugar Topping: In a small bowl, mix
½ tsp. ground cinnamon, ⅓ c. all-purpose flour OR gluten free
flour, and ½ c. granulated sugar OR ¼ c. sugar substitute. Cut in
butter with either a pastry blender or 2-knife method.

Coffee Cake: Mix all Coffee Cake ingredients in a large bowl
except blueberries. Hand mix cake ingredients 1 minute. Fold in
blueberries. Spread the batter into the prepared pan. Sprinkle top
with Crunch and Melt Sugar Topping.

Bake approximately 45 minutes, or until toothpick inserted in
center comes out clean.

Dripping Vanilla Drizzle: Mix all ingredients together. If too thick,
add HOT WATER, 2 drops at a time.
Drizzle onto cake—and enjoy!

TIP: This cake can be frozen, thawed, and warmed.
Recipe by Rebecca M. McLafferty 7-5-2019

EVAH'S CINNAMON ROLLS

Melt-in-your-mouth cinnamon rolls with glazed icing.

INGREDIENTS

DOUGH
1 (¼ oz.) package active dry yeast
½ c. warm water
½ tsp. sugar
½ tsp. salt
½ c. scalded milk (brought to an almost-boil and then cooled) OR warmed in microwave—NOT hot

⅓ c. granulated sugar OR sugar substitute (i.e. Truvia® or Splenda®)
⅓ c butter, melted
1 tsp. ground cinnamon
1 egg
3 ½ to 4 cups all-purpose flour (regular or gluten free)

FILLING
½ c. melted butter (to spread on dough)
¾ c granulated sugar OR equivalent sugar substitute
2 tbs. ground cinnamon
¼ tsp. nutmeg
½ c. raisins (optional)

½ c. walnuts or pecans, chopped (optional)

GLAZED ICING
4 tbs. butter
2 c. confectioners sugar
1 tsp. vanilla extract
4-6 tbs. hot water

Preparation:
Preheat oven to 350°. Grease bottom and sides of 9x12-inch baking pan. Bake time 30 minutes.

DOUGH: In large bowl, dissolve yeast, ½ tsp. sugar, and salt in warm water. Stir in (cooled) scalded milk, ⅓ c. sugar, butter, cinnamon, and egg. Stir in 2 cups flour. Stir in remaining flour until it is easy to handle (not sticky). Knead the dough on a lightly floured surface for approximately 5 minutes. Place in well-greased bowl. Turn the dough over and place back in bowl (the top will automatically be greased). Cover and let dough rise until double in size, approximately 1 ½ hours.

When double in size, punch the dough down and knead briefly to get rid of air bubbles. Roll out on a lightly floured surface, forming a 9" x 15" rectangle.

FILLING: Brush or spoon the melted butter on the rolled-out dough. Mix together the sugar, cinnamon, and nutmeg. Sprinkle on top of melted butter. Add raisins and/or nuts (optional). By hand, roll the dough lengthwise, to form the cinnamon roll log. To keep the filling from leaking out, seal the ends by pinching/squeezing them together with your fingers.

Slice the dough into 12 slices.

Apply butter to pan. Place the slices in the pan. Let rise until dough is doubled in size, about 40 minutes. Bake for 30 minutes or until golden brown.

GLAZED ICING: While cinnamon rolls are baking, mix together confectioners sugar, softened butter, and vanilla. Stir in 1 tbs. of hot water at a time, until it is the desired consistency. Spread over the slightly cooled rolls.

Recipe by Rebecca M. McLafferty 7-5-2019

ABOUT THE AUTHOR

Rebecca McLafferty recently retired from public education, eager to write stories that glorify God.

She married the love of her life, Joseph, whose Air Force tours enabled European travel before raising two children. They treasure five wonderful grandchildren.

Rebecca's country spirit reflects nineteen years in Michigan's Upper Peninsula. After settling in Wisconsin, their alpaca farm became the venue for her annual Country Memories Farm Christian Writers Conference. Attendees benefited from speakers, education sessions, and down-home hospitality.

A member of American Christian Fiction Writers (ACFW) and ACFW-Southeast, Rebecca co-created Pens of Praise Christian Writers Group. She also belongs to Crossway Communicators and contributes weekly to the Fill My Cup, Lord, Blog and monthly to the Fresh Starts ~ Second Chances Blog.

Montana, a favorite vacation spot, is the setting for her first romantic suspense book, Intentional Heirs. Book two of the Sunrise Crik Series is currently under construction. Visit Rebecca's website at www.rebeccamclafferty.com, email rebeccamclafferty4353@gmail.com, and Facebook at https://www.facebook.com/author.rebecca.mclafferty.

Made in the USA
Monee, IL
07 January 2021